CORRUPT PRINCESS

KNIGHT'S RIDGE EMPIRE
BOOK 14

TRACY LORRAINE

Copyright © 2022 by Tracy Lorraine

All rights reserved.

No part of this book may be reproduced in any form or by any electronic or mechanical means, including information storage and retrieval systems, without written permission from the author, except for the use of brief quotations in a book review.

Editing by Pinpoint Editing

Proofreading by Sisters Get Lit.erary

Photography by Wander Aguiar

Models - Liam Black and Joli Irvine

"**F**uck. You've got the most insane pussy I've ever felt, Siren," I groan as her tight, velvet walls engulf me and my grip on her hair tightens.

I fucking knew it would be good from the first time I slipped my fingers inside her when we were dancing back in the Spot.

I had more than a few ideas for where I wanted this night to go as her hips rolled and her arse ground against my aching dick, but I could never have predicted what my best friend had planned for the two girls we managed to find ourselves tonight.

"Nico," she screams as I thrust inside her so hard I actually see fucking stars.

Jesus, who is this woman, and why didn't I find her sooner?

Another cry fills the room, and when I rip my gaze away from the spitfire I've got laid out on the horse in this room full of sin and debauchery, I find the eyes of the girl my best friend is railing from behind.

Pleasure is etched into every inch of her face, her fingers

twisted in the sheet beneath her as Toby fucks her like the savage not everyone realises he is.

"You can join if she's not enough for you," she taunts as I continue watching her lose herself.

The loud slap of Toby's palm against his girl's arse sounds out around the room before he barks, "No one touches you but me," forcing his girl to look over her shoulder and give him some attention.

"Got my hands more than full, man," I say, sliding my palm up Siren's stomach, grabbing a handful of tit just to prove a point.

Her cunt gushes around my cock at my less-than-gentle touch.

"You fucking love it, don't you, Siren? Getting railed by me while my best friend fucks yours. Does having others watch you being a filthy whore get you off?"

"Yes," she cries, lifting her hand to cup her breast and pinch her nipple as I focus on the other.

"Gonna make you come so hard that you're going to spend the rest of your life wishing you could feel my cock stretching you open once more."

"Fuck. Your mouth is filth. I fucking love it. Keep talking," she begs, her free hand skimming down the curve of her stomach until she finds her swollen clit.

Her pussy clamps down on me so fucking hard, I almost spill my load inside her right there and then.

"Jesus, Siren."

She screams as we work her together, and I lose myself in the pleasure flooding my veins right along with the sight of her getting ready to fall before me—all the while attempting to ignore the screaming voice in the back of my head, which is trying to tell me that tonight isn't going to be enough.

But it has to be.

I. Do. Not. Do. Repeats.

Ever.

That just means one thing...

I need to get my fill tonight. I need my cock spent, my body exhausted and my wank bank full of images of this girl for when the next one comes along and predictably doesn't live up to her.

"Nico, Nico, Nico," she chants, clearly doing a much better job of remembering my name than I have hers.

It doesn't matter. Siren suits her much better than anything her momma could have given her.

"Come for me," I demand, thrusting into her with abandon as sweat trickles down my spine and my balls begin to draw up.

I curse out the Johnny that's wrapped around my cock.

I've always been a strong advocate of safe sex, but fuck if I don't want to pull out of this woman and watch my cum run from her cunt. I want to own her, mark her, make her fucking mine.

Wait... what?

No.

No, I never want to—

"Fuck. FUUUUCK," I groan when she throws her head back and screams out my name as her cunt chokes my dick and milks my seed from me. "SIREN."

I suck in a sharp breath as panic slams into me and I bolt upright.

More pain than I've ever experienced before explodes throughout my body as I move. My chest heaves, my vision blurs, and nothing makes any sense.

I was just fucking Brianna. What the fuck hap—

"Nico, fuck, calm down, man," a familiar voice says, although it sounds like he's at the other end of a tunnel.

"What's going on?" I demand as the darkness starts to fade, giving way to blinding lights that make my eyes water.

"You need to calm down. Sit back, yeah?"

A warm hand lands on my shoulder before I'm shoved back onto something soft.

"Where am I? What's going on?" But as I ask that question again, my vision begins to clear.

The stark white sheets that are covering my legs are the first thing I register right before the realisation that I'm not in my own bed.

The tube in the back of my hand is the second clue that shit isn't right.

And then I finally look up and find myself in the middle of a fucking hospital room.

Panic slams into me much like it did when I first came to, but I can't put my finger on why.

I don't remember anything, or the reason why I'm here.

But something is wrong. Really fucking wrong.

"Just breathe, Nico," that familiar voice says again. But despite it being familiar, it's different from what I'm used to. It's... softer.

As I twist my head to the side, pain shoots down my neck.

But it's soon forgotten when I glance at who's standing beside me, looking more concerned than I think I've ever seen him.

"Daemon?" I whisper.

"It's good to have you back with us, man."

"U-us?" I stutter before he jerks his chin to the other side of the room, and when I slowly turn around, my breath catches at the sight of my sister curled up on a temporary bed in the corner.

"She's refused to leave since you got here. She's freaking

the fuck out that you might have been about to leave her, too."

The pain in my neck pales in comparison to the ache in my chest as Daemon confesses that to me.

"Shit. No. Never. I wouldn't," I argue, although I have no idea how true those words are. I don't even know why I'm here. All I do know is that it fucking hurts.

"I know," he says confidently. "I told her that."

A million and one things float around my head that I could really do with right now. The most obvious is that I really don't need to be in a fucking hospital bed.

"You need anything?" he asks.

My eyes catch on the jug of water and an empty glass on the table to my right.

"Drink. You got it."

Reaching over, he pours me a glass, pops a straw into it and then lifts it to my mouth.

Something akin to amusement glitters in his dark eyes, and it makes fire lick at my insides.

"You don't need to enjoy this quite so much, you know," I groan. Now I've been promised the relief of cool water, my throat is raw as fuck.

A smirk twitches at his lips, but he doesn't say anything. Instead, he just nudges the straw against my lips, encouraging me to drink.

I take a few sips but stop the second it hits my stomach, because it makes me want to barf.

After placing the cup back on the table, he drags a chair closer and sits down beside me.

"How are you feeling?" he asks, that concern back and wrinkling his brow. I don't fucking like it.

"Like I got hit by a bus," I confess. "Did I?" I ask, genuinely wondering.

"No. You don't remember?"

Closing my eyes, I try to focus on anything that happened before waking up here.

Steak. I remember eating steak. And drinking Dad's favourite whisky.

Pain slices through my chest at the thought of him. Why is it I can't remember the events leading up to being here, but the grief that has consumed me since the night Dad died is still there and just as oppressive as ever?

"No," I say, keeping my eyes closed and resting my head back.

No one—especially not my sister's fucking boyfriend—needs to see the grief-stricken look in my eyes right now.

There's a reason I locked myself in my flat for so long. It was so none of them could see what a fucking mess I was. Here though, they're going to have full access to the disaster that I've become.

"I have no idea."

"Nico," Daemon says softly and I crack my eyes open, sensing that he's about to say something important, but before any more words leave his hips, the door behind him opens, and a familiar nurse slips in.

"Nico Cirillo, what a sight for sore eyes you are." Janice, the terrifying nurse that we seem to always have the misfortune of being treated by, steps up to my bed. "I thought I told you lot that I didn't want to see you here again."

"Can't say I planned it," I admit on a sigh as she starts poking me.

"How much pain are you in?" she asks.

"A lot. And you prodding me sure doesn't help."

She pauses and shoots me a warning glare.

"I'll increase your painkillers."

"That would be wonderful."

"They'll make you drowsy, though."

No problem. I'd rather be checked out of real life right now, anyway.

"Perfect. Give me everything you've got."

She potters around for a bit, checking my vitals and writing notes on the clipboard at the bottom of the bed—I'm pretty sure anything to delay putting me out of my misery with more pain meds.

I breathe a sigh of relief when she leaves, knowing that she'll bring oblivion back with her.

Movement in the corner of the room catches my eyes and guilt floods me, because going back into a drug-induced coma means checking out on Calli again.

"You want me to wake her?" Daemon offers.

I shake my head. "No, let her rest. I'm assuming she hasn't had a lot in the last..." I trail off. "What time is it? Hell, what day is it?"

"It's almost eight a.m. Saturday morning."

"Right," I reply, as if discovering the day and time helps in any way.

Silence falls between us and I rest back with my eyes closed once more. I have nothing I want or need to say.

Right now, I'm so numb that I don't even have a burning desire to discover why I'm here. I'm sure that whatever it is, is all my own stupid fault.

I've been on a one-way road to self-destruction for a while now. I guess ending up here at some point was inevitable.

The door opening drags me from my black thoughts, but I don't open my eyes, I just allow Janice to do her job. And as the coolness of the drugs works its way up my arm from the cannula in the back of my hand, I pray that I can return to dreams of better times when I was able to lose myself in my siren's pussy instead of drugs and alcohol to drown out the pain.

Thankfully, the darkness comes for me quickly, and I drift off.

But this time, it's not my siren that greets me, but my dad, and that is all kinds of painful.

"What the fuck?" I bark as bright light illuminates my bedroom, making my eyes water even behind my eyelids.

"Get your arse up, soldier," Dad demands, throwing a pile of clothes at me before looming over me with his hands on his hips and a dangerous-as-fuck expression on his face.

"Fuck," I hiss, throwing my covers back and trying to force my body to wake up as quickly as it needs to.

One glance at my alarm clock tells me that it's barely four a.m.

Just like every morning this month.

I knew it was coming. For years, he's warned me that things would step up when I turned twelve.

I have no idea who made twelve the magic age where male members of the family start embarking on their lives as men, as Cirillo soldiers. But I'm right in the thick of it now, and I've gotta say, it's harder than I was expecting.

Dad stands there looking pissed off as fuck as I drag my dark clothes on.

"Not fast enough, boy," he growls when I fail to pull my trainers on with my first attempt and end up bouncing around the room on one foot. "When duty calls, you have to be ready."

I bite my tongue to stop myself from telling him that I'm fucking exhausted and all I want to do is curl up in bed once more.

It's still dark as fuck outside. The last thing I want to do right now is run around the garden, go nighttime target shooting or bounce around a ring as he trains me to fight like a man.

But then I think of him, of my grandfather, and all the men who came before them.

I think of me in a few years.

A man. A soldier. A capo.

The underboss.

Hell yeah.

One day, everything my father has now will be mine.

I'll hold the power right alongside Theo. Screw ruling Knight's Ridge College. Side by side, we'll rule this entire side of the city. And we're going to be fucking good at it, too.

The second I'm ready, Dad marches across the room, pulls my door open, and heads toward the stairs.

Of course, I follow.

It's what's expected of me. To follow in his footsteps, to become the kind of respected man he is.

My eyes flicker to Calli's door.

She'll be curled up in her bed, sleeping soundly. She's completely unaware of what my life has been like recently.

We don't talk about these kinds of things when she's around. It's always been the case. I get it, I think. She's going to lead a very different life from me, being a girl and all that. But I'm not sure her being totally kept in the dark is right. But then, who am I to argue? All I have to do right now is follow orders, pass my training, and make my next steps toward being a soldier and securing my future as part of this Family.

I follow Dad silently out of the house and into the cold, dark night—or morning, I guess.

He leads me toward the shooting range, but just before we get there, I spot two dark figures waiting for us.

I don't need to see the size difference between them to know who it is.

Theo might be a year younger than me, but as the future boss of this entire Family, Uncle Damien decided that twelve was too long to wait, and he started Theo's training the same day I started mine.

It's not often we're brought together, our fathers preferring to train us alone. So the fact we're both here now rings some alarm bells.

We come to a stop in front of them, a weird crackle of tension going through the air that makes my stomach knot.

"Morning," Uncle Damien drawls ominously, and my dad nods in greeting. "We want to see what you two have learned. We're not leaving here until one of you either passes out or taps out."

My breath catches as reality slaps me upside the head.

"You want us to fight?" Theo questions, his brain functioning faster than mine.

"Show us what you've got, soldiers."

My eyes find Theo's, and I recognise the same unease, even in the darkness.

I take a step forward, but a large hand lands on my shoulder, hauling me back.

"You've got this, Son. And remember, no matter the outcome, I'm proud of you."

BRIANNA

"Nico," I scream, jumping from the chair I was lounging in and sending it crashing back as I take off running. My heart thumps in my chest as heavy footsteps follow me, making butterflies erupt in my stomach.

I might be running, but I have every intention of letting him catch me.

Nico has been like a bear with a sore head since the moment he turned up here with the lads.

He knew I was coming—Jodie assured me that Toby had warned him—but that hadn't stopped him from watching me with contempt since the moment he got out the car.

But as the hours have gone on and the alcohol and weed has flowed, that contempt has turned into something else entirely.

Sure, the hate between us is still there. I'm not sure that will ever vanish. Without even speaking, we seem to manage to rub each other up the wrong way. But in doing so, we also tempt each other in the right way too.

And the drunker I'm getting, the more I'm craving the

side of Nico that I've become entirely too addicted to over the previous few months.

"Get back here, whore," Nico demands as I jump from the decking that connects all our tipis where we've been hanging out all evening.

I land with an ungraceful thud, but I recover quickly and take off once more.

But he's closer now, even without looking back, I can sense him. My skin tingles as if he's only seconds away from touching me.

I make it another two steps before his fingers thread into my hair and I'm hauled painfully back to his body.

"Run as fast as you want, Siren. You know I'll always catch you."

"You barbarian. Put me down," I squeal as he throws me over his shoulder, giving everyone we left behind full view of my backside. Curling my fists, I slam them down on his arse, frantically kicking my legs in the hope he'll release me.

But he never does. Instead, he takes off running into the darkness of the trees.

"NICO," I scream. "Stop and put me down this second."

His laughter fills the silence around us, but he never stops. And the longer he runs, the more blood rushes to my head.

Eventually, though, he slows, and when I'm finally placed back on my feet we're next to one of the tipis. His chest heaves with exertion, but his eyes are blown with need, and it sends heat washing through me, making my pussy clench with desire.

He drags me around the side and slams me up against the wall. His lips crash to mine as we continue to ride that familiar fine line of hate and lust, allowing ourselves to be engulfed by both.

"You." Kiss. "Drive." Kiss. "Me." Kiss. "Fucking." Kiss. "Insane."

"Mutual," I confess on a sigh as he kisses down my neck and hooks my leg around his waist, enabling him to grind against my pussy.

Yeah, I might have chosen to wear a skirt tonight for a very good reason. And that reason certainly didn't have anything to do with the heatwave Stella promised us when she booked this trip, because it's bloody freezing. Sure helps having Nico's hands on me, though.

His lips find mine once more as his hand slips down my inner thigh, searching out what he really wants.

"Yes, Nico. I need you inside me."

"Filthy little whore," he groans into our kiss, his fingers finding the soaked fabric of my knickers.

A deep growl rumbles up his throat as he rubs me through the lace.

"Surprised you bothered wearing any when you've spent all night tempting me, Siren."

"When did a pair of knickers ever stop you from getting what you wanted, Nico?"

He tucks his fingers beneath the fabric and slides them through my folds, collecting up my juices.

"I guess we already know it wouldn't be to stop my boys from seeing what you're hiding, would it? You like an audience, don't you, Siren?"

"Nico," I cry when he spears two fingers deep inside me.

"You'd let me carry you back around there right now and allow them all watch me fuck you like the whore you are, wouldn't you?"

"Yes, yes," I chant as his fingers find that magic spot he seems to have exact coordinates to. "Want your cock, Nico."

"Course you fucking do. Bet you've been dreaming about

me filling that tight little cunt since the last time you tempted me into fucking you again."

"Never," I argue, not willing to let him know just how much I do crave his cock and mind-blowing skills. Even if they are as good as his ego believes they are.

Prick.

"Such a fucking liar, Siren."

"No," I cry, immediately mourning the loss of his fingers when he rips them from me, leaving my pussy clenching around nothing.

But it's quickly forgotten when he lifts my fingers to his mouth and closes his lips around them. His eyelids lower and I imagine his tongue lapping at his digits, savouring my taste.

A whimper rips up my throat before I grab his wrist and rip his fingers from his mouth so he can kiss me instead.

The second his tongue sweeps across mine, my own taste explodes in my mouth, kicking my desire up another notch.

Hiking my leg up higher around his waist, Nico shoves his jeans down around his hips, freeing his glorious, thick cock.

Desperate for him, I reach out, needing to feel his hardness beneath my own fingers.

"Greedy whore. You can give him all the attention he deserves when we get inside. But right now, I need to be inside you before I explode," he confesses, his voice raspy with desire. "Now be a good girl and take my cock."

My knickers are dragged aside before the head of his dick runs through my folds as he coats himself in my juices.

"Please," I whimper.

"Fucking love it when you beg for me, Siren," he growls before thrusting his hips forward and filling me in one smooth move.

"Yes," I cry, my heart pounding in my chest, but then... there's nothing.

Warmth that I wasn't aware of before races up my arm as something—someone, maybe—squeezes my hand.

"Brianna? Bri, are you awake?"

The sound of my best friend's voice washes through me, settling the unease that I wasn't aware was there until she spoke.

Jodie.

But as much as I might want to talk to her, to tell her that I'm awake, I can't.

Am I even awake?

Confusion swirls around me as my panic begins to build.

My chest heaves as my heart rate increases.

"It's okay, Brianna. You're okay. I'm right here."

But why is Jodie here?

I was with Nico. He was fucking me against...

But before I even get a chance to finish that thought, everything goes dark once more.

The nothingness of dreamless sleep is welcome.

For many, many years as a kid, falling asleep was as painful as being awake. I'd close my eyes and the nightmares would immediately come. Only, they weren't really nightmares. More memories.

Times when I'd curl up in a ball, desperately trying to ignore the way my stomach growled and knotted in agony from a lack of food while my body trembled with the cold.

It took a lot of years and more than a couple of shrinks to be able to banish those recurring nightmares to allow me to get some decent sleep, something I've never been more grateful for as I continue to drift in and out of slumber.

Most of the times I've come to, it's been silent. I have no idea where I am, or who is here. Other than Jodie, I haven't been able to recognise any of the voices I've heard in the few moments of consciousness.

All I know is that wherever I am, I shouldn't be.

The last thing I remember was being in Twenty-Five, bored out of my brain as Brad talked about something dull.

Why did I even agree to go out with him?

My brows pinch as I think about him.

I haven't heard his voice. Does he know I left?

Why did I leave?

I wouldn't have just walked out. I might have been bored, but I'm not that rude. Not after he spent all that money on me. Usually, I'd let him take me home and—

Bile burns up the back of my throat as the thought of what I'd usually do with him makes my stomach turn over.

"Brianna," Jodie shrieks as I retch.

Her footsteps fly across the room before her hand lands on the back of my head gently helping me lean forward.

"It's okay, I've got a tray," she says as I puke up the contents of my stomach, which, to be fair, isn't all that much.

"I'm calling the nurse," she says when I finally stop retching and lie back.

The nurse?

Why is there a nurse?

But I never get the answer to those unspoken questions, because I drift off once more.

"No, she didn't really wake up. Just came to a bit, threw up and then drifted off again," my best friend says somewhere nearby.

"She's going to be okay, Demon. She was lucky. They were lucky."

They? Who are they?

Me and Brad?

Did we leave? Did we head back to my place or to a hotel? Did something happen on the way? When we got there?

Is Brad okay?

He may never be the love of my life like I believe he wants me to be, but that doesn't mean I don't care on some level. He's a... friend, I guess. A friend I have literally nothing in common with aside from wanting good sex. I mean, it could be worse.

I'll be sad if something bad has happened to him. I won't be heartbroken, though.

"I know. I just... I can't keep seeing my best friends in this position. It's heartbreaking, Toby. All I want for them is the best, and they keep getting fucked over left and right."

Toby doesn't reply for the longest time, his silence confusing me.

"I know, baby. But everyone is going to be okay. They're stronger than this."

Jodie lets out a heavy sigh, and I picture her tucked into Toby's side as he comforts her.

I'm so glad she found him.

After all the loss and heartache she suffered, even if some of it was at his hands, I'm so happy they found a way to work through it all.

"I'm here, Demon. Lean on me all you need."

"I love you," she breathes, her voice cracking with

emotion that makes a lump so huge crawl up my throat that I find it hard to suck in the air I need.

I've always told myself that I don't need that. Call it lingering effects from my childhood abandonment issues. But even after the counselling, I still find having to rely on anyone absolutely terrifying.

The only person I rely on is me. End of.

Okay, and maybe Jodie and Joanne, a little bit. But they've been there for me from the second they turned up at the hospital Mum was taken to, and they both pulled me into their arms and promised me that everything was going to be okay.

With my heart in my throat, I drift back off once more.

3

___

NICO

Everything is beyond fuzzy when reality comes back.

But this time when I crack my eyes open, the room is dark but, more noticeably, empty.

My breath catches as a wave of loneliness I wasn't expecting to feel washes through me.

A lump crawls up the back of my throat, and I swear my eyes actually burn.

What the actual fuck, Cirillo?

Lifting my non-cannulated hand, I try to rub the sleep from my eyes, but the second I make contact, pain radiates throughout my face and down my neck.

"What the fuck?" I mutter, my voice raspy with sleep as I pull my hand away and stare at it like it was the cause.

A toilet flushes somewhere close, but I'm too lost in my confusion of what happened and how I ended up here to really focus on just how close it is until a door opens and light footsteps pad through my room.

The moment I look to the left and my eyes lock on my exhausted sister's, that emotion floods me full force again.

I'm not alone.

"Calli," I breathe.

Relief covers her pretty face for a few seconds before it gives way to something else, something a little terrifying— which is new for my little sister.

"You fucking selfish prick," she seethes, storming over with her fists curled at her sides. "If your face wasn't already fucked up, I'd punch you right in it."

My brows shoot up, causing my formerly mentioned fucked-up face to scream in pain.

What the fuck happened to me?

"How could you, Nico? How could you be so fucking stupid?"

My lips part to respond but no sound leaves my mouth. How can it? I don't remember anything.

"You could have died, Nico. Both of you could have been dead right now just because you're too much of a pussy to deal with life. It was a shock, trust me, I fucking get that. But I didn't go around trying to kill everyone when I found out. Jesus, Nico. I'm not sure I've ever been so fucking furious with you."

I continue staring at her as she paces back and forth beside my bed, but still, no memories come.

Eventually, though, I manage to ask one of the most pressing questions about what she just said.

"Both of us?" I ask, making her stop mid-pace.

She spins around and pins me with a look that almost makes me regret ever waking up.

"You really don't remember?" she asks, coming a little closer.

I shake my head, instantly regretting it when the pain slams into me.

"N-no, I don't."

"Unbelievable," she breathes, throwing up her hands in disbelief. "All of this, all this pain and you don't even remember."

My lips open and close like a fucking goldfish.

"How about I show you? You think you can get your sorry arse into a wheelchair?"

"A wheelchair?" I spit, totally offended that she even thinks I need one. "I can walk."

"Good. I didn't really want to push you anyway." Reaching out, she rips the covers off me and gestures for me to get up.

My eyes clock the stand with the drip on beside me, but the fact I'm attached to it doesn't seem to faze my sister.

"We'll take it with us, don't worry," she sneers.

"Do you think that maybe…" I trail off before I mention anything about a nurse, because knowing my luck, it'll be Janice who will stroll in looking for a victim to hurt.

Running away might be my best option right now.

"Maybe what? You should continue lying here in ignorant bliss over what you've done?"

My stomach knots as the dread that's sitting like a dead weight at the bottom only gets heavier.

Swinging my legs over the side, I shuffle forward and place my feet on the cool floor.

"Come on then," my sister demands, getting impatient with how slow I am.

For someone who apparently hasn't left this room since I was brought in, she's not being all that caring.

The second I push my weight onto my feet, my knees threaten to buckle beneath me.

Calli watches me with a raised brow.

"Want me to get that wheelchair now?" she quips as I slowly sit my arse back on the edge of the bed.

I say nothing. I don't need to. My sister can read me well enough.

"It's a fucking good job I love you, Nico Cirillo," she hisses before storming out of the room.

I hang my head, the throbbing ache in my face not getting any better for the move as I continue trying to drag up memories of how I got here. But everything is dark, as if nothing in the run-up to being here even actually happened.

Calli is back in a flash, pushing a goddamn wheelchair toward me like I'm a cripple or some shit.

"Get in, arsehole," she whispers ominously.

"You know, I think I would have preferred to wake up to Janice," I hiss once I'm seated.

"You'd be so lucky."

She tucks me in with a blanket like I'm a little old man who's about to catch a chill before wheeling my drip stand over.

"Make yourself useful and hold this," she demands.

"Where are we going?"

"Next door."

My heart pounds as she pushes me forward.

Other than her, the only other person I've seen since waking up is Daemon. It could be anyone in that room.

"Where's Dae—"

"Shush," my sister chastises before I even get a chance to say his whole name.

"I sent him home. It's too risky, him being here."

"What time is it?"

"Three a.m."

"Was this the Italians?" The second the question rolls off my tongue, I regret it.

Calli immediately stops pushing and steps in front of

me. She studies me with her eyes narrowed and anger coming off her in waves.

I've never seen my sister looking quite so fierce. It's a little terrifying.

"No, Nico. It was you. All of it was you."

With those ominous words, she shifts around me once more and continues toward the door next to mine.

"Open the door then," she demands when I'm right in front of it, forcing me to lean forward and suck in a breath as my ribs smart.

She pushes me into the dark room. Just like mine, the first thing I see is a person curled up on a camp bed on the other side, but I have no way of telling who it is from my position, and it becomes clear that it is isn't who my sister brought me in here to see the second she spins me around and a hospital bed fills my vision.

If I thought I felt emotional when I believed I was alone, then it's nothing compared to the heart-stopping moment when my eyes land on the woman in the bed.

"Siren," I breathe, my voice cracked with emotion.

She's fast asleep and despite the dark eyes, the bruises and dried blood, she looks as beautiful as ever to me.

Only...

I did that.

I'm the reason she's lying there with her arm bandaged up and held in a sling around her neck.

"Closer," I demand, not content with just sitting at the end of the bed, watching her.

Calli wheels me around to the side with her good arm and brings me to a stop.

I immediately reach out for Brianna's hand, although I hesitate before I make contact.

If this truly is my fault, then she's not going to want me anywhere near her, let alone touching her.

But in the end, my need for her overrides my thoughts as I take her hand in mine.

She doesn't move or react in any way, and it cuts my chest straight down the centre.

"Tell me what happened, Calli. Please," I beg quietly, not taking my eyes off my siren.

"You had a drink, you got angry, and you forced her into your car before you drove like a fucking moron through the city and aquaplaned straight into the side of a fucking building."

All the air rushes out of my lungs.

"I did this?" The words are so quiet I'm not convinced she'll hear me, so when she responds, I jump like a pussy.

"Yes."

"Why? I would never hurt her."

Calli scoffs, and it cuts me so fucking deep I'm not sure I'll ever recover from it.

"Not like this, Cal. Never like this."

"What did you really think was going to happen, Nico? This thing between you has been futile since it first began. It was obvious to everyone that you were going to hurt her eventually."

Her words trail off as I lose myself in my own dark thoughts.

Is she right? Was this always how it was going to end?

No.

Brianna was never meant to end up in a hospital bed because of me.

The games we've been playing.

They're just that... games.

We both get off on them as much as each other.

Just because the others don't understand our dynamic, that doesn't mean it doesn't work for us.

Not that there is an us.

That's the whole point.

Neither of us wants an us. It's why it's so much fun.

Isn't it?

"What's wrong with her?" I force out through the lump in my throat.

Calli pauses, and I'm sure it's just to build the tension to ensure the knot in my stomach tightens to the point of pain.

"Concussion. Mostly cuts and bruises."

"But her arm?" My eyes drop to the sling and bandage that sneaks out of the ugly hospital gowns we're both wearing.

"She's got some bad cuts down her upper arm. She had to have surgery to remove the glass."

"Shit."

"Yep. She's going to be left with a reminder of that night, and you, for the rest of her life. Well done, big bro. I hope you're fucking proud of yourself."

"Fuck," I breathe, dropping my head into one of my hands, refusing to release Brianna to make use of the other.

Pain and regrets drip through my veins as my grip on Brianna's hand tightens.

I have no idea how long I sit there with thoughts of all the people I've let down recently before rustling hits my ear.

"Nic?" a deep, familiar voice says.

Glancing over my shoulder, I discover that half of the lump in the camp bed belongs to my best friend.

Despite the room being in darkness—aside from some emergency lighting and the moon seeping in through the cracks in the blinds—his eyes widen at the sight of me and he sucks in a sharp breath.

"Shit, you've looked better."

"Felt it too," I mutter, hating the bitter rejection that swamps me at the realisation that he hasn't visited me to see it before.

It's the right thing to do. Brianna deserves all their support right now.

Not me. The arsehole who caused all of this.

"Pretty sure my girl is going to rip you a new one when she wakes, man."

"She's more than welcome," I say on a sigh as he gently sits up without disturbing Jodie. "I fucked up."

"Yeah, man. You really fucking did."

Silence falls around us as I return to watching Brianna sleep.

"Has she woken up yet?"

"Not really, no. The anaesthesia is still wearing off. The doctors aren't worried."

"G-good." I think.

I scrub my hand down my face once more, scrubbing at the roughness of my jaw.

"I'm sorry," I whisper, my chest cracking in two all over again as those words spill from my lips.

"It's not us you need to be saying that to, man."

"I know. But it seems like the right place to start."

"Nico?" a sleepy voice says.

"Yeah, Demon. He's here."

I look over just in time to see her flip over.

Her eyes collide with mine and narrow in anger.

"I'm glad you survived so that Brianna can kill you herself when she wakes up," she seethes, anger laced through every word.

"I'm sorry, Jodie. I never meant to—"

"You could have killed her, Nico," she shrieks, getting to her feet and glaring pure hate at me. "What did she ever do to you?"

My lips part to respond, but Jodie quickly cuts me off.

"Nothing, Nico. Nothing is the answer you're looking for."

"Okay, baby," Toby soothes, getting to his feet behind her and pulling her into his body.

"I'm just so fucking angry," she says as he kisses her neck.

"I know. But throwing abuse at Nico isn't going to get us anywhere. I think his broken nose is a painful enough reminder that he fucked up."

Broken nose. Well, I guess that makes a lot of sense.

"Let's go get coffee," he says, tucking her into his side. "And some fresh air."

"B-but—"

"Brianna will be safe with Calli."

"What about me?" I blurt, regretting the words instantly. I blame the painkillers.

"What the fuck about you, Nico?" Jodie spits. "I wouldn't trust you with a fucking hamster right now. You're a fucking liability. Damien needs his head testing if he's seriously considering allowing you to move up through the ranks."

"Come on, baby." Toby pulls Jodie through the door before she gets a chance to spit any more painful truths at me, although it doesn't stop her, her voice carrying until the door finally clicks closed.

Silence fills the room as the weight of my actions presses down on me.

"She's never going to talk to me again, is she?"

Calli moves about behind me before she drags a chair to Brianna's other side and rests her hand on her leg.

"Do you think you deserve for her to?" she asks, looking up at me, her tired eyes holding mine.

"No," I whisper.

"Why did I do it, Cal? What happened to make me lose control?" I ask, because that's the only explanation here. There's no way I'd ever put Brianna in danger unless the red haze of anger descended and I lost my shit entirely.

Calli's lips part to respond, but she swallows whatever she was going to say and instead shakes her head.

"I don't know the details, Nico." Her eyes finally shift from mine as she fidgets on the chair. "That's something you're going to need to talk to Brianna about. It's not my place to guess."

When she looks back at me, my eyes narrow in suspicion.

"You're lying to me, Calli. What do you know?"

She lets out a heavy sigh. "Nothing that I'm willing to discuss right here and now."

I want to argue, to demand she tells me everything, but when she looks at me again, I know it would be pointless.

"Fine. But when we get out of here, I want to hear it all."

"Fuck you, Nico. I don't owe you anything."

Tension crackles between us. My teeth grind, making my face ache like a motherfucker, but I'll take the physical pain over the weight of my regrets and the confusion over not knowing what happened any day.

The air is thick between us as we fall into an awkward silence.

I probably should go back to my room. But I figure that I haven't done anything that I should have when it comes to

Brianna before. She really shouldn't expect anything else from me.

Eventually, Calli starts drifting off, damn near folded in half with her head resting on her arms on Brianna's bed.

"You should go home and get some sleep," I say, remembering Daemon telling me that she'd refused to leave my side.

"I'm not leaving."

"Calli," I sigh. "I'm fine. Brianna is going to be fine. You've got school. Exams."

"It's Sunday," she argues.

"Exactly. You have school tomorrow. You might have decided against uni, but I'm not letting you fuck this up."

"You're not letting me do anything," she snaps, although it's much less fierce with her exhaustion than when she tried ripping me a new one earlier.

"Go, or I'll get Daemon to come and drag you out," I threaten.

"You wouldn't."

"Try me," I warn, more than aware that she won't want to put Daemon at any more risk than he already has been, being here with her.

"Fine," she spits, "but only because I'm so tired, I can barely keep my eyes open."

"Pass your phone. I'll call one of the guys to take you."

"Do I look like a fucking patient to you?" she sasses. "I can sort my own lift. There's a mean-looking security detail who seems to be following my every move. Pretty sure he'll deliver me back safely."

"It's for your own safety."

"Do you see me arguing? All I want right now, Nico, is for all of us to be okay and to be able to move on from this bullshit. And if that means we all need a shadow, then I'll shut up and take it. Not sure Stella and Emmie will agree, but I figure I'll let them find this out on their own. I've got enough of my own shit to be worrying about."

"Like?"

"My shit, Nico. Not yours, remember."

Pushing to her feet, she steps closer to Brianna and gently tucks a stray lock of her hair behind her ear.

"If you need me, call me. I'll be right here," she promises. "And if he gives you any shit, I'll get the guys to ensure he can't leave his hospital bed again." She shoots me a look with that warning. "Can I trust you with her? Or do I need to get Jodie and Toby back before I leave?"

The words dance on the tip of my tongue, but I swallow them down because really, can anyone trust me at this point?

Jodie's right.

I'm a fucking liability.

And not just to the Family, but to everyone connected with me.

I'm a ticking time bomb, and it seems I got very close to finally exploding on Friday night.

If only I could remember what it was that pushed me to pull the pin.

4

BRIANNA

The second my senses start to come back to me, I know that something is different.

I might still have my eyes closed, but everything is clearer. I no longer feel like I'm trapped in a tunnel with no way of climbing out.

I'm groggy and tired but almost... normal.

The only sound that hits my ears is that of someone breathing.

Jodie.

She's been here this whole time. I might not have been able to see her, or even hear her, but I've felt her. Her love, her support.

She's my rock, has been for years, and I don't think she really has any idea how much she's helped me overcome everything I have, to be where I am now.

If it weren't for her and Joanne, there's no way I'd have finished school, let alone be accepted into uni. I owe them everything.

Needing to see her, to tell her how much I love her, I force my eyes open.

I have no idea how long I've been asleep, but it feels like someone has attempted to glue my lashes together. Pretty sure I even rip a few out when I finally manage to lift my eyelids.

Sunlight streams in through the open blinds, searing into my eyeballs and making me wince, but I'm unable to focus on that or the room I'm in because my attention is immediately drawn to the person sitting beside me and holding my hand.

It's certainly not Jodie, and as I stare at his broken face, images of the events that led up to this point start playing out in my mind.

My heart begins to race as I think about him following me to the bathroom, fucking me against the wall and then...

My stomach turns over as I picture him staring down at my phone with what I now know was Calli's scan image on the screen.

"Oh God," I breathe, trying to reach for the sick tray on the wheelie table beside my bed.

I miss by a mile and instead hit the water jug. The entire thing goes crashing over, spilling water everywhere.

"Holy fuck," Nico barks, jumping to his feet in fright as cold water lands in his lap. "Brianna."

"Sick," I manage to somehow force out in the panic, still trying to reach for the tray.

"Fuck. Yeah. Shit, Siren."

He manages to get it in front of me right in time, and I retch unattractively into it. I guess holding my sick bucket is the least of what he owes me at this point.

Barely anything comes up. Hardly a surprise really, seeing as I haven't eaten anything for... an indefinite amount of time.

"W-what day is it?" I force out after pushing the tray away.

Nico holds it out in front of him, looking utterly terrified, before he gingerly shuffles around the bed to the door in the corner which I assume houses the bathroom.

It's not until he's got this back to me, or more so his bare arse, that I register he's wearing a hospital gown too.

"Sunday," he says when he slowly walks back.

He hesitates beside me, looking utterly unsure of himself.

It's the first time I've ever seen it, and I'm not a fan.

I like strong, powerful, in-control-of-everything Nico.

Not this weak, concerned, and confused version.

It's at odds to almost everything he's ever tried to show me about himself.

I'm not an idiot. I know that almost everything he's allowed me to see about him is an act.

He's only been truly real with me a couple of times over the past few months, but none more so than last week when I went to his flat to tell him about Knight's Ridge and he broke in front of me.

That one moment is why he's been so vicious since.

I get it. He's scared.

Hell, I am too, most of the time, but I'm not so determined to hide it that I push everyone away from me.

His eyes hold mine and I swear I see something, a softness, within them that I've never seen before.

I'm so lost in them that I don't realise he's moved until he's right in front of me and his hand is cupping my cheek.

"Siren, I'm so fucking sorry."

His eyes glitter with moisture that makes my heart skip a beat and my chest ache uncomfortably.

He's a mess. His nose is covered in an ugly bandage that

does little to hide the bruising. Dried blood paints his chin and his neck, his hands too. One of them has a cannula in, which I can only assume is attached to something I've failed to notice.

He looks about as broken as I feel.

I'm still drowning in his dark eyes when a door opens and the squeak of someone's footsteps approaches.

"Whoa, I was not bargaining on walking in on that, Mr. Cirillo," a soft voice says. "Although I must confess, I've seen far worse in this job."

A weird possessiveness washes through me the second I realise she's talking about his arse that's no doubt sticking out of his gown with the way he's leaning over me. And thankfully, I manage to swallow any comment I have about her checking him out.

I shouldn't care. I'm here because of his unbearable and unreasonable arse.

Ripping his eyes from mine, Nico reaches behind him to cover up before he lowers himself slowly into...

Shit. A wheelchair.

He must be even worse than he looks if he's resorted to allowing someone to push him around.

"Does it hurt bad?" I ask, keeping my expression neutral.

"Pretty bad, yeah."

"Good," I spit.

All the air rushes out of his lungs, his brow crinkling in confusion.

"Seriously?" I hiss. "You're surprised that I'm pissed? You could have fucking killed us, Nico."

My throat burns as I shout at him.

"Okay, Brianna. Please try and stay calm," the nurse soothes, stepping up to me with a blood pressure monitor in her hand that really isn't necessary. I already know it's sky fucking high.

"You remember what happened?" Nico asks me, still looking like a broken, confused puppy.

"Yes," I hiss.

"I think it's probably time you left me to care for my patient, Mr. Cirillo."

Nico's chin drops as he looks from me to the nurse in shock.

"B-but—"

"Do as you're told for once in your life, Nico, and fuck off."

Lifting his hand, he scrubs his jaw, staring at me as if I'm talking an entirely different language.

Just when I'm about to repeat myself, he speaks.

"Fine," he huffs, wrapping his fingers around the tube that disappears into the back of his hand and tugging.

My stomach convulses as it comes free and a little blood trickles over his skin.

"Nico, that's not—"

"I don't care, Janice. I don't fucking care, okay?"

Before he's finished talking, he's shuffled himself toward the door.

"This isn't over, Siren," he says ominously before fleeing the room, once again leaving both of us with the image of his naked arse.

"Well," the nurse—Janice, I guess—says, still looking at the door. "Not sure that arse makes up for his attitude."

I have no idea if it's whatever drugs they have me on, but for two minutes, I forget about all this bullshit, and I throw my head back and laugh.

And fuck does it feel good. Even if it makes everything hurt like a bitch.

"You needed that, huh?" Janice says once I've come back to reality.

"Like you wouldn't believe. So what's the deal here?" I ask, gesturing to myself.

"Good news. You're going to be totally fine. You've got a concussion, so you'll probably suffer with the effects of that for a few days. Headache, sickness, dizziness possibly."

"What about this?" I say, nodding toward the sling wrapped across my body. "Is it broken?"

"No, sweetie. The surgeon just put that there to support it while you slept. You had some glass fragments go quite deep. They had to remove them and stitch up the lacerations."

"Oh," I squeak, tears stupidly filling my eyes.

Somehow with all the shit that's gone on in my life, I've managed to avoid any serious injuries or surgeries, and I hate that Nico was the one who forced this crap on me.

"Will it scar?" I ask quietly.

I'm not against scars. I truly believe they show strength of character, but I'm not sure this is what I want as a permanent reminder of how much I've overcome.

"I haven't seen beneath your bandage, sweetie, so I can't really say. But I would think there will be some scarring, yes."

"Cunt," I hiss. "Shit, sorry."

She chuckles lightly.

"You're in the Cirillo wing of this hospital. I've heard worse."

I let out a heavy sigh and rest my head back against the pillow while Janice continues to do her job.

"How's your pain?"

"Hurting."

"Out of ten?"

"I dunno. Like... seven. It's bearable." The pain in my chest knowing that Nico did this to us is worse.

"Okay, well I'll give you some more relief, but if you ever feel like it's too much, just tell me, yeah?"

"Sure," I agree.

"Would you like to try eating something?"

I shake my head. "Just water would be great."

I glance over at my toppled jug, not feeling at all guilty about the fact Nico is wearing most of it.

She pours me a glass of water from a bottle she had stashed in her bag and allows me to take a sip, but that's all I manage because the second it hits my empty stomach, I'm convinced that I'm going to barf again.

"If it gets worse, I can give you something for it," Janice promises me.

"How long do you think I'll need to stay here?" I ask, ignoring her offer of more drugs.

"Hopefully just a few days. The doctor will want to ensure your concussion has subsided and your wounds are healing nicely."

"What about Nico?" I ask with a wince.

"That knucklehead can leave whenever he's ready," she scoffs.

"So he's... he's okay?"

Her expression softens at my words. "Yes, he's okay. If you're lucky, the knock to the head might have woken up a few brain cells too."

"We can only hope, huh?"

She tidies her things up and gets ready to leave, but I stop her before she gets to the door.

"Was anyone else hurt?" I ask, a vague memory of someone walking in the road in front of us hitting me.

"No, sweetie. The only witness was thankfully

unscathed and confessed to the whole thing being his fault when he walked out unexpectedly."

My brows pinch in confusion, because all of this was certainly not some random drunk guy's fault.

But as she finally excuses herself from my room, I figure that this is how shit works when you're tied up with the fucking mafia. Murder, extortion and corruption are as everyday as popping to the shop for some milk.

Another of my pained sighs fills the air before I close my eyes.

But I don't drift off for a long time. I can't. My head is spinning with thoughts of the barely dressed guy with the broken nose who left not so long ago with his shoulders slumped in defeat.

5

NICO

"Whardware what the fuck happened in here?" Toby asks a second after the door to my room opens and heavy footsteps sound out. Although, he stops abruptly when the crunch of broken glass fills the air.

Turning around slowly from the chair I'm sitting on that looks out over the hospital grounds, I scan the devastation that is my room.

Janice is going to have a fucking cow when she comes in and finds it.

I lost my shit. Being sent away from Brianna after seeing her so weak and vulnerable broke something inside me. I had—I have—no idea how to handle it other than to lash out.

I was already barely holding it together when I stepped back in here, and then I caught sight of the flowers sitting on the side and the card that was tucked into the top.

Get well soon.
Mum.

The dark and angry beast that lives inside me, that I'm struggling more and more to contain, just erupted, and the next thing I knew, the room was spinning around me as I clutched the wall for support and everything was trashed. The flowers were strewn across the floor along with smashed glass and water. Everything—furniture and medical equipment—was in disarray, some broken, others just flung across the room in sheer frustration.

How dare she fucking turn up here and drop flowers like it shows she cares?

I, obviously, was asleep. But what about Calli?

Was she sleeping too when the bitch turned up?

I bet she thought all her Christmases had come at once when she realised she didn't have to deal with us.

Lucky fucking her.

"I'll go and get something to clean this up," Toby mutters, not hanging around for a verbal response from me.

He doesn't need one.

He knows me well enough to be able to read into things. Most of the time, I fucking hate it. But right now, I don't have the energy to explain or to try and convince him that it had nothing to do with the state I found Brianna in, or the reaction I had to her telling me to leave.

Rejection burns through me. The memory of the resoluteness in her voice cuts through me as if she's saying the words right now, and I sag back into the chair.

My face and body ache, but the pain of that is easy enough to ignore.

What is going on in my chest, though, hurts in a whole new kind of way that I've never experienced before.

Every single inch of me wants to go storming back into the room next door—as much as I'm able to storm anywhere right now—and refuse to leave until she's told me everything that happened in the lead-up to our crash and I've convinced her of how sorry I am.

Although I must admit that right now, fear is dripping through my veins that what I did is going to be unforgivable.

What if I really fucked it up this time?

What then?

What will happen if she does walk away?

Like she should have done weeks, if not months, ago, a little voice says in my head.

A loud growl rips from my throat at the same time Toby pushes back into the room.

"Things are going well, huh?"

I let out a sigh as the sound of him cleaning up my mess hits my ears.

Guilt floods me, but I make no effort to move as the glass clinks as he sweeps it up.

"She kicked me out," I confess.

"Can't say I'm surprised, man."

"I just... I just want to know what happened. I can't remember anything."

"And that's why you're pissed? Because she won't explain?"

"Yeah," I agree with a wince.

"You're so full of shit." He moves around behind me, dumping the glass into the bin and righting other bits of the room. "There is nothing wrong with caring about her, worrying about her."

"I know that," I scoff, my fingers wrapping around the arm of the chair with a forceful grip.

"Sure you do."

Silence falls between us as he continues tidying up before he lowers his arse to the chair opposite mine and places a coffee and panini on the small table between us.

The second I see it, my stomach growls loudly.

"Thought you'd be hungry."

"Janice is withholding food," I mutter, needing to blame someone else.

"She probably decided that you deserved it. Where's Calli?"

"I sent her home. She was wiped."

"Hardly surprising. What happened with Brianna?"

"She woke up, got pissed at me and made me leave."

He stares at me, searching my eyes for the truth he knows I'm withholding.

"I apologised. She wouldn't hear it," I confess painfully.

The last thing I expect him to do is throw his head back and bark out a laugh.

"What?" I demand, confused as fuck.

"She's lying in a hospital bed, Nico. Turning up looking like shit and telling her that you're sorry for being a total fucking idiot isn't going to get you anywhere."

"She saw my arse, too."

"Fucking hell," he mutters, scrubbing his hand down his face. "I swear to God, if you offered to let her suck your—"

"I'm not that fucking stupid. Although if it will help, I'm all for it."

"Jesus fucking Christ, this is going to be harder than I thought."

"What is?"

Leaning forward, he rests his elbows on his knees and holds my eyes.

"Tell me the truth, Nico," he begs. "Do you want her?"

"In my bed, yeah. She's fucking—"

"No," he booms, making me flinch like a fucking pussy.

"I don't mean in your fucking bed, Nic. I mean in your life. Do you want her? Or just what's between her thighs?"

"Like, forever?" I ask, my face screwing up like I'm chewing on a bitter lemon.

The thought alone is fear-inducing.

Spending the rest of my life with one woman. One pussy.

Yeah, the best one you've ever had, and the only one you've wanted since you got a taste of it that night in Hades.

"Yes, dickhead. Forever."

My lips open and close like a fucking goldfish, but no words come out as I sit there staring at my smug-as-fuck best friend.

"You tell me that you want her, that you're serious about her, and I'll do everything I can to help you. But if this really is all just about the fucked-up game the two of you have going on, then you're on your own. I won't stand by and watch as you hurt someone my girl loves like a sister."

"So you're choosing her side in all of this?" I ask, needing confirmation of what I'm hearing.

"I'm not choosing fuck all here, Nico. Although if I were, after everything you've done, I can't deny I'd be leaning her way right now. You fucked up. All you've been doing since the night we first met them is fucking up."

"She doesn't want me," I argue.

This thing between us worked—or not, depending on how you look at it—because neither of us wants anything serious out of this.

"Are you sure?" he asks, effectively tugging the rug out from beneath me.

"Uh..."

"See?" he says, throwing his hands up in frustration.

"You don't even know what she wants because you've never taken a second to listen to her."

"Nothing wrong with preferring to make her scream," I argue.

"You need to make a decision," he says, pushing to his feet. "You either want her, or you don't. Make her yours, or let her go."

Fire licks at my insides as he offers me that ultimatum.

"Oh, so it's come to that now, has it?"

"Yeah, Nico. It has."

Toby hung around for long enough for me to eat the panini he brought, but the atmosphere between us was less than pleasant.

He's pissed at me, I get it. I'm fucking pissed at myself for putting both of us in here, but there's fuck all I can do about it now.

He left with very few words said between us. He didn't need to tell me where he was going. It was obvious that he'd prefer to spend time with Jodie and Brianna than me.

Hell, I'd rather not spend time with me if I didn't have to.

At least the room looked almost back to normal by the time he left, which will hopefully stop Janice from going apeshit at me on her next delightful visit.

I sit there in pain but refuse to do anything about it for the longest time. I deserve it. Whatever went down Friday night was entirely my fault. I know that for a fact. Every time a nurse pokes their head in, I send them away again. Thankfully, most are easier swayed than Janice, who seems to have gone off shift.

Thoughts of Brianna only being next door taunt me the whole time I sit there, but as much as I might want to force myself into her room, I don't. Not yet, anyway.

Voices outside are my first clue that my peaceful and silent torture is coming to the end about three seconds before the door busts open and Theo, Seb, and Alex pile into the room wearing football shirts and covered in mud and sweat.

"Glad to see you've all been enjoying yourselves," I mutter as they steal any scrap of food that I've left, drain my water jug, and make themselves at home on the two free chairs and my fucking bed.

"Well, we didn't think you needed us turning up pointing out all your fuck-ups first thing. The state of your face should have done the job well enough," Theo muses.

"Fuck you."

"Nah, man. Not when you're injured." He grins at me, making himself look like a fucking maniac.

"So how's it going? Janice taking good care of you?" Seb asks, throwing a grape into his mouth. Fuck knows where they came from or how they survived the carnage I caused earlier.

"Oh yeah. She's treating me with a nice gentle touch," I mutter.

"I fucking bet she is. I hope you've told her that your girlfriend is next door," Alex teases, making my teeth grind.

"She's not my girlfriend," I growl.

"Sweet," he sings, hopping to his feet. "I should probably be in her room, making her feel better then."

"Sit your fucking arse back down, Deimos."

A smirk covers his face as he does as he's told.

"It wouldn't matter anyway, she's already full of my cum," I taunt as a memory of me fucking her in the bathroom at Twenty-Five slams into me like a truck. I gasp as it plays out in my mind, lifting my hand to push my hair back as my blood begins to heat. "Fuck." That was hot as shit. How the fuck could I forget something like that?

"Thought you couldn't remember anything," Theo mutters.

"I-I couldn't. That just... hit me."

"Of course he'd remember getting his dick wet over everything else," Seb laughs.

"Shut the fuck up," I bark. "It's not fucking funny, I have no idea why I lost my shit and ended up in that building."

Silence ripples through the room.

"You really don't remember anything?" Alex asks, looking a little more concerned now.

"No."

"Christ, you finally hit your head so hard your brain fell out," Theo quips. "I mean, it's always been quite small so..."

"Anyone packing?" I growl, glaring pure hate at my cousin.

"Seriously, bro," Alex says, leaning forward with a deep frown marring his brow. "You don't remember anything?"

I sit back, trying to force my brain to come up with something.

The image of fucking Brianna into the wall in that bathroom plays out on repeat in my head, causing my cock to swell under my less-than-attractive hospital gown.

"We were in Twenty-Five," I confirm. I don't know how I know. It's not like I've ever been in the ladies' toilets there before, but I know.

"You took her on a date?" Seb asks, almost sounding impressed.

"Does that really sound like something I'd do?"

"No, probably not."

"Probably?" Alex snorts. "Nico wouldn't know dating and romance if it smacked him in the face."

"And you would? Bet you can't even remember the last time you got laid," I tease.

"I can assure you, my memory is a hell of a lot better than yours right now."

"Okay, so who was she?"

"She?" he asks, wiggling his brows like a freak. "Don't you mean they?"

"Fucking hell," Seb groans. "As much as we might all want Alex's dirty secrets, can we focus on the task at hand? You were in Twenty-Five, not on a date with Brianna..." he continues.

"No idea why either of us was there or why I kicked off to the point I drove my car into a building."

When both Alex and Seb look at Theo, I do the same, hoping he can fill in some of the blanks.

"For fuck's sake, throw me under the bus why don't you?" he scoffs.

"What? You were the one who grilled her security until he squealed."

"I didn't grill him. His job is to protect Brianna. He just didn't know he was meant to be protecting her from one of our own."

"So?" I hiss, more than ready to discover the truth about all of this.

"Brianna went out on a date with Brad. She—"

"Brad the bellend," I mutter to myself.

"Yeah, sure, whatever. He took her to Twenty-Five. You followed them."

"I accused her of being a whore because he'd dressed

her up in designer gear and paraded her around like he owned her."

"You watched them eat, then organised for one of our girls to entertain Brad while you followed her to the toilet."

"And now we all know what happened in there," Seb says with a smile.

"So what happened after?" I urge, needing the end of this story.

"We don't know. Phillip said you dragged her out of the building like the place was on fire. It took him a bit of time to catch up with you, but by the time he did, it was too late."

"So what happened in the bathroom, Nico?" Seb prompts.

I think back, but my memory is capped at being inside her.

"I have no idea."

"Did she do something?" Alex asks. "Tell you something?"

I look up, finding his eyes as he silently urges me to think, but I swear I see something else there.

"You know something?" I accuse.

"What? No. I have no idea. None of us did until I woke up to Daemon pounding on my front door."

"Daemon? How did Daemon know?"

"Brianna managed to call Calli."

"Why Calli?" I ask, frowning. Surely if she were going to call anyone for help, it would be Jodie.

"No idea, man."

"Fuck," I hiss. "I fucking hate this."

"Brianna is the only one with the answers," Theo points out helpfully. "You're going to need to stuff down your macho bullshit and figure out a way to get her to talk to you."

"Of course you already know she kicked me out," I mutter.

"We didn't need to be told. It was pretty obvious what her reaction was going to be."

"Just be glad you've got a bed. When I was kicked out in this place, I slept on a row of chairs for a week," Seb reminisces.

"Maybe I'm just not as pathetic as you," I counter as Alex pulls his phone out and taps at the screen.

"Pfft, I fucking doubt that. You were in here sulking like a little pussy when we turned up."

"Yeah, about that. Why the fuck are you here?"

"Isn't it obvious? To see your beautiful face." Seb grins.

"Is it that bad?"

"Yeah, it's that fucking bad," Alex announces happily. "Excuse me," he says before slipping from the room.

"Where the fuck is he going?" Theo asks while Seb keeps his attention on me.

"You haven't looked?"

"No," I confess. When I shuffled my way into the bathroom earlier, I made a point of keeping my eyes on the floor, although it had little to do with the state of my face and more to do with the regrets I'd find lingering in the depths of my eyes if I looked in the mirror.

6

———

BRIANNA

he door closing rouses me from sleep.

Just like before I closed my eyes, Jodie and Toby are sitting beside me, cuddled up on one chair.

I tried to tell her that I was okay, but she wasn't having any of it.

They're leaving tonight, though. Both of them need to sleep in their own bed, not the makeshift one they've spent the last two nights on.

If I didn't already know that Toby was it for my best friend, then I would now, having experienced just a little bit of his support through this. He's barely left her side, and I appreciate the fuck out of him for it.

First the truth about her father, then Sara, and now me. Poor bitch seriously needs a break.

Opening my eyes, I force a smile onto my face in greeting as Alex walks into the room.

If he were wearing anything else, it might take me a moment to figure out which twin it is, but something tells me Daemon wouldn't be seen dead in a Spurs shirt.

"Hey, how's the patient?" he asks, making his way over.

"Yeah, you know. Feel like I was slammed into the side of a building."

He comes closer and, much to my shock, leans over and drops a kiss to my forehead.

"Glad you're okay, Bri," he says quietly before lowering his arse to the spare seat.

"Apparently, I'll be right and rain in a few days, with just some kick-arse scars as a forever reminder of what a dickhead Nico is."

Alex snorts a laugh. "Like he'd ever let us forget that, anyway."

The urge to ask how he is sits right on the tip of my tongue, just like it did when Toby returned from his room earlier, but I swallow it down. I shouldn't care.

"He's okay, Bri," he says, making me question whether those words fell from my lips without my knowledge. Damn drugs. "I can see you want to ask."

My mouth opens to tell him that I don't, but he talks before I get a chance.

"He's in there trying to remember what made him lose his shit."

"Oh," I sigh. It's something every single one of my visitors has asked me in the past few hours. But as of yet, I haven't uttered a word about what made him go nuclear.

Alex knows the truth, though.

He's the only other person in this friendship group who does.

"Jojo?" I ask. "Is there any chance you could go and get me one of those iced frappes from the coffee shop? My throat is raw as fuck."

"Yeah, of course," she agrees, scrambling from Toby's

lap at the chance of doing something useful. "Do you need anything else?"

I open my mouth to respond but quickly close it again.

"Anything," Jodie urges.

"Okay. Could you get me the frappe? Then go home, shower, and take some time for yourselves. But before you come back, could you swing by my place?"

Guilt washes through her expression. "Shit, I should have already got your things."

"Jojo, it's okay. You've been here. I can't ask for anything else. But I'm okay. Alex will keep me company for a bit, won't you?" I say, shooting him a look.

"Of course. And I'm sure the others will find their way in here when they've stopped berating Nico next door."

My stomach knots as I think about him being so close.

"We'll keep him out if you don't want him in here, Bri. You don't need to worry about him."

"I'm not," I lie. Although I'm not sure if I'm more worried about him than I am seeing him. And I hate him even more because of that.

"Is there anything you specifically want?" Jodie asks, dragging my mind back to the task at hand.

I rattle a few things off that I want including my dressing down, slippers, clean underwear and facial products. I'm pretty sure she'll nail it, though.

Silence falls when they finally walk out and it's not until the door is securely closed behind them that Alex finally speaks.

"He found out, didn't he?"

I swallow nervously before confirming what he already knows.

"Yeah. Calli went for a scan—"

"She had a bit of bleeding and Daemon was freaking the fuck out," he supplies helpfully.

"She sent me a photo of it. Nico picked up my phone and it was right there with her name. He lost his shit. Dragged me out, threw me in his car and took off like a lunatic. He wasn't drunk, though, like they've told him he was."

"I know. He was tested. And the guy who walked out has taken full responsibility."

I nod, aware of this fact. "They shouldn't have told him that he'd been drinking when he woke. That was mean."

"He needed a wake-up call, Bri. He's been losing his shit for weeks. Something like this was always going to happen."

"You could have warned me," I mutter.

"You knew it just as well as us, if not better."

"I know. I just wish..." I trail off, not really sure what it is I do actually wish. I probably should be saying that I wish I'd never met Nico freaking Cirillo. But that's not true at all. Sadly. Mostly, I just wish he were hurting less. Or that there was something I could do to make it better.

"We all do," Alex agrees, resting back in the chair and propping one muddy trainer against the lowered rail on my bed.

"Really?" I ask, screwing my nose up.

"Trust me, you don't want me to take them off."

"Lovely."

"So what happens now?" he asks.

"I need to talk to Calli, find out what their plan is. Nico could remember any minute. Is that better or worse than her announcing it to everyone?"

"Umm... pass. He's going to blow his top regardless."

"Surely the second time can't be as bad," I muse.

"Maybe we should take him to a padded cell or something so he can't hurt himself."

"He needs to get the fuck over himself. Calli is an adult who is able to make these kinds of decisions and have everyone who loves her support her."

"I have no doubt that he'll support her, Bri. He loves her something fierce. He just... he's still holding on to the little girl she used to be. Back then, life was easier. He had Evan, Cassandra wasn't the world's biggest bellend, and the weight of the world wasn't pressing down on his shoulders."

"Well, he needs to get over it."

"You know all of this, but everything he's done is because he cares, right?"

"Pfft, Nico doesn't care about me until I'm on my back with my legs open."

Alex chuckles. "Sure, that's a part of it. But there's more. He's refused to accept or acknowledge it, but it's there."

"You're seeing things."

"I'm not," he states confidently. "You wouldn't still be a part of his life if he didn't want you here."

"He's doing a good job of trying to get rid of me."

"Nah, he'd freak the fuck out if you actually turned your back on him," Alex says confidently.

"Well, maybe we're about to find out, huh?"

"For real?" he asks, sitting forward, looking more concerned than I've seen him in a while.

I shrug. "I'm not making decisions while I'm high on meds. I'm hoping things will start to clear soon and I'll have an epiphany."

"If you do, send one my way," he says absently. I'm not sure I'm actually meant to hear it, but I do.

"What's going on, Alex?"

"Shit," he hisses, averting his eyes as he pushes his fingers through his bedraggled hair, dragging it back from his brow. "Nothing. Forget I said anything."

Refusing to look at me, he keeps his eyes locked on my bed.

"I'm not going anywhere, and I literally have nothing else to do if you need an ear. You know I can keep secrets."

Finally, he looks up at me, but just as his lips part, the door opens.

"Brianna, what a sight for sore eyes," Seb sings with a wide smile.

Alex breathes a sigh of relief that he's been saved from having to tell me anything as Theo follows Seb into the room to greet me.

I keep my eyes on the door for a beat too long, cluing them all into what I'm thinking.

"He's not coming. A nurse turned up to give him an intimate wash," Theo laughs.

"She looked fucking terrifying, I'm not sure I'd want her anywhere near any of my intimate parts," Seb adds as he hops up on the end of my bed while Theo takes the cot Toby and Jodie were in.

All three of them study me as if I'm about to offer to go and wash Nico's balls.

"So you lot couldn't be bothered to shower before visiting, huh?"

"We thought you'd be missing us too much to care," Seb says, squeezing my ankle in support.

"Not sure I'd quite say that."

The three of them fall into easy conversation around me. To start with, I join in, offering a few words here and there, but eventually, my eyelids start getting heavy again and I have no choice but to close them.

"We should go," Theo says, noticing that I'm half asleep.

"No," I say, reaching my hand out for someone but also no one at the same time. "Stay. I like having company."

"The girls are heading over in a bit. They've been at Mickey's."

"Great, so they're going to turn up as sweaty as you three then."

"Here's hoping," Seb says, and without opening my eyes, I can picture the shit-eating grin on his face as he rubs his hands together in delight.

"Addict."

"Takes one to know one. I know what you've been doing in the lift of our building, Miss Andrews."

My eyes pop open just in time to see Theo smack him around the back of the head.

"He didn't," I breathe, although I'm not sure why I bother because of course he fucking has.

"Uh…" Alex starts, rubbing the back of his neck awkwardly. To be fair to him, he's the only one who has the decency to look any kind of embarrassed about it.

"Oh come off it. You literally fucked right in front of Toby and Jodie the night you met," Seb announces. "You don't have a shy bone in your body."

"Maybe not, but I like to be the one who chooses what to show others. Don't tell me, you've seen the videos from the library too?"

Silence falls around the room as the three of them stare back at me in shock.

"The library?" Seb asks, looking half shocked and half impressed.

"Fucking hell," I mutter. "I should just let you leave."

"What did Nico do to you in the library, Bri?" Alex asks

eagerly, sliding to the edge of the chair in his excitement to hear the answer.

"Nothing you need to be watching."

"Damn, Miss Andrews, that's—"

"Going to get me fired?" I interrupt.

"What? No, never. The boss practically owns Knight's Ridge. He'd never let Middleton kick you out for something as trivial as fucking Nico in the library."

"Trivial?" I blurt. "We're not two students going at it in a moment of passion. I'm his fucking teacher."

"Nah." Alex waves it off as if it's nothing. "It'll be cool, Bri. Don't even sweat it."

"This is my job. Literally, the only thing I've ever wanted to do and—"

"Nothing is going to happen, Brianna," Theo assures me. "You will finish your training at Knight's Ridge without any issues, no matter how hard Nico tries to make your life."

"Great," I mutter. "Maybe I should just defer the rest of my training to next year." Even as I say the words, disappointment floods me. I don't want to do that. I want to be working my first real job in September, not still training. But with everything that's happened, and now this accident, I can't help but wonder if it's what's going to have to happen.

"Don't talk shit. We'll make sure you pass no matter what happens."

"Oh no," I say, staring dead into Theo's eyes. "I'm not accepting any easy ride just because my best friend is fucking one of you."

"I'm not offering you a free ride, and if I were, it wouldn't be because of Toby and Jodie. You're one of us now, Brianna."

"But—"

"I don't give a fuck about what's going on with you and Nico. That will sort itself out one way or another. But you're not going anywhere anytime soon, so you'd better get used to it."

My lips open and close like a fish as I stare back at the enigma that is Theo Cirillo before I concede on this argument and whisper, "Thank you."

"Not necessary. We look after our own, Brianna. Now, we're going to let you get some rest. If you need anything, even if it's to get rid of that idiot in the middle of the night, call us, yeah?" he says, nodding to my phone on the table beside me.

"Okay," I agree.

"Hey, is the video of the two of you—"

"Shut the fuck up, Deimos," Theo snaps, reaching out and dragging him to the door by his arm.

"See you soon, Bri."

I'm pretty sure that the second the door closed after the guys, I passed straight out.

When I come back to again, it's dark out and my room is quiet, although there is evidence that Stella and Emmie have been here like the guys promised.

Sitting on my table is a whole array of chocolates, sweets and other treats along with a ripped-out page of a sketchbook. At the top it says, 'flowers die but ink lasts forever'. Beneath it is the most stunning black pen drawing of lilies and roses, along with a pretty small flower I can't name. There are skulls, crowns, and what I think is snake skin all intertwined and the words, 'Be fierce. Be unstoppable. Be you', laced through it.

My eyes are glued to it for the longest time, picking out all the intricate details. It's incredible. Emmie's definitely inherited her father's talent and is going to make a fantastic artist one day—if she's not too busy popping out little Cirillo heirs, that is.

I'm busy chuckling to myself as I picture Emmie as a doting housewife and mother when the door opens and a nurse I'm yet to meet invites herself in.

"Hi, Brianna. I'm Maria. I've come to change your dressing."

I fall quiet, still clutching Emmie's drawing in my hand as she goes about what she needs to do.

I tell myself not to look when she's lowered my gown and pulled the dressing from my shoulder and upper arm, but I can't help myself.

My gasp of shock rings through the room and Maria's eyes instantly shoot to mine.

"It's not as bad as it looks, I promise."

Ugly stitches cover my red, blood-stained, swollen skin.

"I find that hard to believe," I choke out as she discards the old dressing and pulls a clean one from its packaging.

"It will scar, Brianna. But you'll be amazed by how quick it will improve."

I blow out a breath as I fight to keep my tears from spilling down my cheeks.

"Here, it's time for some more painkillers." She passes me a small white cup with some tablets inside and I make quick work of swallowing them down. With any luck, they'll send me back to sleep, and when I wake, I'll be in my flat and all of this will have been one big nightmare.

"We'll get you up and washed tomorrow," she tells me after cleaning up.

There's a part of me that wants to argue, to tell her to do

it now and then go and get my discharge papers, but there's a bigger part that's too exhausted to even bother trying, so when she leaves with the promise of bringing me some dinner soon, I just let her go.

I'm only alone for five short minutes before a knock sounds out on my door, and a head that I wasn't expecting pokes into the room.

"Brad?" I baulk.

"Hey, baby. How are you feeling?"

Something seriously uncomfortable settles heavily in my stomach as he walks inside and closes the door behind him.

The last time I was with him, he was about two minutes away from being seduced by that hooker. The fact he never came to find me only leads me to believe she did her job in distracting him.

He moves across the room silently, but his eyes hold mine firmly. If he's feeling any kind of guilt over what happened, then he isn't showing it.

"So the Cirillo wing?" he finally asks after lowering himself to the chair closest to me. "You've sure got some friends in the right places, huh?"

"I-I—"

"It's okay, baby. I'm glad you're being looked after."

He sits forward and takes my hand in his.

"I'm sorry, Brianna. If I had any idea that you weren't feeling well then—"

"W-what?" I stutter, thrown for a loop by his words.

"I spoke to Jodie. She said you left because you were sick."

"Right," I mutter.

"You should have called me," he says softly as if he

wasn't all over some glamorous blonde two seconds after I left the restaurant.

"I didn't want to ruin your night."

"Taking care of you would never ruin my night."

My lips part to say something. Surely, he doesn't really believe the bull that's falling from his lips? It's been two days since we were in Twenty-Five, and as far as I know, this is the first time he's tried to see me. Guilty much?

I probably should feel some kind of jealousy, knowing that while I was in surgery having my arm stitched back together, he was probably balls deep in some hooker. But honestly, I just don't care. I'm mostly shocked he fell for it. Although, knowing Nico, he wouldn't have hired someone who would have been easily cast aside if he was serious about keeping me away from Brad.

"I came by yesterday," he confesses as if he can read my thoughts, "but you were sleeping. I brought those, though," he says, nodding to a vase of flowers I hadn't really paid any attention to.

"Thank you."

Over the past few weeks, there's been a disconnect growing between us that wasn't there when we first met, but now, as we sit here awkwardly, it's only getting wider.

"What did you do with the rest of your night?" I ask, unable to let it lie.

"I ran into an old friend. I'm ashamed to say that I didn't come looking for you as fast as I really should have. I came by your flat, but you weren't there. Then yesterday morning, I had a message from Jodie saying there had been an accident and you were here. How are you feeling?"

"I've been better," I confess, although I quickly realise that isn't just because of what's happened, but also the company.

7

———

NICO

After the guys left, I gave up fighting my exhaustion and crawled onto the bed, although sleep didn't come as quickly as I was hoping.

I didn't take the last lot of painkillers and it was starting to show.

But I was done feeling drowsy, even if sleeping did make it all go away.

It was time to stop hiding like a pussy and try to sort my shit out.

And that needed to start with talking to Brianna.

I just wasn't sure how that was going to happen.

For all I knew, she had a security guard on her door to stop me from seeing her. The guys never said anything, but I wouldn't put it past one of them to agree to protect her. She seems to have them all wrapped around her little finger just like she does me these days. Alex especially seemed keen to see her, something that's still pissing me off.

I know he wouldn't do anything like he threatened, but the thought of him hanging out in there with her makes fury bubble away in my stomach. I want to be the one in there making sure she's okay. It's my fault she's here in the first place, I want to try to make it up to her in any way I can, and if that means being her little bitch while she recovers, then so be it.

When I wake, the lights are on, illuminating the room, and there's a nurse pottering around.

"Ah, good evening, Nico. How are you feeling?"

"Great," I lie. Truth is, I ache like a bitch and all I want to do is curl up in a ball and block it out. "Any chance of getting discharged? I'm done here."

"Uh…" She looks like she's on the verge of saying no, but something about my expression must change her mind. "As long as you've got someone who can keep an eye on you at home, I don't see why you can't be recouping there instead of taking up one of our rooms."

"Careful, you're starting to sound like Janice. It's not possible for you to hate me that much."

Her chuckle lets me know that she's aware of Janice's distaste of all of us.

"I'm sure she'll be thrilled to see that you're off her patient list when she clocks in in the morning."

"Hey, you might even get a raise out of it," I tease.

"Let me check you over, then I'll go and get the paperwork sorted. You have clothes, right?"

"Sure do," I agree, glancing at the bag in the corner of the room that I found after the guys left.

They might be pissed off with me, but that didn't stop—Theo, I guess—from swinging by my place and grabbing me some things.

"You can shower, and I'll redress your nose when I come back."

I sit still while she does her thing and before long, she's leaving me alone once more, not wanting to waste a second more of my time in this room, I pad through to the bathroom and turn the shower on.

Finally, I shed the ugly fucking gown and step under the water.

A groan rumbles deep in my chest as the hot water hits my skin, and I stand there for the longest time letting it pound down on my shoulders. If only it could wash the events of the last few days down the drain with it.

Part of me not wanting to take those painkillers was the hope that more memories might return. I thought that remembering taking Brianna in the bathroom was going to be the beginning of the night emerging for me, but even after Theo explained what he knew, I was no clearer as to why I left that place like it was about to blow up around us, dragging Brianna behind me.

What happened inside that bathroom, Nico?

But no matter how many times I ask myself that question, the answer doesn't come.

The nurse comes back not long after I emerge from the bathroom, fresh and ready to take on the world. Or at least, ready to attempt to get myself back into Brianna's room. That's about the only battle I've got the energy to fight right now.

She redresses my nose as promised, something that I think is totally unnecessary, but she point-blank refuses to let me leave without it. So, I sit back and humour her, grinding my teeth to the point that I'm sure I'm about to crack one every time she even gently touches my nose.

It's not the first time I've broken it. When you find yourself in the middle of fights as often as we do, it's kind of inevitable that it'll go eventually. But I swear it's never hurt this fucking much. It brings tears to my eyes, something I have no desire for this nurse to witness.

The second she's done, I stuff my pitiful few possessions into a bag and walk out of the room without looking back.

The corridor is empty as I turn toward the room next to mine.

I'm fully prepared to just march in and give her little choice but to talk to me when her door opens and a man in a sharp navy suit emerges.

With the lingering effects of the drugs flowing through my veins, it takes me a couple of seconds longer than it should to recognise him as Brad the bellend.

The moment I do, my grip on the bag in my hand tightens until my nails are digging into my palm and I have no choice but to lean against the wall beside me to keep me up.

Sensing my presence, he looks over his shoulder.

His eyes immediately lock on mine, and the fire in them makes my breath catch.

He can't know what I did Friday night. Lola is one of our best girls and she knows her life wouldn't be worth living if she betrayed us. But that doesn't mean he hasn't figured me out.

Hell, for all I know, he could have clocked me long before I made my presence known to Brianna.

But so what if he did? The boring fucking banker is hardly going to go up against me. He might be dull as fuck, but something tells me he's not stupid.

Without a word, or even slowing his pace, he turns back toward where he's going before rounding the corner and leaving me standing there as if I just imagined the whole thing.

The moment I recover, I move toward Brianna's door. Finding it not quite closed properly, I press my palm against the wood and push it open.

What I find inside cracks my chest right open.

She's sitting on her bed with her head in her hands, her shoulders shaking as she sobs, her soft whimpers filling the silence of the room around her.

"Siren," I breathe, my legs carrying me deeper into the room long before my brain has registered the decision. She just calls to me on that kind of level.

Without asking permission, I lift her covers and climb into bed with her, twisting her around so she's half sitting on me as I wrap my arms around her trembling body and tuck her head beneath my chin.

I'm not sure I've ever comforted anyone before. Okay, maybe Calli when she was a kid, but that's different. I have never, ever comforted a woman I've been fucking. I'd be more likely to send them away crying. Hell, I can guarantee I have.

"It's okay, Siren," I soothe quietly, silently terrified that the sound of my voice will break through her distress and she'll immediately release me and demand I leave.

Thankfully, though, that isn't what happens.

Instead, she clings to me harder as her tears begin to soak through the fabric of my shirt.

"I've got you, Bri," I say, dropping a kiss to the top of her head, holding her as tight as I dare with that massive bandage I know she's rocking on her upper arm. The thought of hurting her terrifies me despite the fact it's too little too late.

Eventually, she calms down, but much to my surprise, she doesn't release me. And after a few minutes of quiet, I shift painfully so that I can lie back on her bed and bring her with me.

She rests her head on my chest, right over my heart, listening to it pound embarrassingly fast beneath her ear.

Her hand slips under my shirt, the heat of it burning me from the inside out as she holds me. She throws her leg over mine, linking us together in every way possible. But still, no words leave her lips.

There are a million and one things that are going unspoken between us, but it seems for right now, she's content on just having this moment. And I can't lie, I'm pretty fucking happy with it too.

Eventually, her breathing evens out and her body goes limp as she drifts off into sleep.

But I can't. I can't take my eyes off her or let my mind settle.

Is this what Theo, Seb, Toby, and Dae—nope not going there—have every night? Do they literally cuddle up to the same person and fall asleep like this?

If it is, then I gotta say, it's not as bad as I thought it would be.

Fuck. Who am I right now?

I've slept with women before... Okay, that's a lie. I've slept with Brianna before. Everyone else has been sent away the second I was done with them. But we've always just passed out on our own sides of the bed in sated, sweaty, exhausted heaps. Most of the time, I've forgotten she's there until she scares the shit out of me the next morning, or I wake up with a hazy memory of her presence but find that she's already escaped, like she's been prone to doing recently.

But this... this is... nice?

A silent laugh peals from my lips as I laugh at my own ridiculousness.

Maybe I should have just taken those pills.

But my own thoughts are nothing compared to the

amusement I get when both Jodie and Toby slip into the room a little while later with bags in their hands.

Jodie's eyes open so wide I'm sure they almost pop right out of her head at the sight of me with Brianna in my arms.

"Did someone give her a lobotomy while we were gone?" she finally whispers while Toby just studies our position with interest.

"You're funny," I hiss back.

"She literally wanted to kill you the last time I so much as mentioned your name. How did you go from that to… this?"

I give her a one-shouldered shrug, because fuck if I know.

"Brad the bellend came to visit," I confess quietly. "I saw him leave and then found her crying."

"He made her cry?" Toby asks, frowning.

"Nah," Jodie says. "There's no way he made her cry. She doesn't care enough about him—"

"Aside from his magnificent cock," I point out, quoting what Brianna has said to me many, many times when taunting me with her regular fuck buddy.

"I'm not sure even that is good enough to make her cry."

"Anyway, she fell asleep like this, so…"

"You look cute," Toby says, amusement dancing in his eyes. "How's it feel to finally discover the joys of snuggling?"

"Fuck you," I hiss, although there's no heat in the threat, and if his smile is anything to go by, he hears every single one of my unspoken words.

Yes, I'm enjoying this, dickhead. Get over it.

"Okay, well, we just brought her some things. If you're okay with her, we're going to head home, but I'll be back before I start work tomorrow."

"Do you have any idea when she's going to be discharged?" Toby asks.

I shake my head.

"Can you find out?" I ask, needing her out of here just as much as myself.

"Sure. And we'll set up our guest room."

"Wait, what?" I blurt.

"We're not letting her go home while she's still recovering," Jodie says, rolling her eyes at me as if it's obvious.

She's right. The thought of Brianna going back to her flat alone doesn't sit well with me either. But honestly, Toby and Jodie's place isn't much better.

So what would you prefer? That she moves in with you?

"Got any other suggestions?" Toby asks with a knowing smirk.

"N-no. I guess I hadn't really put much thought into what happens once we're out of here." Lies. Such lies.

"Sure you hadn't. If you think of any, do let us know," he teases.

"Just go, before you wake her up," I hiss, more than ready to be alone with my siren once more.

8

BRIANNA

I wake hot with sweat coating my skin, my cheek pressed up against something that isn't a pillow, and my fingers wrapped around—

"Oh my God," I gasp as my brain wakes up and I realise exactly what I'm holding.

I tug my hand free, but it gets stuck against the elasticated waistband pinning my wrist down.

A deep growl rumbles beside me, and my heart jumps into my throat as reality slams into me.

"Fuck," I bark, tugging harder and successfully freeing my hand from Nico's sweats and moving it as far away from his rock-hard cock as I can get it.

"Party pooper," he grunts, his voice rough with sleep.

I blink a few times, letting my vision clear properly, and I find that for the first time since waking here, I actually feel a little more alive.

But then I remember the reason I've woken up so hot, and I turn to my bedmate.

"What the fuck do you think you're doing?" I snap, desperately trying to ignore how hot he looks with eyes puffy from sleep, the longer-than-usual stubble on his jaw and his full li— *Do not go there, Brianna. He is the reason why you are here with stitches in your arm.*

"Siren—"

"No, don't fucking *siren* me. Get the hell out of my bed," I demand.

"Babe, come on."

"Babe? Are you actually fucking serious right now? Do you think that just because I was hugging your dick in my sleep, I've forgiven you? That all of this is okay and we can just go back to how things were?"

A deep frown forms in his brow, and I swear whatever hope that might have been in his eyes dissolves into disappointment. My God, did he actually think that? The sight sends a pain shooting straight through my heart. But it's nothing compared to my lingering headache and pain from my stitches, so it's easy to push it aside.

"You're unbelievable. Your dick might be good, Nico. But it's not that fucking magical," I spit, then frown as a smirk twitches at his lips. "What?"

"You seem to be feeling better this morning, Brianna," Maria says with an amused lilt to her voice.

"Oh for the love of God," I sigh, falling back on the bed. "I haven't done anything with his dick," I confess as she pulls my notes from the end of the bed and studies them.

"It's not my place to judge if you have. Just remember those stitches are only so good."

She glances up at me, her eyes crinkling as she fights the smile that wants to break across her face.

"That sounds like all the permission I need."

"I thought you were leaving, young man," Maria says, turning her eyes on my bed buddy.

"He is," I confirm, giving his shoulder a less-than-gentle

shove. "He's not welcome in here. I don't know when he snuck in."

Maria glares at him.

"Janice is in. I can get her if you need—"

"N-no, that won't be necessary," Nico stutters before rearranging himself beneath the sheet and climbing out of bed.

Maria winks at me as she comes closer.

"How are you feeling?"

Ignoring the elephant in the room who decides against leaving as requested and instead lowers his arse to the chair, I focus on my nurse.

"Better, actually. I... umm..." I hesitate, not wanting to confess this. "I feel like I slept better."

I don't need to look over to know he's got a smirk pulling at his lips.

"That's great. Are you ready to get up and washed?"

"Yes," I sigh, more than a little desperate to clean all this sweat and grime off me.

"Need any help with that, Siren?" Nico asks.

"I think I've got it, thank you. But if you could, you know, fuck off, that would be great."

Maria snorts a laugh, and much to my disappointment, she doesn't immediately follow my lead and kick him out.

Great, he's also got the staff under his control.

I swing my legs off the bed and press my feet to the floor. Thankfully, my body complies, allowing me to shuffle toward the bathroom, forgetting that I'm returning the favour of flashing my arse at Nico as I go.

"Damn, Siren. You really know how to torture a guy," he groans behind me.

My fingers twitch to reach up, release the bow holding the gown together and let the whole thing drop to the floor to really punish him. But fear of the sight of my bandaged arm ruining the whole thing stops me. I fucking hate it. I've never been scared to make a stand, but this is what he's reduced me to.

"What are the chances that I'll find you gone when I emerge?"

"Slim, Siren. Really fucking slim."

Thankfully, Maria closes the door behind us, stopping Nico from hearing the growl of frustration that rips from my lips.

"If you really want him gone, I can make it happen in a heartbeat. But something tells me that—"

"You're on his side?" I hiss.

"What? No. I don't know enough to even consider joining a side here. I just sense that the two of you need to talk."

"Why did I need to get the hopelessly romantic nurse? I bet Janice wouldn't have been so sympathetic." Honestly, I don't know which nurse Janice is, but I've heard her name mentioned a few times. There are few people the guys are wary of, but she's one of them. I like her already.

"Oh, guaranteed. He'd already be out in the car park if she had anything to do with it."

I allow her to untie my gown and gently pull it from my body. Then she wraps my dressing with something akin to cling film before gesturing for me to sit on a stool in the middle of the shower.

I want to argue and insist that I can stand, but something tells me I'm going to need all my energy to deal with Nico once this is over.

The warm water rushing over my skin feels incredible, and I lose myself in the sensation for the longest time. But eventually, Maria ruins it.

"Do you want to talk about it?"

"About what?" I ask innocently.

"Him. I popped in a couple of times overnight. He was just lying there, watching you sleep. It was the sweetest thing."

"Nico doesn't do sweet, so you can get that thought out of your head right now."

She sighs as she sets to work on washing all the grime out of my hair with the finesse of a damn good hairdresser.

"Every guy can do sweet for the right girl, Brianna."

"Then I'm not the right girl. What Nico and I have, it's... toxic. Hence, how we ended up here."

"It was an accident," she argues, having probably heard the bullshit they're all spewing about what happened.

"Sure."

"The way he looks at you, Brianna, there is no way he'd ever do anything to hurt you."

"Trust me, Maria, you don't know him like I do. Hurting me is his favourite hobby." Her fingers still in my hair. "Oh shit, no. Not like that. You don't need to be calling the cops on him or anything. He's just a dickhead boy who only thinks with his cock."

"If you look a little deeper, you might find there's more to him than that."

"Yeah, a fuck load of hurt and anger that he tries to hide from the world."

"But you've seen it. Doesn't that tell you something?"

"Yeah, that I'm a fucking fool who can't help myself. If only he was useless in bed," I muse, much to her amusement. "You're enjoying this too much."

"Not at all. But you weren't wrong earlier. I am a hopeless romantic, and I always root for the bad boys, because it's true what they say. They can be tamed, but only by the right woman."

I look over my shoulder and narrow my eyes at her.

"You've got a bad boy, haven't you?"

She chuckles. "Yep, he wears a cut and rides a motorcycle."

I shake my head. "Reaper?"

"I had a suspicion you might have heard of them."

"I guess that explains why you're willing to treat all these twisted motherfuckers."

"That's my life in a nutshell," she laughs. "I think you're done here. Ready to go and deal with your bad boy?"

"No, not really."

"Well, you've got a few hours to make a decision, then I'm getting you discharged and you'll be able to lock him out of your life if you want."

"If only it were that easy."

"If he fights for you, you know he's the one."

"Or he's as blinded by my pussy as I am his dick."

Maria laughs. "If it doesn't work out, you'd fit right in with the Reapers."

"I think having one corrupt organisation in my life is enough. Thanks, though."

"I can see why you and Emmie are friends."

"Did you see her yesterday?"

"Briefly. I was just starting as she left. She's the perfect example of what I mean about taming the bad boys."

I throw my head back and laugh. "Oh yeah, she has Theo right where she wants him."

"So put his cousin in the same place," she says, letting me know that she's more than aware of the family dynamics going on within the Cirillos.

After Maria changes my dressing, I dress in a pair of

leggings, a bralette, and an oversized zip-up hoodie that Jodie apparently dropped off for me while I was sleeping last night. Someone else who knows exactly how comfortable I was cuddling into Nico's side.

I remember Brad leaving after an awkward-as-fuck visit where I knew that he'd fucked a whore Friday night, and he tried to make out like he didn't. I should have just called him out on it. I don't care where he's sticking his dick, as long as it isn't in me. But forcing him to be honest would mean that I'd need to offer him the same in return, and I had zero desire to talk about my life truthfully.

A rush of cool air floods the room when Maria pulls the door open, and my stomach knots and my heart jumps into my throat as I think about walking out there and facing Nico once more.

I was exhausted when Brad left, and I don't know if it was just that or hormones or what, but I broke. It was coming. I'd felt more and more unstable every time I woke up, but watching him walk out was the final straw.

I just don't remember ever allowing Nico to be the one to comfort me. But I know he did.

Part of me loves that he was there when I needed someone. But there's another part that hates it. And that part understands why he freaked out like he did last week when he crumbled in my arms.

Sucking in some confidence, I hold my head up high, pulling the door wider, and step out.

Only... he's not here.

I stop in the middle of the room, watching as Maria plumps my pillows and tidies up.

"Have faith," she says, able to read the expression on my face.

"He did the right thing," I force myself to say, all the while fighting those tears back once more.

What the hell is wrong with me?

Unless it has something to do with Jodie, I don't get emotional over people. Ever.

Avoiding the bed—the memories of how I woke in it with him are still too fresh—I take myself to the reclining chair that Maria has returned to, looking out the window.

"Here," she says softy. "It's time to step back into your life."

She places my handbag on my lap, and I let out a heavy sigh.

"Nothing can be worse than being stuck in here, Brianna. Pull up those big girl knickers. You'll have people who care who want to hear from you."

I don't argue with her. What's the point?

"I'll be off shift soon, but someone will be back with breakfast shortly," Maria says as I focus on the bright summer morning beyond the window. I yearn to feel the warmth of that sun on my skin, have the sweet scent of the flowers and fresh grass in my nose instead of the sterile hospital air.

"Thank you," I whisper, still battling with my emotions.

"Hopefully, you'll be gone by the time I'm back later on. Good luck, yeah?"

I sigh.

"Have faith," she repeats. "There's no way he left you."

"He should. It would be easier for both of us."

"Nothing worth fighting for is ever easy, Brianna."

With that ominous bit of advice hanging in the air between us, she squeezes my good shoulder in support and leaves my room.

Silence wraps around me like an unwanted hug, and I quickly find myself pulling my phone from my bag as a distraction from the ache in my chest from knowing he escaped the second my back was turned.

It's dead, and after a root around the bag Jodie delivered, I find the charger and plug it into the wall and wait for it to power up.

It starts buzzing almost immediately with messages, emails, and social media notifications.

I have messages from Calli assuring me that help is on the way and to just hold on, that nothing matters other than us both being okay.

There are guilt-filled ones from Brad telling me that he'll come visit as soon as he can and that he's sorry. All of it feels totally pointless. If he cared, surely, he'd have ignored that woman's advances and come to find me instead of allowing me to be dragged out of that place by a raging bull.

I have ones from Joanne letting me know that she's thinking of me and assuring me that she's here for anything I need, but that Jodie has told her I'm okay and to give me space, which I appreciate.

I scroll through my socials, more of a distraction than anything else, because the less I think about Nico leaving, the better.

I hate him for what he did. For how he freaked out and almost got both of us killed. But I'm finding it harder than ever to convince myself that that is true.

Admitting defeat, I drop my phone into my lap and rest my head back against the chair, anxiety flooding me as I think about what's going to happen next.

But before I get too lost in the what-ifs, the door opens and the scent of coffee hits me almost immediately.

My mouth waters and I look over, expecting to find a

nurse standing there with a tray, but the image that appears before me is very different.

"You left," I blurt like an idiot as Nico's long legs eat up the space between us.

"To get you a decent breakfast."

My eyes drop from his exhausted and bruised ones in favour of what he's holding, and I gasp at the box I find.

"B-Betties?" I ask, the memory of ordering a boxful on Friday morning hitting me.

"Your favourite, right? And a skinny caramel latte with an extra shot, because I thought you would probably want the boost."

My mouth opens and closes as my heart tumbles in my chest.

Damn him for being so sweet.

He drags one of the chairs over before lowering his arse to it and ensuring his knee bumps against mine.

Sparks immediately shoot up my legs from the innocent touch.

Prick.

My eyes shoot to him once more, just in time to catch the smirk that covers his face.

Damn him, he knows exactly the effect he has on me even when I'm actively trying to despise him.

"How do you know I like Betties?" I ask.

"Things might be hazy, but I haven't forgot everything, thief." Unlike when he previously accused me of stealing from him, anger doesn't darken his eyes. Instead, I'm pretty sure there's pride within them.

"You owed me," I state. "I'd had the world's worst hangover because of you and that fucking stunt you pulled in the library."

"You loved it." He smirks again as he opens the box and offers me first pick of the pastries hiding inside.

"Why am I not kicking you out?" I mutter to myself.

"Because you know I'll take these with me. And let's be honest, you'd be lonely and we both know how much you like looking at my pretty face."

"Pretty?" I scoff. "Have you looked in a mirror recently?"

His amusement instantly vanishes.

"No, actually. I haven't."

"Why? I thought you'd want to see how 'hard' you look," I tease.

He sucks in a breath that's full of a million secrets I don't think he has any intention of letting free.

But then he shocks the shit out of me by quietly saying, "Because all I'll see is a fuck-up staring back at me."

"Nico," I breathe, instantly regretting sympathising in any way.

Jesus, this man fucks with my head.

Ripping his sad eyes from mine, he thrusts the box at me again to force me into making a choice before he steals a croissant and stuffs it into his mouth.

A tense silence falls between us while I battle with demanding that he keeps talking and kicking his arse out.

"The nurse is discharging me."

"I know. I've already spoken to Toby and organised a lift back for you."

"You don't need to do that. I'm more than capable of getting an Uber home."

9

NICO

The second I confessed to being a failure, I knew she wasn't going to kick me out.

Sure, she wanted to. But she wouldn't.

She couldn't.

Because for as vicious as she can sometimes be, Brianna cares. She cares more than I think she'll ever admit, but I see it every now and then. And even more so when she's feeling vulnerable.

Her walls are lowered right now. Maybe not as low as they were last night when she allowed me to comfort her, but still lower than normal.

"You're not going home, Siren."

Her breath catches as she reads between the lines of that statement.

"I am not going to your place," she snaps.

"Wouldn't even have suggested it, babe."

"Can you quit with that?" she demands. "I'm not your babe, your siren, your anything."

Her words cut, but I can hardly argue with her.

I've spent all these months trying to convince myself

that she's nothing to me. I have no idea why things feel so different just because we've both had something akin to a near-death experience.

Now, I'm not suddenly saying that I want her to be something. I guess I'm just less against it.

I'm pretty sure I hit my head harder than the doctors think I did in that crash.

"Sure," I mutter, reaching for another pastry just to give me something to do and an excuse not to leave.

My face hurts like fuck while chewing, but even with that I can admit that these are the best pastries I've had in my life. No wonder she risked my wrath to order some last week.

"Jodie wants you to stay at her and Toby's place for a bit while you recover." I expect some kind of response, an argument, but she just sits there picking at her pain au chocolat.

The silence stretches on. I want to say it's uncomfortable, but it never is when we're together. Even if shit is tense like it is now, something still feels right.

She's still withholding secrets, and while it might piss me off, I know I'm not in any position to start making demands.

"I haven't forgiven you," she says eventually. "Last night... Last night was a lapse in judgement fuelled by painkillers and exhaustion."

"Sure. Yeah. I know," I say, trying to keep any of the hurt that's slicing through my chest at bay.

Holding her last night, watching her sleep, knowing that in some small way I was helping was... well, it was everything. I knew it wouldn't go very far in the grand scheme of things. That she would wake up and regret it. Much like I did in the moment I discovered that breaking down in her arms not so long ago was real and not a dream—or nightmare—like I'd first believed.

"Nothing about any of this is okay, Nico. I need you to know that."

"Trust me, I do. I'm going to make it up to you, though."

"You don't even know what you're making up for. You don't remember what you did and why."

"I'm sure I'll figure it out eventually. I'm starting to remember bits."

"Oh yeah?" she muses with a mouthful of pastry.

"Yeah. I remember railing you against the wall in the bathroom and how fucking incredible your cunt felt wrapped around my cock."

A bitter laugh falls from her lips.

"Of course that's what you remember."

"Fucking heaven, ba—" I swallow the rest of that word when she shoots me a cutting look. "Just saying that I'd never forget getting inside you for long."

"Not really the most important part of the evening though, was it? How about the woman you paid for to distract my date? Or the fact you sat there all night stalking me like a grade A creep? The whole situation was fucked up long before you even tried to kill me."

"Trust me, I wasn't trying to kill you. I'd never—"

"Could have fooled me. It was fucking terrifying, Nico."

"I'm sorry."

"It doesn't fix anything though, does it?"

I shake my head. "I don't know what else to say, to do."

"There isn't anything. You fucked up. Over and over again, you fucked up, Nico. Until you sort your own shit out, there will be no making up for any of the crap you did to me. You're a mess. And I'm not just talking about your face."

"I know," I whisper as the door opens on the other side of the room and a nurse walks in, quickly followed by Jodie and my sister.

Calli's eyes narrow as she studies me sitting here with Brianna. They swirl with anger and relief, but that relief isn't enough to stop her being pissed with me.

I get it, I do. But when the fuck did she decide to take Brianna's side over mine?

"You're all good to go, Brianna," the nurse says softly as Jodie and Calli step deeper into the room.

"What are you doing here?" Calli snaps.

"Nice to see you too, Sis," I quip.

"He brought me breakfast," Brianna explains. "I'm humouring him."

"Ouch," I say, lifting my hand to cover my heart. Although, damn, it's not all an act.

"You're barking up the wrong tree if you want sympathy, Brother." Calli scowls at me before turning to Brianna, her face morphing into a smile. "Ready to blow this joint?"

I can't help but snort a laugh.

"You're not bad-arse enough to talk like that."

She flips me off over her shoulder but otherwise ignores me.

"We've got a car waiting for you downstairs, and Jodie's guest room is ready for a queen."

"Can't I just go home?" Brianna asks, although I can't help feeling like it's the last place she really wants to be right now.

"No," Jodie states. "I want you close. So does Mum. She's been freaking out."

Brianna's lips part to argue, but she clearly thinks better of it.

I watch as the two of them get all of Brianna's things packed away and prepare for her to leave.

To take her away from me.

My eyes trail my sister around the room as something niggles in the depth of my mind. There's a memory there wanting to break free, but whatever it is, it's just out of reach.

"What?" Calli snaps, sensing my attention.

"N-nothing."

Her eyes shoot to Brianna, practically confirming what I'm suspecting.

Whatever happened Friday night had something to do with my sister. And something tells me that it involves whatever she refused to tell me about when I stormed into her flat last week.

Unease tugs at my insides.

I know that Calli is right. Just because I'm her brother, it doesn't mean I need to be party to all her secrets. But when it's something serious enough to make me damn near kill myself, then yeah, I think I deserve to know.

I continue looking between the two of them as they finish up.

"Ready?" Jodie asks Brianna as she steps up to her.

"Yeah, I'm ready to get away from all this."

She holds my eyes and I hear her unspoken words loud and clear.

She wants to get away from me.

I force myself to hold her stare as she practically shoves her hand into my chest and rips pieces from my heart.

"Let me get the bags," I say, needing to be some kind of useful.

"We've got it," Calli says, throwing Brianna's duffel over

her shoulder. "In case you hadn't noticed, we don't actually need men."

I stand there like a spare part as Calli holds the door open and Jodie loops her arm through Brianna's as they turn to leave.

I watch them go, my heart sinking into my feet.

"Siren?" I say right before they disappear around the corner.

She pauses, and for a second, I don't think she's going to acknowledge that I've said anything.

But then, right when I'm about to give up hope, she looks over her shoulder.

"I'm sorry. For all of it."

She holds my eyes for a beat before lifting her chin in defiance and turning to walk away.

"Fuck."

———

My finger hovers over the button for Toby's floor in our building, aware that that's exactly where she is right now.

The temptation to follow them, to demand I ride back here with them was massive, but I stuffed it all down and stayed exactly where I was until they had to have been in the lift and making their way out of the hospital.

I stumbled back, dropped my arse back in the chair and lowered my head into my hands.

That's where the nurse found me sometime later when she returned to flip Brianna's room ready for another patient.

With very few words, I grabbed my very few belongings and headed out.

Unlike Brianna, no one was here to pick me up.

Everyone was at school, or looking after her. It's where they should be, but I'm not sure I've ever felt their absence quite so strongly.

Where's your mum, Nico? a little voice asks.

If Dad were here, I wouldn't be alone right now.

Although... none of this would have happened if he were still here. Losing him was what started this domino effect of disasters in my life. He was the trigger. The huge black hole of loss that's still growing inside me is the reason for all the hate, anger, reckless decisions, and brutal acts against Brianna.

It's wrong, all of it.

But I need it. I need the thrill, the excitement, the risk. I need it to feel alive. That rush when I took her in the library, the buzz of adrenaline that someone could catch us. I fucking crave that.

The fear in her eyes when I threatened her future. As fucked up as it was—as it is—it made me feel alive and reminded me that while I might be drowning, I'm still here.

Although, ultimately, my obsession, my addiction to her almost killed both of us.

Despite her actions last night and this morning, that final look held a thousand words, and 'stay the fuck away from me' was right up there with some of the most important ones.

Am I going to be able to do it, though?

Can I walk away knowing that she's living right beneath me, suffering because of me? Can I do the right thing and give her what she's asking for?

Probably not, no.

Thoughts of her, of all the things I've put her through, is the final thing I need to convince me to lift my hand and press my finger to the button for the top floor of the building instead.

She doesn't need you, Nico.

Doing the right thing for once, I leave her the fuck alone.

I push through my front door with a heavy heart. It feels like a lifetime since I was here, not only three days.

As I shuffle through the hall and emerge in my impressive penthouse, it doesn't take me long to realise that it's spotless. Jocelyn must have spent almost all weekend here.

That thought only makes the ache in my chest that much worse.

She might not have been sitting by my bedside, but she was here for me. Here in a way others haven't been. She really is a fucking angel.

Abandoning my bag on the table, I head for the kitchen.

Tins line the counter, and I don't need to pop the tops to know that I'll find an array of my favourite homemade goodies.

Instead, I zero in on the note.

Nico,

Calli told me what happened. Silly, silly boy.

I can hear her voice as clear in my head as if she was standing right beside me. I hang my head in defeat, because she's not wrong.

I hope you're feeling better, even if the regrets of your actions are smacking you upside the head right now.

I've made your favourites for your recovery. You will find more in both your fridge and freezer. If you need any more or fancy anything different, you know where I am.

I've also organised something for you for tomorrow morning. Your buzzer will go off at 9 a.m. sharp. Be up, be ready, and be brave.

Everyone needs you right now, Nico. None more so than Calli.

If you need anything, call me.
All my love,
Jx

"Fucking hell," I mutter, my voice cracked with emotion as tears burn my damn eyes.

I'm not sure Jocelyn will ever truly understand what she means to us.

The fact she's standing by us right now while our worlds are turning to shit is everything.

I might hate that she's still working for our mum, but I can only assume that there's a reason. Jocelyn isn't stupid. She also isn't greedy, so I know she isn't hanging around for the money. Hell, Calli and I could match her pay and keep her for ourselves, but something tells me she wouldn't be up for it. For some reason, she loves her job and is more than willing to put up with our mother. It's more than can be said for her own children.

Finally, I pull the lid off one of the tins and stuff a homemade chocolate chip cookie in my mouth before starting my coffee machine and taking myself through to my bedroom.

The worst of the nightmare I caused this weekend might be over, but there's still a fucking long way to go until I'm going to feel anything like my old self again. Honestly, I don't even know where to start to try and dig him out. But I know I have to.

This weekend was a wake-up call that I really shouldn't have needed.

If I continue on this angry, self-destructive path, then I'm only going to end up in one place.

The ground beside Dad. And while there might be parts of that fantasy that sound all kinds of appealing, it's not enough to make me want it more than life.

I'm not ready to give up yet.

I've got revenge to deliver on the Italians and a woman who deserves the best apology I can give her... If I can figure out what that might look like.

10

BRIANNA

"We've got you," Jodie whispers in my ear as we step inside the lift, feeling me trembling beside her.

"I know," I say weakly.

Honestly, I know that walking away from Nico like that was the right thing to do. Really, I should have sent him away the second I woke and found him beside me, but for some reason I couldn't do it.

But letting him escort me back to his building really wasn't going to happen.

I haven't forgiven him, and I certainly haven't forgotten, and I have no desire to allow him to believe that could happen anytime soon. Right now, I'm struggling to forget just how reckless he was Friday night after he dragged me into his car.

He was pissed, I get that.

I've been keeping a huge secret from him. But it wasn't my place back then, and it's still not my place now to tell him what I know.

But I also can't deny that I should never have allowed him to find out quite so easily.

Leaving my message previews on was stupid, and I was asking for trouble. But hindsight is a great thing.

The second Calli hits the button for the ground floor, she comes to stand on my other side.

"He deserved that."

"Yeah, I know. Doesn't mean it was easy, though." A pained sigh slips past my lips and the three of us ride the rest of the way in silence.

I'm guided out of the lift and straight through the double doors where there's a blacked-out SUV waiting at the curb.

Memories of trying to walk out of the lift in their building not so long ago and walking straight into Nico slam into me. Despite knowing that he isn't here, that he couldn't have possibly beaten us down here, the temptation to turn around and check burns through me.

"Brianna?" Jodie questions, and it's not until her voice flows through my ears that I realise I've stopped.

Finally, I look back. But just like I already knew, he's not there.

He hasn't followed me.

And he's not going to either.

He read my silent warning loud and clear, and he hasn't come to chase me.

Pain cuts through my chest as I picture his face before I turned away from him.

"S-sorry. Let's go."

Her eyes narrow as she studies me. She might think I'm crazy for caring about him, but also, I know she gets it. What she went through with Toby was... less than conventional, so I know she'll never judge me for doubting my decision to walk away from him. But that doesn't mean I'm going to voice it right now.

"You sure?"

"Yeah. I'm ready to be done with this place."

She leads me toward the car where Calli is waiting with the door open. There's a suited driver standing just a few feet away, but he's paying us little attention. Instead, his eyes are everywhere.

The thought of us being in danger makes my heart jump into my throat.

"Ignore him," Calli whispers when I get closer. "The guys are just being overprotective."

As I awkwardly slide into the back of the massive car, I can't help but think of everything I've done since that Italian strike the night of Calli's mum's birthday. I've been walking around the city like everything is normal.

That was really stupid... wasn't it?

"Are you okay?" Calli asks, climbing in beside me.

"H-has something happened?" I whisper. "With the Italians?"

"No, not that I'm aware of, why?"

"That guy, he looks like security."

"He is." She leans in a little closer. "Don't tell Stella or Emmie, but the guys have details on all of us right now."

"What?" I gasp as Jodie joins us.

"Take it as a compliment," she says, squeezing my hand in support.

"Even me?" I ask, my brows knitting together.

"Who do you think found you both so quickly on Friday night?"

I open my mouth to respond, but there are no words.

The second our driver drops into his seat, he pulls away

from the curb. But one glance over my shoulder lets me know that we're not alone.

Another blacked-out SUV trails behind us.

"This is serious, isn't it?"

Calli reaches forward and presses a button that makes a screen appear, blocking us from the driver.

"It always has been," she says finally when we're in the privacy of our little cocoon. "But with every day that passes, the risk of something happening is getting higher."

"The guys are getting antsy. And finding out about you and Nico hasn't helped," Jodie adds, proving she's listening. Not that she couldn't while we're stuck in the back of a car.

Guilt rushes through my veins, but I refuse to apologise for something that was not my fault. I wasn't the one who lost my shit Friday night and drove through the city like a madman.

"Something needs to happen before they all blow."

"Can't they make the move?" I ask, totally unaware of anything involving what's going on now.

"They could. But they don't want to."

"So we're just sitting ducks?"

"Pretty much. They're testing out how good their leak is by allowing false intel to go back to the Italians. Only time will tell if the leak is a part of the Family who've been informed."

"Check you out, Miss Cirillo," I say, trying to force a little lightness into my tone. When we first met, she was a frustrated, sheltered princess desperate to embrace the mafia blood that runs through her veins. It seems that with the help of a certain bad boy, she might just have got her wish.

"I love not being kept in the dark," she confesses. "And Daemon tells me everything. Well, probably not everything but I trust him, and I know there will be things that he can't divulge, even to me. But I finally feel like I'm where I'm meant to be, that I've found my place."

"Well, it looks good on you. You're glowing," I tease, making her eyes almost pop out of her head in panic.

I can't help but laugh at her.

She can freak out all she likes, but she's on borrowed time, and she knows it.

"This all feels like it belongs in some *Die Hard* movie," I mutter, going back to the most pressing issue.

"Get used to it," Calli says. "Something tells me that it's going to be worse before it gets better."

Silence falls between us, the weight of the danger we're all in sitting heavy on my shoulders.

"What happened with Brad?" Jodie suddenly blurts, leaning around Calli to look at me.

"Umm..."

"Nico said you cried when he left."

I can't help but laugh. "I wasn't crying because he left, I can assure you of that."

"What did he say?"

"Was his usual charming, apologetic, boring self."

Jodie chuckles while Calli frowns.

"Who is he?"

"Some guy I've been hooking up with for a few months. He's..."

"Boring?" Jodie offers.

"Boring but a great fuck. He's easy. And he—"

"Wants to marry you and have his little boring babies with you."

"Seriously?" I hiss at my best friend.

She shrugs innocently. "You know it's true. He's totally smitten with you."

"So smitten he was too busy getting distracted by a hooker Friday night to come and rescue me?"

"Bri, you can't expect him to suddenly be the exact kind of man you've always told him you don't want just because you got cornered by Nico."

"I..."

"You know he's about as faithful to you as you are to him. He probably—and mostly correctly—assumed that you'd hooked up. Hell, for all we know, he could have seen Nico before you did."

"No chance. He would never have let me leave if he did."

"Well, whatever happened, he bought my lie about you being sick and leaving easily enough."

"Probably because he knows it's bull. He might be dull as duck shit, but he's not stupid," I mutter.

"Shouldn't you just end it?" Calli asks innocently.

"You think I haven't tried? He's persistent as fuck." When we... well, fuck, and I'm reminded of his better bits. "Maybe I should just leave. Start over somewhere new and leave all these irritating men behind me."

"You're joking, right?" Jodie snaps.

"Maybe. Seems like it would be a good solution."

"No it wouldn't," Calli states before Jodie gets a chance. "And anyway, I'm pretty sure my brother would follow you to the end of the Earth."

"No he wouldn't," I scoff, refusing to believe her words are true.

"Did you not see his face up there when we left? I've only seen that much hurt on it once before, and that isn't a night I ever want to repeat."

A heavy silence falls around us, I'm sure all our

memories go straight back to that night. The rubble, the scent of death and destruction.

I squeeze my eyes closed as I remember watching Nico drop to his knees beside his father and bow his head as reality slammed into him and disbelief and grief gripped him in a tight hold.

It was agonising to watch. Something I wouldn't wish on my worst enemy.

"This is going to eat him alive, Bri. Hurting you... it's going to fuck him up even worse than he already is."

"It's his own fault."

"No," she says sadly. "It's mine."

"Why? What did you do?" Jodie asks in disbelief.

Calli shakes her head as the blacked-out car we're sitting in pulls into the underground garage of the guys' building.

"It's what I haven't done," she confesses before the engine cuts out and the door is opened for us.

I make sure to get a good look at the four suited men who are standing around the garage, ensuring our safety, as a sense of foreboding washes through me.

"Are we even safe here?"

"One of the safest places in the city, Miss Andrews," one of the guards confirms.

I want to say his words make me feel better, but I'm not entirely sure they do.

We're ushered toward the lift, leaving the guards behind.

As we ascend, a pained sigh leaves my lips, and Jodie reaches for my hand.

"I know you'd rather go home. But I can look after you."

"I know," I whisper. Not to mention that I'm probably safer—something I really don't want to think about.

The second we step inside Jodie and Toby's flat, Joanne comes rushing toward me and pulls me in for a tight hug.

"I'm okay, Jo," I say lightly as I rub her back, sensing that she needs the support more than I do right now.

"I know. I know. Doesn't stop me from worrying though. You're one of my girls," she says with a smile and tear-filled eyes as she moves back.

"I promise, I'm okay. Who doesn't love a few bad-arse scars anyway?" I ask, hoping my voice doesn't give me away.

I'm scared about what my arm is going to look like. I know it's vain and that it's only skin. But I can't help it.

What if it's ugly?

What if Nic— no. What if it freaks guys out and scares them off?

Forcing those depressing thoughts down, I allow Joanne to wrap her arm around my waist and lead me further into the flat.

"We have the guest room all ready for you. Everything you could possibly need is in there. Toby tried buying Jodie a nurse's outfit for you, but you'll be glad to know I put an end to those discussions."

"Oh yeah?" I ask, shooting a look over my shoulder at my best friend. She returns my knowing smirk with one of her own. Oh yeah, she has that little outfit.

"They've promised to be very well behaved while they have a guest. Haven't you, Jojo?"

"I have no idea what you're talking about, Mum," Jodie says innocently.

"You can't fool me, child. I remember all too well what life with a bad boy is like."

"Jesus," Jodie mutters while Calli and I snigger.

"Where would you like to rest?" Joanne asks me. "Sofa or bed?"

"Is it just us?" I ask.

"For now. The guys are at school."

"Out here then. I'm not sure I've got enough energy to deal with everyone yet."

Joanne gets me settled on the sofa with more pillows than I know what to do with and a thick fluffy blanket that would probably be too much in winter let alone this time of year.

The girls rally around me, plying me with drinks and snacks and keeping the conversation light while Joanne is listening. But as nice as it is to spend time with them, the elephant in the room that is Nico never leaves.

As the minutes tick on, all I can think about is where he is, what he did after we left, and if he's okay.

I hate it. I should be able to shove him aside. All of this is his fault.

But he never leaves.

I guess I should expect it really. It's been the same way since the first night we met. It wasn't just my body he got inside that night. It was my head too.

If only he would leave as fast as he entered.

Eventually, school comes to an end and Toby, Seb, Alex and Theo appear to check in on me.

I appreciate the gesture, but I don't hang around long, favouring hiding in the luxury that is Toby's guest room. This one room is bigger and fancier than my entire flat. But as nice as it is, I long for my own space. Peace to allow myself to try and process what happened Friday, and to figure out a way forward.

I figure I'll give myself today to mope, then tomorrow, I

need to pull up my big girl knickers and figure out a way to get back on with life.

Just because I've spent the weekend in the hospital, it doesn't mean that the world has stopped. I still have a school placement and my final assignment to worry about—assuming what happened last week hasn't come to light, and I've been thrown out of both Knight's Ridge and my course.

"The boss practically owns Knight's Ridge. He'd never let Middleton kick you out for something as trivial as fucking Nico in the library." Alex's words from the other day come back to me, and all I can do is hope they're true.

Just a few weeks and then the next chapter can start.

Despite knowing that the guys are back from school, no one knocks on my door or even pisses me off by letting themselves in.

It hurts. But I get it.

They were all with Brianna in Toby's flat, I have no doubt.

And they should be. She deserves all their attention and support right now.

Despite still being exhausted and emotionally and mentally drained after the past few days, I barely got any sleep.

Every time I closed my eyes, I could see Brianna's defiant 'don't fuck with me' expression before she walked away from me. It's literally haunting me. And knowing she's so close and easily accessible is the worst kind of torture.

I have full access to every single flat, cell, and torture chamber in this building. I could easily slip into Toby's place and into his guest room without anyone knowing.

I wouldn't even need to wake Brianna. I could just sit and watch her sleep like I did in the hospital.

"Jesus," I mutter, scrubbing my hand down my face.

I'm so fucked.

If I thought I was losing my mind when it came to this woman before, it has nothing on what's going on in my head now.

My need to see her, to know she's okay, to fucking apologise again and to beg forgiveness is growing more and more out of control. They're things I've never even considered doing before now.

I'm still lying there God knows how long later, being a pathetic arsehole, when my buzzer goes off.

My heart jumps into my throat. My first thought is that it could be her on the other side of my door. It's a pointless fantasy but one I cling onto for a few seconds before Jocelyn's note from yesterday comes back to me.

"Shit," I hiss.

If anyone had left me instructions like that, I'd ignore them. But this is Jocelyn, and I can't.

I drag on a pair of sweats and pull a clean t-shirt from my drawer. I'm still wrestling my arms into it when I get to the front door, and I pull it open without checking the peephole.

"Uh..." I stutter when I find an attractive young woman standing before me, wearing what is obviously a very expensive suit and carrying two takeout coffees.

"I understand that yours is a cappuccino with an extra shot and one sugar," she says matter-of-factly before brazenly striding into my flat without an invitation.

"Uh..." I say again like an idiot as I close the door behind her and follow her down into my living room.

"Nico?" she asks, turning to me after placing the takeout cups and what I now see is a bag of pasties—not from Betties—on my coffee table.

"Y-yeah."

"I'm Jade, Jocelyn's niece. I'm also a bereavement counsellor."

My heart thunders so hard in my chest, I'd be surprised if she couldn't hear it from the other side of the room.

My lips part to argue, but she cuts me off as if she can read my mind.

"I know you don't want me here, Nico, and I know that you're going to fight this. But I also know that Jocelyn wouldn't have called me in if it weren't entirely necessary."

"I'm not sure you should even be in the building," I confess.

"I've been fully vetted, and I'm under a very, very strict NDA. You don't need to worry. I've worked with the Cirillo Family before. You can trust me."

"Can I though?" I don't mean to say the words out loud, but if Jade is offended by them, then she doesn't show it.

"Here," she says, holding her phone out to me. "Call your boss if you're sceptical. He knows I'm here. I spoke with him personally yesterday."

"Fucking hell," I mutter as I march over and drop onto my sofa.

She doesn't say anything for the longest time, and with my eyes closed as I rest my head back, it's almost possible to believe I just dreamed all that and she was a figment of my imagination.

But then she shatters that illusion when her voice fills the air around me.

"I understand that things have been rough recently, Nico."

I scoff at her words.

"And I also know that talking to me is probably the very last thing that you want to be doing right now. But I can promise you, talking about this, about your dad and your loss, will help."

My fists curl, my short fingernails digging into my palms until I'm almost certain I've drawn blood.

Lifting my head, my eyes find hers and she silently encourages me to say something.

I suck in a breath, remembering those words on Jocelyn's note.

Be up, be ready, and be brave.

Easier said than done, Jocelyn.

Then I think of Brianna downstairs, possibly still in bed and suffering because of me, and before I know what's happening, my mouth opens and words start pouring out.

Jade stays all morning. Mostly, she just listens as I talk about Dad and the giant black hole he's left in my life, but every now and then she'll ask a question that forces me to think hard, to feel more, and to rip the already painful wound open even deeper.

It's fucking agony, talking about everything I've lost, the hatred and anger it's left me with, and all the stupid fucking decisions I've made since that night—most of which revolve around one woman.

By the time she pushes to her feet to finally leave, I'm emotionally drained in a way I'm pretty sure I have never been before.

My heart aches, my muscles are all so tight I'm sure some of them are on the verge of snapping, and my head is spinning. If I didn't know any better, I'd think I'd just woken up with a killer hangover with the way the room is spinning.

"Jocelyn has booked me in for weekly sessions with you," Jade informs me, much to my horror.

Although I can't deny that despite my pain, there is a part of me that feels lighter from having spoken to her.

"Okay," I say, as much to her shock as it is mine.

She pulls her diary from her handbag and we schedule weekly sessions on Thursday evenings.

She lets herself out of my flat with only a few more words, leaving me on the sofa.

And that's where I wake up later that afternoon with my skin slick with sweat from the ray of sunshine I'm lying in.

My heart still hurts as I replay everything I spoke to Jade about. I want to hate Jocelyn for setting that up, for forcing me to open up and spill some of the ugliness that lingers inside me, but I can't find it in me to do so.

So instead of being angry, I roll off the sofa and pad through to my bedroom where my phone is still sitting on the bedside table.

Ignoring the notification and messages from the guys, I find my chat with Jocelyn and shoot her a simple message.

Nico: I was brave. Thank you.

As if she's waiting for it, the message shows as read immediately and the little dots start bouncing.

Jocelyn: I'm proud of you, Nico. I know you might not feel like it right now, but you're going to come out of this stronger.

A small smile twitches at my lips because, despite everything, I'm able to begin to believe that she might be right.

Closing down her message, I open up the group chat with the guys, read through the jokes and memes they've sent throughout the day, and then go to Toby's chat.

Toby: How are you feeling?

Toby: Bri is good. Jodie is taking good care of her.

Toby: But she still hates you.

"Arsehole."

Nico: Thanks for that. I hope you've had a shitty day.

Lowering my phone, I stare across the room at my reflection in my mirrored wardrobe doors.

I chose them specifically because they give me full view of the bed. I knew they'd supply me with endless enjoyment as I railed nameless, faceless girls night after night. But as my own reflection blurs to nothing, there's only one woman I see there.

Memories from the past few weeks slam into me and I forget about the world as I watch us roll around my bed together. My cock hardens as I picture myself spreading her thighs and eating her until she's screaming, then flipping us over and letting her ride me until she falls apart once more, her pussy clamping down on my dick as she uses me for her own pleasure.

"Fuck, yeah," I grunt, falling back in my bed and pushing my hand beneath my waistband.

My length is like steel as I wrap my finger around it, precum already leaking from the tip.

I pump myself a few times, losing myself in the

sensations as I force my body to believe it's not my hand but the images of my siren that are playing out in my mind.

I'm almost at the point of no return when I suddenly stop. I release my grip and blow out a long breath.

What I did earlier, confessing my vulnerability and inability to deal with my loss, was for her.

I promised myself in that hospital that I'd find a way to make this right, to prove to her, and the others, that this won't beat me.

Pulling my hand free of my sweats, I push to my feet, my hard cock taunting me from behind the tented fabric as my balls scream in frustration with my lack of release.

But there's something I need to do more than jerking off along like a loser.

I rummage through my school stuff until I find a notebook. Grabbing a pen, I sit on my bed and rest the pad against my thighs.

"Fuck it," I hiss. I've already allowed myself to bleed out once today. Why should I allow the pain to stop so soon?

I tap my pen against the top of the paper for a few seconds before I force myself to stop overthinking what I need to say and just write.

Siren...

My heart is racing and I'm sweating once again when I finally lower the pen and notebook to the bed.

I stare at my own messy writing, second-guessing myself.

She probably doesn't care about any of it.

Hell, I might never be brave enough to even allow her to know it exists, but I do feel better now I've got it out.

Leaving it where it is, I push from the bed and walk into my bathroom, only to find another mirror that brings back more memories of her.

My cock is aching once again by the time I've shaved the mess covering my jaw and stepped into the shower, but still, other than cleaning up, I don't touch myself.

Is it some fucked-up kind of self-torture? Yeah, most definitely. But fuck it. It feels like the right thing to do. The next time I come, I want her to be in control of it. And not because I've given her little choice, but because she wants to. I want to say because she's forgiven me, but I'm not sure that's ever truly going to happen. But I can't see a future for us where we're not going to have to see each other, so she needs to be able to put up with me in some kind of form, and that includes the pleasure we both love taking from each other so much.

I'm redressing when my phone buzzes on my bed.

Walking over, I find a message in our group chat. I almost ignore it, assuming it's just another bad joke from Alex, but when I spot Theo's name as the sender, I pay it a little more attention.

Theo: My place now. There's news.

My heart jumps into my throat and my hand trembles like a pussy as I unlock my phone and tap out a quick message that I'm on my way.

I pocket my phone before folding up my letter, scribbling Brianna's name across the front of it and stuffing it into my jeans.

Theo's flat is in silence when I let myself in. I'm hardly

surprised that I'm here first, seeing as I'm the only other person on this floor.

As I make my way down the hallway, I start to wonder if he's even here, it's so quiet, but when I emerge into the living space, I find him standing in his kitchen with his palms on the counter and his head bowed.

Nothing about the way he's standing fills me with any kind of joy.

"What's going on?" I ask, hating how unsure my voice sounds.

He startles at my words, letting me know that he wasn't aware of my presence, but by the time his eyes meet mine, he's pulled his mask on and gives nothing away.

It's too late, though. I've already seen it.

He looks behind me as if he wants to wait for the others to get here.

"Fuck them, bro. Just fucking tell me."

"They've taken the bait."

All the air rushes out of my lungs at his words.

"They believe Daemon and Ant are at the other location?" I ask, just to confirm I didn't miss something else while I was out of it this weekend.

"Yep. Enzo has heard them talking... planning."

"When? How? What are they—"

A door slams behind me before voices fill the space, cutting off my questions. They're going to have exactly the same ones in about thirty seconds, so I may as well wait.

"Hey, what's poppin'?" Alex asks like the moron he is.

Seb, Toby, Daemon and Ant spill into Theo's flat behind him, all their eyes landing on Theo who's now walked out of his kitchen.

"The Italians are getting ready to strike."

"Oh fuck, seriously?" Seb asks almost in disbelief as he

drops onto Theo's sofa as if he hasn't just announced we're about to go to war.

I guess it is almost an everyday occurrence at this point.

"Enzo just fed back the intel," Theo says, nodding at Ant.

"So what's the plan? Ambush at the warehouse?" Daemon asks.

"Warehouse?" I ask, realising that they've been working on this while I've been out of action.

"I believe so. Boss is working on a plan."

"Are we one hundred percent sure they've actually fallen for it this time?" I ask, hating that I need to vocalise the question at all. But after our last shit show of a plan, I think we should all be seriously sceptical of anything we're sent into.

"Yes," Theo states confidently. I want to believe him, I really fucking do, but I lost the most important person in the world the last time we walked confidently into a what we believed was a well thought out plan.

My eyes fall on Daemon. He was the only one who was suspicious of the night of my mother's birthday party.

If only we'd listened to him.

"D?" I ask.

Theo's back instantly straightens at my simple question. But fuck him. I'm not willingly putting anyone else I love at risk. It is not happening.

Daemon nods.

"Okay."

"Unbelievable," Theo hisses.

"I'm sorry. Did you want to run into another ambush that we might not walk away from?"

"We get it, man," Alex says, trying to defuse the

situation before I poke the bear too hard. "But this is solid. Enzo has our backs."

"Fucking hope you're right."

"So what's the plan?" Toby asks, trying to steer the conversation back instead of my insecurities.

I guess there's something else I can talk to my new shrink about.

Fuck me, what is my life coming to?

12

BRIANNA

Despite my arguments that I was fine, Jodie insisted on having the week off work so that she could look after me.

Totally unnecessary. I'm more than capable of looking after myself. And it's not exactly like I've been good company. I've spent most of the past few days locked in her guest room.

The guys have been here to hang out. The guys minus Nico. It's been nice, I guess. But I can't help feeling like an outsider.

It's not their fault. They've all fully embraced me as a part of their little family. But I hate that he feels like he can't hang out with his friends because of me. I mean, I'm assuming that I'm the issue.

I've almost asked about him a million times, but for some reason, the words get stuck on my tongue. So now, he's turned into an even bigger elephant in the room than he was before.

My final image of him in my hospital room still refuses to leave me. Calli was right. He looked wrecked as I turned my back and walked away from him. But what was he really expecting? He'd almost killed me.

I blow out a breath as I stare up at the stark white ceiling above me.

I want to go home. I want to restart my life, but every time I mention leaving, Jodie gets this sad look in her eyes and I buckle.

For the most part, I've kept my phone turned off since getting back from the hospital. Everyone important knows where I am, and I've been in contact with both my uni tutor and Melissa via email.

Thankfully, both of them just wished me a speedy recovery and said they're looking forward to my return. I guess that's something to smile about.

It's about the only thing.

Whatever is going on with the guys and the Italians is getting serious.

They haven't said anything around me, and when I've asked Jodie, she doesn't have much more detail either. Whatever is going on is top secret, and to be honest, I'm happy with that.

I have zero desire to dive deeper into Nico's dangerous world.

At some point, Jodie knocks on the door to deliver me a hot chocolate before she heads to bed with Toby.

I say all the right things, but I don't really feel it. I'm shutting down, and the longer I keep myself locked inside this room, it's getting worse.

She can see it too, but her concern over me being alone is overriding it.

I've told her that I'll stay until Sunday, but then I'm returning to my life and my job.

I've already lost more time at school than I want to; I

refuse to miss any more and risk not completing my training.

Grabbing my laptop from the end of the bed, I pull up the job hunting I started earlier.

I've earmarked a few teaching jobs that caught my attention. Now, I need to figure out if I'm actually brave enough to apply for any.

I study each school's website until my eyes burn.

The rest of the flat is in silence. I know that Jodie and Toby are being courteous because they have a guest, and I hate that they're putting a stop on their usual wild sexploits so I don't have to endure it. I'm grateful, though. There's no better way to really nail home how little action you're getting than listening to your best friend get railed across the hall.

My phone taunts me on the bedside table when I lean over to turn the light off.

I hesitate, questioning myself over whether I should turn it on or not.

Would he have even bothered to message?

He sure hasn't tried to force his way in here to see me, so I don't know why he would.

In the end, my curiosity gets the better of me, and I reach for it, powering it up.

The second it connects to Toby's WiFi, messages and notifications begin popping up.

But there isn't a single one from Nico.

Unfortunately, most of them are from Brad and his guilty conscience.

"Get a grip, Brianna. He doesn't care," I hiss at myself, hoping that hearing the words will stop me from obsessing over him.

It's been three days since I laid eyes on him. I should be relieved.

I swipe at my screen angrily to turn my phone back off again, irritated that I lowered myself to that level in my need to hear from him.

You are a strong and independent woman, Brianna Andrews. You do not need validation from Nico or any other man.

I know that. I do. But I also just want to check in on him.

I glance over at the door. It would be so easy to slip out of the flat and head upstairs.

Is he even in? Or has he already forgotten all about me and is out with Alex trying to find a woman to spend the night with?

It certainly would have been what he was doing when we first met.

A lot has changed since then, though. And as much as I might want to tell myself that he's out living his life, something tells me that he's not.

He's not the same person as he was the night he fucked me six ways from Sunday in Hades.

Hell, I'm not the same person either.

I fall back onto the bed, my eyes on the ceiling once more, wondering if he's up there. And if he is, what he's doing.

I don't remember drifting off, but it happens faster than I was expecting seeing as I've barely left this room for the past two days. Apparently, healing from my near-death experience is a full-time job.

The first thing I sense when I begin to come to is that I'm being watched.

My heart jumps into my throat and my body immediately begins to burn up.

But then, a deep, rumbling growl rips through the air, one I'd recognise anywhere, and I relax. Although, not a lot.

Cracking my eyes open, I find that the room is almost too dark to even see him. I can just make out his dark form in the shadow.

I fight to keep my breathing even so he doesn't realise I'm awake.

What the fuck is he doing here?

He groans again, and my eyes drop to his crotch, expecting to find him jerking off like a creep over my sleeping body.

But despite not being able to see where his hand actually is, there is no movement.

He just... sits there.

My eyes are heavy as fuck as I lie there in the dark, watching him watch me.

The temptation is so fucking strong to let him know that I'm aware of his presence, but I don't move a muscle despite the fact my body is burning up beneath the duvet.

My lower stomach clenches with desire, my pussy getting slick with arousal like it always does when he's around.

He's like fucking kryptonite.

I don't want him. Most of the time I can't stand him. Yet my body speaks to his like no other I've ever met.

I shift slightly, holding my breath as I test the water.

I've no idea if the movement is too slight, if it's too dark, or if he's not really paying attention, but he doesn't so much as flinch.

Does he not care about being caught?

"I'm so fucking hard for you, Brianna," he says so quietly I almost think I'm imagining it. "I miss you."

I suck in a sharp breath at that confession. It hits so much different from his first one.

"Nico," I sigh, his name nothing more than a breath on my lips as I brazenly roll on my back, kicking the covers off my heated body.

"Siren?" His raspy voice is a little louder this time.

"If you're going to watch, I might as well give you a good show, huh?"

I slide my hand down my stomach, tucking my fingers beneath the lace edging of my knickers.

"Oh fuck," he grunts, sitting forward and lifting one hand to push his hair off his brow.

A gasp rips from my lips when my fingers find my swollen clit.

Pushing lower, I dip my fingers into my pussy before dragging them back up and spreading my own juices over my heated flesh.

"Nico," I moan, knowing that it'll drive him crazy as my back arches.

A growl rips from his lips. "You're a tease, Siren. Show me properly," he demands.

But to his irritation, I don't follow orders this time. Instead, I up my pace.

I have plenty of experience with getting myself off, and I know exactly how to touch myself to ensure I'm heading toward that cliff in only seconds.

I rub my clit harder, my pussy aching to be filled.

My free hand reaches up and cups my breast, pinching my nipple when I find it hard against the confines of my tank.

"Fuck. You're mesmerising, Siren."

"Nico," I cry, getting closer and closer to that ledge.

"Are you going to come while I'm sitting here watching you be a filthy whore?"

"Yes, yes," I cry, my body locking up as I prepare to throw myself right over that cliff.

But just before I freefall, everything comes to an abrupt stop.

I blink against the darkness as my hand is ripped from my underwear and thrown to the side, no longer needed, before my knickers are dragged down my thighs. He pulls one of my feet free but leaves them hanging on the other as he presses his palms to the inside of my thighs and spreads me wide for him.

"Fucking missed you, Siren. Been dying without you," he groans, blowing a cool stream of air against my sensitive skin.

"Please," I beg, reaching for him and twisting my fingers in his soft locks in the hope of dragging his mouth closer to me.

"So impatient, Siren. Anyone would think you missed me too."

"I hate you," I gasp when he blows my clit once more.

He chuckles. "Sure you do. Just not my tongue or my cock, right?"

"And your fingers," I confess, rolling my hips temptingly.

"Anyone would think you only keep me about for one thing."

"I don't keep you about, Nico. I can't get rid of you."

"There's a reason for that, Siren. We're just too fucking good together."

Before I get a chance to respond to that, he dips his head and finally licks up the length of my pussy.

"Fuck, yes," I cry, throwing my head back into the pillow as my fingers twist in his hair, keeping him against me.

"Your fucking mouth should be illegal."

"I'll take that," he growls against me. "Now, focus. I want you coming all over my face, and I want to fall asleep with your taste coating my tongue."

If he didn't immediately spear two thick fingers inside me, I might argue that I want to be coming all over his cock too, but when he finds my G-spot, I lose all sense of anything and just do as I'm told.

His tongue laps at my clit as his fingers brush over that magic spot inside me again and again, building me up to what I know is going to be a mind-blowing release. It always is with him. It's why I'm not protesting about him taking over. I know that tomorrow, I'll regret it. It's going to make him think that I've forgiven him.

I haven't. Not by a long way, but I am only so strong.

And what's my other option—aside from my own fingers right now? Call Brad? Yeah, no. I don't think so.

"Nico," I cry out when my release is in touching distance.

"Come for me, Siren. Give me everything."

His words slam into me, fear racing through my veins that he's demanding more than I can give, but it's too late. I'm too far gone, and one more lick of his skilled tongue and I'm soaring.

"NICO," I scream as pleasure explodes through me, shooting through my limbs and making the tips of my fingers and the ends of my toes tingle with its intensity.

My chest heaves as wave after wave of pleasure

overtakes my system, leaving me a sweaty, sated mess before him.

"Fuck, that was good," I confess on a breathy moan. "You might be a cruel prick, but you've got some mad skills."

His chuckle fills the air, clearly not offended in the slightest—standard—but before I get a chance to say or do anything else, my exhaustion takes over and darkness comes.

Fucking painkillers.

As of tomorrow, I'm done with them.

Fuck the pain. I want to be living.

***

I awake with a start. My eyes fly open so wide they hurt, but I can't see anything. The blackout curtains are too good.

I scan the darkness, looking for evidence of what happened the night before. But there is nothing. The chair is empty—well, aside from the clothes I've thrown on it over the past few days. And more importantly, when I slide my hand out to the other side of the bed, it's also empty. And cold.

"Shit," I hiss, rolling onto my back.

Something tugs at my ankle, and when I reach down, I find my knickers twisted up around it.

Fuck.

What was I thinking?

A noise out in the flat catches my attention, and when I look over at the alarm clock, I find that it's long past when Toby should have already left for school.

Swinging my legs over the edge of the bed, I try to ignore the ache that sits heavy in my stomach.

I might have got off last night, but it was nowhere near enough.

He didn't even fuck me with that delicious cock of his.

Why did he think that abandoning me without the full Nico Cirillo experience would leave me feeling more likely to forgive him? Not that any number of orgasms will ever be enough to forgive his actions. But still. A good railing would have helped.

Maybe he didn't want to hurt you, a little rational voice says in my head, but I squash her as quickly as she pops up. Nico isn't that considerate. If he wanted to fuck me, nothing would stop him.

Shit. Was it just a pity orgasm?

Was he sitting in his flat feeling guilty over what happened and thought I could use a good time to make me feel better?

"Arsehole," I hiss, gripping my toothbrush a little harsher than necessary.

I clean up and throw myself through a quick shower. I've still got a dressing over my shoulder, but with every day that passes, I'm less and less careful about getting it wet. Today especially as I stand there under the waterfall shower in Toby's guest bathroom.

I want to believe that by washing any evidence of his visit down the drain, my memory might go with it. It's wishful thinking; I know that before I even attempt to forget.

Ignoring the soaked, half-peeling-off wet dressing, I pull on a pair of booty shorts and a vest and head out in search of a much-needed coffee.

Jodie is sitting at the dining table with a laptop open before her. She's completely distracted, tapping away.

It's not until my shadow falls over her that she realises she has company.

A small gasp rips from her lips before her eyes lift to mine.

"What?" I ask when something wicked dances in her eyes.

"Oh nothing. Nothing at all."

I frown at her, trying to figure out what's going on.

"Do you want a coffee?" I ask.

"Please." She slides her mug toward me for a refill. "I'd make yours with a double shot if I were you."

I mean, yeah, I fucking need it, but— realisation slaps me upside the head.

"You heard me." It's not a question; it doesn't need to be. The answer is written all over her face.

"Babe, it was hard not to. Do you know how loud you can scream?"

"Do we have to?"

"I thought someone was trying to kill you, Bri. I woke up terrified and already halfway to your room, ready to fight for you."

"As much as I appreciate that, it really wasn't necessary."

"No. So I saw when I threw the door open."

There isn't much that embarrasses me these days, especially with my best friend, who has literally seen it all before, but my body defies me and heat blooms on my cheeks.

"Jesus Christ," I mutter, stalking toward the kitchen while she laughs at me.

"It's nothing to be ashamed of, Bri. We all have needs."

13

———

NICO

I went back to school today. I didn't want to. I wanted to do the exact fucking opposite, but my time hiding in my flat is over.

Hell knows I've done enough of that in the past few weeks.

So instead, I had a solid word with myself, pulled on my uniform, ran some wax through my hair, and tried to forget everything else.

I have exams. I need to focus. I want to say that I'll have the summer to fuck about. But I won't. The second my exams are done, I intend to dive head first into my soldier role. I don't care if Damien doesn't think I'm underboss material. I already know I'm not. But I have every intention of proving to him that one day, I will be.

One day, I will step into my father's shoes, and I will make him proud.

I want that. And for the first time in my life, I don't think that's all I want, either.

"Mr. Cirillo?" Mrs. Hendrix says, dipping down low to get into my eye line.

"Huh, sorry. Can you repeat the question?"

Her brows knit in concern as she continues staring at me.

After a silent couple of seconds, she pulls a chair closer and sits down opposite me.

It's not until she does that that I realise the room is empty. The lesson is over and I'm... still sitting here.

Shit.

"I'm sorry, I totally checked out."

"How is she?" Mrs. Hendrix asks softly.

"H-how is who?"

"Nico, I'm no fool, and I'd appreciate if you didn't treat me like one. I know that you and Brianna... know each other."

"Y-you knew?" I ask, a frown forming on my brow as she nods. "Why did you schedule her in this lesson?"

Hell, I might have been the one to do the damage where Brianna is concerned, but Mrs. Hendrix put her right in the line of fire.

"Because I'm worried about you. I'd hoped that her being here might help you focus."

I can't help but laugh.

"It worked, too, didn't it? I've seen the work you've given her from your revision sessions. You want to impress so you're putting the effort in."

"Risky game you're playing there, Mrs. Hendrix."

"Because you never play dirty," she teases, making me swallow nervously.

"Things between us... they're..."

"Complicated?" she asks when I trail off.

"I was going to say toxic, but yeah, that works."

"You care about her though, don't you?"

I swallow once more.

"You don't need to answer that. I can see it in your eyes." She gives me a soft, encouraging smile. "Whatever you've done, Nico, she'll forgive you. She just needs time. That and not to be thrown into a building at a million miles an hour."

I narrow my eyes at her.

"Who are you?" I ask, more than suspicious of how we might be connected.

"None of that matters," she says, waving my concern off. "You need to focus on you, and her."

I slump down in the chair and let out a heavy sigh.

"She won't see me," I confess, scrubbing my hand down my face.

"How hard have you tried?"

My lips part to say something, but I soon realise that I have no decent answer to that question.

"Try harder, Nico. No battle was ever won by sitting back and letting everything happen around you."

With that ominous statement ringing in my ears, she returns her chair to its rightful place and quickly sets about tidying up, leaving me slumped there, lost in my own head.

"Please send her my love when you see her. I'm looking forward to having her back next week."

"Next week?" I blurt.

"That's what her last email said, yes."

Unease rushes through my veins at the thought of her leaving Jodie and Toby's flat. While she's locked up with them, she's safe. Protected. But once she's out again in the wild, anything could happen. Anyone could happen. And I don't just mean Brad the bellend.

I never put all that much thought into it before, but if the Italians are getting ready to strike, then they'll be watching us like hawks. And the easiest way to disarm us is to use our girls.

The thought alone makes my stomach twist up until I'm sure I'm about to puke on the pristine carpet of this classroom.

But as much as I might want to bundle them all up in bubble wrap and keep them safe, I know I can't. And if I ever stand a chance of Brianna talking to me again, I really need to take a step back. Smothering her with my fears and insecurities right now isn't going to help.

"Th-thank you for... this," I say, finally pushing to my feet and heading toward the door.

"Brianna is one in a million, Nico. Don't let her get away. You'll regret it."

I have no words to respond to that, so I just nod and continue walking out of the classroom and then the school.

As I expect, Toby is sitting in his driver's seat waiting for me.

"Hey, you had a good afternoon?" he asks innocently.

"Who is Mrs. Hendrix?" I bark.

"Umm... English teacher?"

"She's Cirillo."

"What?" he blurts, clearly not expecting those words to come out of my mouth.

"She knows about me and Brianna," I confess. "Has done all along."

"I have no idea. I can look into her, though."

I nod despite thoughts of him snooping into her life not sitting quite right with me. More than anything, I need to know who Brianna is working with.

"I'm sure it's nothing to worry about. We'd already know if it was."

"I guess," I mutter as he pulls the car out of the space.

"So," he starts the second we're off Knight's Ridge grounds, "are you going to talk to her tonight?"

I rub my hands down my thighs. "I can't," I confess.

"Why the hell not? She misses you, man."

"Does she though?"

"You know just as well as I do that she does."

"That's not the same thing," I mutter, my cock swelling inside my trousers just thinking about what she really misses. I fucking do too. But I don't want her just because she's desperate for my cock.

I want...

I want more.

"Fucking hell," I mutter, scrubbing my hand down my face and staring out of the window. "I can't tonight anyway, I'm busy," I stupidly confess.

"Oh? Hot date I don't know about?"

"Something like that."

He glances over, his stare burning into the side of my face as he waits for me to elaborate.

I don't want to, and I silently chastise myself for saying anything.

"Jocelyn has set me up with her shrink niece."

"Oh?" Toby asks, his eyes popping open in shock.

Seeking help in the form of therapy or counselling isn't really the Cirillo way. Generally, we focus on the task at hand and spill enough blood to work through our issues. But apparently, Jocelyn is forcing me to be a rebel and figure this shit out the 'normal' way. I get it. I know why she's doing it. It's not just for me, but for Brianna too. Because she deserves it. And that is exactly why I'm putting up with it.

"Apparently, I've got issues."

"Dude, you don't need a shrink to tell you that. I could have done it for free."

"Funny, prick," I mutter.

"Seriously, though, I think it's a good idea. Hell, we could probably all do with a bit of it. We're all fucked up enough."

I mumble some kind of agreement. What else can I do? He's talking the truth.

"So what's the plan here? Try to sort your head out and then make some big gesture?"

"Who says I have a plan for her?"

"You're so full of shit. I'm assuming this shrink is going to try and prove to you that you care about her? All this denial isn't good for your soul, man."

"Of course I care, dickhead. She's... Brianna. But that doesn't—"

"Oh, come off it, bro. You've been in love with her since the night she allowed you inside her knickers and we all know it. She has you wrapped so tight around her little finger that she's never going to release you. And do you know something else?" he quickly adds before I manage to get a word in. "You fucking love it."

"You have no idea what you're talking about. I don't want that. What you guys all have. One woman for the rest of my life. Ugh." I force myself to physically shudder, but it's fake. All of it.

The truth is... I think he might just be right.

"Just talk to her. And I mean with real words, Nico. Not late-night promises of pleasure I know you're so fond of."

"Arsehole," I scoff.

But all he does is chuckle in return.

"At least try and talk to her before all this shit kicks off."

"Have you heard anything?"

"No. But I can't imagine they'll sit on this intel for long. I'd put money on it being this weekend."

"Same," I agree.

"You need to be ready, Nico. What time is your shrink coming? We should hit the gym."

Training in the gym with Toby and then the session with Jade are about as tortuous and painful as each other. By the time Jade lets herself out of my flat later that night, I'm both emotionally and physically spent.

I'm still wearing my gym clothes, my skin still covered in stale sweat—which I'm sure Jade enjoyed immensely—but I can't find the energy to move. And I still have revision to do.

I figure that's going to have to wait as I slump down on the sofa, my eyes closing before my head has even hit the cushion.

Darkness comes for me fast, and I quickly fall into my trusty dreams of a curvy blonde who consumes every second of my life these days.

I knew she was different from that first night we met, but I never could have imagined that it would come to this.

The second she moves past my table, I'm on my feet, my heart hammering in my chest as I watch her study the woman I've lined up to entertain her date while I steal back what belongs to me.

Her arse sways in the most tempting way as she closes in on the bathrooms in that skintight dress that prick has wrapped her in. If I didn't hate him so much, I might just thank him for it.

It'll be such a shame to burn it to nothing but dust later when I finally peel it from her body.

After Brianna has passed her, Lola's eyes lock with mine.

One almost unnoticeable nod assures me that she knows the task and has it more than under control.

I have no doubt in her skills. She's worked at the Empire for as long as I can remember. She takes her jobs seriously. She knows too well what would happen if she failed.

I catch the bathroom door just before it closes and wait for a minute for Brianna to shut herself in a cubicle. I shoot a look at Raoul, who's watching me from the end of the hallway, and slip into the room and hide in the one beside her.

The wait for her to emerge again is excruciating. But I know it's going to be worth it.

My cock strains against the confines of my trousers, desperate to be let out to play.

It's been too fucking long since I've been inside her body. The videos I've got of us together and my own hand only gets me so far.

My heart jumps into my throat when she finally flushes the toilet and unlocks the door.

I count down from ten before I emerge.

A smirk kicks up at the corner of my mouth the second her gasp of shock rips through the air when her eyes land on mine in the mirror before her.

"W-what are you doing?" she breathes when I'm almost in touching distance.

"I could ask you the same question, Siren," I growl, the image of her sitting out there with that prick ensuring my anger continues to bubble under the surface.

She lowers her phone to the side as our eyes continue to hold.

"You shouldn't be here," she hisses.

"And you shouldn't be here with another man," I throw back.

Her chest heaves as I stalk closer, my fingers curling into fists to stop me from reaching for her.

"It's just Brad," she argues as if it's going to make this any better.

It does the fucking opposite, and my anger, my jealousy only burns hotter.

"I don't give a fuck if it's Jesus. He's spent all night eye fucking you in this dress, planning what he's going to do once he gets you out of it. Touching you."

My voice is rough, deep. I sound unhinged as I struggle to keep a lid on everything that's trying to explode within me.

"Careful, Nico. You sound awfully jealous."

A loud growl rips from my throat and I suddenly surge forward.

I'm on her before she's registered I've moved. Wrapping my hand around her neck, I haul her back against my body. A groan rumbles deep in my throat as her arse grinds against my cock. Sliding my free hand over the curve of her waist, I grip onto her hip, stopping her from escaping me.

Goosebumps prick her skin as I breathe against her neck. Her visceral reaction to me only makes my grip harder.

"No one else is allowed to touch my toys, Brianna," I warn dangerously.

"Fuck you, Nico. I don't belong to you. I never have, and I never will. I'm nothing but a cheap whor—"

I have her twisted around and pressed back against the wall before I even really register her words. All the air rushes from her lungs before my hand finds its home around her throat, squeezing in warning, making her lips open wider.

Making the most of it, I slam my mouth against hers, licking deep into her mouth as she fights me. But it's not going to work. There is nothing she could do right now that would stop me from having what's mine.

"Stop fighting, Brianna," I warn into our kiss.

"Fuck you," she hisses.

"Yeah, Siren. That's the fucking idea."

I tighten my grip on her throat once more and finally, she gives into this fire between us and kisses me back just as violently as I do her.

Finding the split in her dress, I slide my hand up her thigh, hooking it around my hip as I continue to explore beneath the fabric.

My entire body tenses when I discover she's not wearing anything beneath this sinful dress.

"Siren," I growl through gritted teeth. "You've been sitting out there with him like this." My entire body trembles with pent-up aggression.

The fact that I haven't stormed out there and laid the motherfucker out is a fucking miracle.

"He told me not to wear any," she breathes, making the situation worse.

"And you listen to everything that motherfucker says, huh? Maybe we should get him in here, let him see what a filthy little whore my siren really is."

Her eyes widen in shock.

But it's pointless. Her not-so-loyal little pet is out there having his ego stroked by Lola as we speak.

"What's wrong? Worried about what he'll think about the real you? The corrupt teacher who gets off on fucking her student?" I snarl.

"I don't give a fuck what he thinks of me."

"Can you afford to lose him, though? Or is this one of the ones I bought?" I taunt, glancing down at her dress.

She tries to fight her reaction but fails massively. I see it all burning in the depths of her eyes. And all it does is feed the monster inside me, desperate to get out.

"So what is it you do here... let him buy you designer clothes and dress you up as his little doll before you lay back and open your legs to pay him back?"

Crack.

That bit of pain is all I need to free the beast.

My lips crash against hers so hard the taste of copper fills my mouth as my fingers find her cunt, two of them plunging deep inside her.

"Nico," she cries as I fuck her like a savage

We continue spitting insults at each other, but we both know this only ends one way.

With me so deep inside her cunt neither of us has any idea where one of us ends and the other begins.

Exactly as it fucking should be.

"More. Nico. I need more," she begs.

"Beg like a good little whore and you might just get it, Siren."

I pull back a little, watching her close in on her orgasm with my cock aching, weeping for a release.

"Fuck me, Nico. I need your cock."

My fingers tighten on her throat, enough to cut off her air this time as I continue thrusting my fingers inside her.

It only takes a couple more seconds for her to shatter, and it's fucking beautiful. She milks my fingers just like she will my cock in only a few minutes.

Her screams of pleasure bounce off the walls around us as I rip my trousers open and shove them down my hips, freeing my cock. But I don't take my eyes off her. I can't. She's so fucking beautiful when she gives into this connection between us.

It's not until I'm lined up at her entrance that she comes back to me.

"Good," I state when her eyes find mine. "I didn't want you to miss this."

I thrust inside her, filling her in one quick move. Her wet, velvet walls hug my cock, her muscles still spasming from her release and sucking me deeper.

It. Is. Every. Fucking. Thing.

"Fuck, you never look better than when you're impaled on my dick, Siren," I confess, unable to keep the truth trapped inside.

She tries to fight me, to stop me from taking her like this in the bathroom while her date is being entertained out in the restaurant. But it's futile, and she knows it. And before long, we're both succumbing to our releases, my cock jerking violently inside her cunt, marking her as mine and mine alone.

And just to really make my point, I release her throat and sink my teeth into the already marked skin.

"Did you want to piss over me too, really drive your point home?" she hisses angrily as the high of what we've just done begins to seep from me.

My deep chuckle fills the room as I pull back and sadly remove myself from her body. My cock has barely softened, more than prepared to go again already.

"I don't think that's really necessary. We both know the truth," I state confidently as I tuck myself away.

"Oh yeah?" she asks, tugging her dress down, stopping me from seeing the evidence of what we just did slipping down her thighs. "And what's that?"

"You belong to me."

She doesn't take that statement as seriously as I do, her laughter filling my ears as she moves toward the cubicle.

Her words go in one ear and out the other. We both know she's going to be spending the rest of the night with me instead of that pussy out there. What just happened in here was merely a taster of what we're capable of when we collide.

Her phone vibrates on the counter as she locks herself in a cubicle and I turn around to look at it instead of walking out like she demands.

I don't have any intentions of reading her messages, but a part of me hopes it's the bellend letting her down easy for the night in favour of his new little pet.

Unfortunately, that isn't what I find.

14

NICO

I awake with a start. My heart is racing and my skin is covered in a sheen of fresh sweat, but it's the image front and centre of my head that I focus on.

A scan picture.

My sister had sent Brianna a scan picture.

A baby scan.

My head spins as I sit there with my chest heaving.

It was just a dream... wasn't it?

But even as I think those words, I know they're not true.

It wasn't just a dream.

It's reality.

That's why I did what I did.

I was trying to get to Calli.

I'm on my feet before I realise I've made a decision and I'm storming out of my flat.

Ignoring the lift, I fly down the stairs much like I did the night I stopped Brianna from leaving. Only this time, I have a different target in mind.

Pressing my trembling hand to the biometric scanner, I

shove the door open the second the green light flashes at me and storm into the flat, the door crashing back against the wall behind me.

It's not until I come to a stop in the middle of the living room that I realise it's dark.

What fucking time is it?

I'm still pondering that question when a door opens and I find myself on the wrong end of Daemon's gun.

"Nico, the fuck?" he barks when he recognises me a beat later and thankfully lowers his piece instead of firing off the clip into my head.

"Nico?" Calli asks sleepily before emerging behind her boyfriend.

She hits the light switch, making them both wince as the brightness sears into their eyes and allows me to see my sister standing there, wearing one of Daemon's wide-armed tanks.

Fuck my life.

"What the hell is going on?" Calli demands, hesitantly stepping a little closer.

Guilt is etched into her expression. Without me saying a word, she knows that I know.

My fists curl as my anger surges forward, a move that Daemon doesn't miss. He steps up behind my sister and wraps his free arm around her shoulders, not releasing his piece in the other.

"Y-you're," I stutter like an idiot. "You're p-preg—"

Calli's sob cuts my words off, and before I know what's happening, she's broken free from Daemon's protective hold and thrown herself into my body.

My arms wrap around her on instinct, one hand holding the back of her head, the other on her back as she trembles against me.

"It's okay, Cal," I whisper against the top of her head before my eyes find Daemon's just a few feet away.

He's finally put his gun down and crossed his arms over his scarred chest as he leans against the wall.

"I should be the one pointing the gun at your head," I growl as the weight of this situation presses down on my shoulder.

"But you won't," he states confidently.

"You seem a little too sure about that, Deimos."

"Of course I am. She loves me and she's carrying our little blob."

All the air rushes out of my lungs as he confirms my dream.

"It's really true?"

Calli pulls her head from my chest and looks up at me with her big, tear-filled blue eyes that have melted my heart from long before I can remember.

"I'm sorry," she whispers. "We wanted to wait until — I'm sorry," she says, cutting off her own explanation.

"You don't owe me anything, Cal. I get it," I say through gritted teeth.

I'm not a fucking moron; I know people don't just go announcing these things the second they find out. And she has even more reason to keep her mouth shut with everything going on recently. We're already worried about the girls' safety with the Italians sniffing around. Add this into the mix...

Fuck.

My grip on my sister tightens as my possessiveness and need to protect her gets even stronger than ever.

"I should have told you. I just knew that you'd flip your lid and—"

"You were right. I would have. I did. Fuck. I'm so fucking sorry."

Releasing her, I push her gently in the direction of her boyfriend.

I have no right to be comforting her right now. I'm the one who's fucked up so badly that she felt like she couldn't even come to me with this shit.

We've lost Dad. Mum's checked out and—

"Brianna knew all this time?"

Reluctantly, Calli nods.

"The day I realised… It was the morning of Mum's party and she found me freaking out in the bathroom at the spa. She calmed me down, made up some bullshit excuse so she could go to the pharmacy for me to get a test.

"I took it before the party, but I never got the chance to see the result.

"Then everything happened and I was left without you, Daemon, Dad, and I had the reality of this sitting in my handbag.

"Brianna and Jocelyn, they held me up, kept me going. Then you came back but Dad left us and everything just went to shit. You were so angry, so—"

"Broken?" I finish for her.

"Yeah, but I was too. I thought I was going to have to do it on my own. Alex promised me—"

"Alex knows?" I ask, hurt laced through my voice.

"I'm sorry," Calli whispers. "You were unpredictable, Nico. Volatile. I was terrified that it would make everything worse if you found out, and it was already a massive fucking disaster.

"Then Daemon came back, and I just wanted us to have this together before everyone else—"

"But half of them already know," I argue.

"Just Bri and Alex. They kept me going, Nico. Without them—"

"Without me," I correct, regret twisting up my insides that I wasn't there when she needed me the most, that she didn't feel like she could trust me. It fucking shreds me up.

"Nico," she starts, but I don't let her say anything else.

"Can I see?"

Her brows pinch in confusion, but Daemon understands.

"The scan, Angel. Show him our little blob."

The second he releases her, she rushes back into their bedroom while the two of us glare at each other.

But this time, I'm not angry. I'm not livid that he's knocked my teenage sister up. I'm relieved. Relieved that she has his total dedication and support. His love.

I see it shining in his dark and deadly eyes. He loves her like he's never loved anything in his life. She literally comes above anything and everything else.

"Here," Calli says softly, handing me a row of small black-and-white images. "These were taken on Friday. I had a little bleeding and Daemon freaked out and demanded we have a scan the second we turned up at the hospital."

"As he should," I agree. "You're carrying precious cargo. These things need checking."

"See?" Daemon says smugly, making my sister roll her eyes.

"How far are you?"

"Almost nine weeks. Due twenty-eighth of December."

"That's some Christmas gift," I mutter, staring down at the almost indecipherable image before me.

"He's there," Daemon points out, his fingertip landing exactly where I'm looking.

"Yeah. I see... him?"

"Obviously," Daemon states. "Cirillos' next best underboss hanging out in there."

"Next best?" I ask, my brows hitting my hairline.

Daemon snorts in a very un-Daemon-like way before he slaps my back.

"With a father like me and an uncle like you, what else is he going to be?"

Can't really argue with logic like that but—

"My little sister is growing the devil's child," I mutter under my breath as he marches toward the kitchen.

"You're all missing something," Calli says, snatching her scan images back.

"Oh yeah?"

"Yeah, your future underboss is a girl."

"Nah, I'm with Daemon on this. Definitely a boy."

"Nope. We're in the twenty-first century, it's about time the mafia was taken over by a bad-arse female. Just think, if Emmie and Theo have a girl first, the entire Family could be under female control," Calli muses.

"Uh... that isn't how it works, Cal. It's a firstborn boy who gets the power."

"Right now it is. But things can change. You and Theo will have the power. And if Emmie has anything to do with it, she'll squeeze Theo's balls so hard he won't have a choice but to give his baby girl all the power."

"There's a lot of ifs in this plan, Cal."

She shrugs, not fazed by this crazy arse idea that's running around her head. "I'm confident."

I look over at Daemon for some kind of backup. There's no way he'll want his baby girl—if that's what they have—anywhere near that kind of danger, but he looks equally as relaxed as Calli right now as he pulls a smoothie from the fridge.

Realisation hits me upside the head, and I feel like a moron for not putting two and two together faster.

"That's why your fridge looks like a health food shop threw up in it."

"Only the best for our boy," Daemon teases.

"Nine weeks," I muse. "So we have what... like, thirty more to argue like this?"

"Depends if we decide to find out," Calli says.

"And will you?"

"Yes."

"No."

I shake my head at them as Calli yawns.

"Shit, what time is it?"

"Two a.m.," she says, padding over to Daemon and stealing the bottle he's drinking from.

She snuggles into his side and tips it to her lips while he watches her with a look of complete adoration on his face.

"I'm sorry for barging in," I say quietly.

Honestly, my head is still reeling with this discovery, but seeing them together, happy, it makes some of my anger over the whole thing dissipate.

It might be Jade's influence, but I'm dealing with this way better than I did last week. That or nearly killing both of us has given me somewhat of a reality check.

There could be a hell of a lot worse things to happen than my sister being blissfully happy and pregnant in a relationship.

When she yawns again, I'm reminded that I should be leaving.

"I'm gonna let you go back to bed."

Calli studies me as I move toward the door.

"You're really calm," Calli says, her brows knitting

together. "Should we be worried that you're about to leave and throw yourself off the building or something?"

I can't help but laugh.

"No. I'm okay, Cal. I'm... I'm happy for you." A lump crawls up my throat. It's so huge that I almost don't manage to get the next few words past it. "Dad would be really happy for you."

Tears immediately flood her eyes.

"Does Mum know?" I ask, although I'm pretty sure I already know the answer.

"No. And I'm happy for it to stay that way."

"You've got it. She doesn't deserve it, anyway. Your little soldier is going to be surrounded by people who love him. He doesn't need her either."

"Please don't tell them yet either," Daemon says. "We wanted you to know first, and now you do, we'll announce it."

"Whatever you want."

"And please, don't go too hard on Brianna because of this. She's been like the sister I never had." Her words are like a solid punch to the heart. "So if you could man up and make that situation a reality, I'd be totally here for it."

"Jesus," I mutter, combing my fingers through my messy hair. "She won't talk to me right now, let alone marry me."

The widest, most genuine smile lights up Calli's face.

"You didn't argue or deny you want it," she breathes, and I immediately realise my mistake.

"Cal," I warn darkly. "Stop letting that imagination of yours run away with itself."

"But—"

"No buts. Brianna and me... it's—"

"Inevitable?"

"A bit of fun. Now you're popping out heirs, I don't need to, so the pressure's off, right?"

I'd have thought those words would come as a relief. I'm sure if I had said them any time previously, then they would have been. But right now, all I feel is the pang of disappointment.

Do I want that? A future with a wife and kids. Do I want to make my old family home my future family home and try not to make the same mistakes our parents did with us?

"Are you going to kick Mum out and move in so you have space?" I blurt, a weird panic hitting me that we're going to fight over that place.

"Hell no. We're good here."

"But it's a flat," I argue for some unknown reason.

"It's bigger than most London homes. We're good."

"The house is all yours. You just need to off your bitch of a mother first," Daemon sneers.

"Surprised you haven't taken her off my hands as well," I deadpan.

"Nah, that bitch is all yours when you feel the time is right."

I shake my head, wondering for the millionth time what my father was thinking, putting up with her cold arse for so long.

It makes me wonder if she was always so detached. I don't remember it to the level we've experienced recently, but she was never exactly a hands-on mum, preferring to leave us in the hands of nannies and housekeepers. But I'm sure she used to show us she cared. Or is that just my twisted imagination?

"Thanks. Such a gift," I mutter before saying some

words I never thought would leave my lips. "Take my sister back to bed. She's exhausted."

"With pleasure, man. It's my favourite place to be."

"I'll talk to you tomorrow, Cal." She smiles sleepily at me before Daemon sweeps her up into his arms and carries her down toward their bedroom, leaving me standing there with an unrelenting ache in my heart.

I leave their flat only a few seconds later.

I should turn toward the lift to take me back upstairs. But I don't. While my head might tell me to go that way, my legs take me in an entirely different direction.

I enter Toby's flat a little calmer than I did Daemon's. But that doesn't mean my heart is pounding slower or my hands aren't shaking.

My sister is pregnant. With an actual fucking baby.

And Brianna knew this whole time and never so much as hinted a word.

I suck in a calming breath as I try to squash the anger that continues to threaten.

I am pissed, but I'm also aware that she was right with what she hissed at me as she fled the library last week.

My sister is proof that we can trust her.

She could have sold us so far down the river by now that we'd have all long drowned. But she hasn't. She's here. She's with us.

She's one of us.

I'm a nervous fucking wreck by the time I reach out and wrap my fingers around the door handle.

Darkness greets me as I slip inside and pad toward the chair in the corner that's angled to allow me to watch her sleep.

With my eyes locked on the lump in the bed which is my siren, I lower my arse and rest back.

My eyes burn with exhaustion and my head spins with the revelations of the night, but just being in her presence settles everything that's rioting inside me. I have no idea at what point she started having this calming effect on me, but now I've discovered it, I'm getting even more addicted.

The flat is in silence. All I can hear is her shallow, sleeping breaths, my own racing heart, and the blood that is forced past my ears.

Seconds tick away as I sit there. I can't even really see her in the darkness. But I know she's there, and that's enough.

"Were you here last night?"

Her sleepy voice scares the shit out of me as it fills the room. My heart jumps into my throat as I study her shadowed form.

"Yes," I confess, my mind going back to last night.

Spreading my legs wide, my hand drops to my crotch as my cock hardens.

Hell yeah, I was here last night. And it was as fucking amazing as it was torturous.

Her gasp of shock rips through the air.

"D-did you... did you touch me?" she asks hesitantly.

A wicked chuckle falls from my lips.

"Nico," she snaps, although there isn't much fire behind it.

"Do you want me to say that I touched you?"

A whimper I'm pretty sure I'm not meant to hear spills from her, giving me all the answers I need.

"What is it you need, Siren?" I ask, sliding toward the edge of the chair.

"From you? Nothing," she spits.

"Oh yeah?" I growl. "Are you sure about that?"

"More than sure. I meant what I said, Nico. We're done.

You can sneak in here like a creep all you like. I'm not falling into your trap again. I'm here for my best friend, and that is it. You no longer appear in any of my thoughts."

"You're lying," I state confidently.

"You're delusional."

"And you're a lying whore."

"Oh, goodie," she quips. "We're back to that."

Pushing to my feet, I move closer, her scent getting stronger as I close in on her, making my mouth water for a taste.

"But there's no question this time. I know for a fact that you are lying."

"Bullshit."

She doesn't move as I step up beside her and bend over. Planting my hands on the pillow on either side of her head, I get lower until I'm right in her face.

"It's not, though, is it?"

"We're over, Nico. I want you to get the hell away from me and leave me alone." But as she says this, she makes no move to force me to go anywhere. If anything, she only draws me in as her voice gets deeper.

"Is that why you got off last night while screaming my name, Siren? Because you don't want me?"

Sucking in a sharp breath, her eyes narrow.

"I told you I was here last night," I growl. "I watched it all. But I never touched you. Whatever you were experiencing was all your own imagination. Now tell me, Siren. What were you picturing me doing to you to make you scream my name so loudly?"

"Nothing," she lies. "I wasn't picturing you."

I can't help but laugh at her blatant bullshit.

"You keep telling yourself that, babe. But we both know the truth, don't we?"

"Y-you need to leave," she says weakly.

"Lies, lies, lies. Such pretty little lies," I sing, resting my weight on one hand and moving the other so I can trail one finger down the side of her face.

She flinches as if my touch burns, but she does little else to stop me.

Her arms and legs are free. If she really wanted to, she could fight me.

I'd win. We both know that. But she could at least try.

Her neck ripples with her thick swallow when I get to the soft skin beneath her ear. My mouth waters with my need to dip down and suck on her, but I hold steady, too lost in watching her eyes darken with desire.

"I meant it, Nico. We're done."

"I know," I breathe, tracing the strap of her vest top.

"Then why are you still here?" she demands, misunderstanding my words.

I let my eyes drop to her lips. They're parted, her breaths rushing past them as I tease her.

Dropping lower, I find her chest heaving, and I watch as I hook my finger beneath the duvet and pull it down, exposing her body to me.

It's dark, but now my eyes have fully adjusted, I can see everything I need to prove that her body is fully on board with what I'm doing.

Her nipples are hard, pressing against the thin fabric of her top, desperate for my touch.

"Look at you, so needy for me."

"In your dreams."

"No, babe. In yours, remember?"

"What was I doing?" I dip lower, pressing my lips to the corner of her mouth, ignoring the burn from my nose as it presses against her cheek. "Was I kissing you here?"

She doesn't respond.

"Here?" I ask, nuzzling her neck and grazing her skin with my teeth.

A violent shudder rips through her body and a moan rumbles in the back of her throat.

"No? Maybe this, then."

Dragging down the top of her vest, I free her breast and immediately suck her hard nipple into my mouth.

"ARGH," she cries, her back arching off the bed as her arm finally lifts from the bed, but it's not to push me away. Instead of following her head's orders, she loses herself in her body's cravings and twists her fingers in my hair, holding me in place as I lap at her.

"Yeah," I say, flicking her peak with the tip of my tongue. "That's more like it, isn't it?"

"Nico," she whimpers, making my cock weep in my sweats.

"Fuck, you're so sexy, babe," I confess, revealing her other breast and giving it the same treatment as my cock tries to rip through the fabric it's hiding behind.

"Is this what you were thinking about while you were getting yourself off last night?" It sure as fuck was one of the things I was thinking about doing as I watched her work herself into a frenzy.

"No," she cries, finally admitting the truth as I bite her sensitive flesh.

"No? So what was I doing?"

Her lips slam closed, refusing to give me what I want.

Nah, Siren. That's not how this game goes.

I bite the side of her breast hard enough to break the skin. She screams as the taste of blood fills my mouth as her fingers twist so tightly in my hair, I'm sure she just pulled the lot out.

"Tell me, Siren. Tell me what I was doing."

She still refuses.

"NICO," she cries when I give her other breast a matching brand.

"I can do this all fucking night, babe. But in the end, I will get the truth and you will be screaming my name loud enough to remind this entire building who you belong to."

"I don't belong to anyone."

I laugh as I shift down her body and press my lips above the lace of her underwear.

"Was I down here?"

Her whimper is all the confirmation I need.

"Did I spread your legs wide and eat you until you forgot your own name?"

"Please."

"Fuck. You wreck me, babe," I confess as I hook my fingers beneath her knickers and drag them down her legs. I unhook them from one of her ankles but leave the other as I press my hands against her knees and spread her wide for me.

Even in the darkness, her pussy glistens for me.

"So wet for me," I murmur, sliding my hand down her inner thigh. I drag my finger through her folds.

"Nico," she begs when I begin circling her entrance, teasing her with what I can give her.

"How badly do you need me, babe?"

"P-please," she whimpers.

"Not good enough."

Dipping my head, I nip the skin of her inner thigh before I begin a trail of kisses that lead toward what we both want the most.

Her scent fills my nose as I drag my tongue along her smooth skin.

"So fucking hard for you, Siren. All I can think about is you."

"My pussy, you mean?" she corrects.

"No," I state, looking up and holding her eyes. "You, Brianna. All of you."

Her breath catches as shock covers her face. But she recovers faster than I was hoping for and she pulls her impenetrable mask on.

I immediately drop to my front and push her legs as wide as they'll go.

Fuck. I missed this.

I dive for her before she's able to demand that I leave and lick up the length of her pussy before focusing on her clit and sucking it into my mouth, making her scream. My face burns with pain, but it's worth it. So fucking worth it to taste her again.

"That was it, wasn't it? You got yourself off last night to the image of me eating you like my favourite dessert."

I barely move away from her, allowing her to get the benefits of my voice's vibrations before spearing my tongue deep inside her.

"Yes," she screams, her thighs tightening around my head. "More."

"For you, anything," I say honestly, although I'm not stupid enough to think she hears my confession; she's too lost to the pleasure I can deliver.

Addicted to her taste, I don't stop eating her. I can't. I have no idea when I might get this close again.

I hold off giving her more for as long as I can to prolong this, but eventually, I have to cave.

She screams as I push two fingers into her wet pussy, curling them to find her G-spot. Her muscles clamp down on me, desperately trying to suck me deeper, and my cock jerks in irritation that he's not buried deep inside her.

"Nico. Nico. Nico," she chants, making me feel like a fucking king as I work her toward her release.

"Come for me, babe. Show me how much you love me eating your pussy."

I suck her clit before grazing it with my teeth and she goes off like a rocket. Her screams bounce off the walls. She's so loud that there's no chance Toby and Jodie don't know what's happening in here.

I don't stop playing her until she's spent.

Finally, I sit up and wipe my hand across my lips before lifting the two fingers that were inside her and sucking them clean.

Her pupils dilate as she watches me.

"Addicted, babe."

She stares at me with her chest heaving, her skin covered in a sheen of sweat, exposed to me and looking like my perfect little whore.

15

BRIANNA

My heart pounds so hard it makes my vision blur as my body comes back down from the high of my orgasm.

The realisation that he didn't touch me last night makes a lot of sense, especially after what Jodie said to me. But... it felt so real.

He stares at me, his expression so different from what I'm used to. Pain flickers through his dark eyes, and I hate that guilt floods me. I shouldn't care after what he's done to me. But I do. I always do.

He's shed his mask of indifference and he's looking at me as if he's waiting for me to either rip his heart out or make all his dreams come true.

My head screams that I should be sending him away.

He's volatile and angry at the world. A barely restrained bomb that's going to finally explode, probably taking me down with him. He is going to hurt me. I'm as sure as that as I am my own death one day.

But my heart and my body... they're on an entirely different page.

My body craves him just like it always has. And my heart, that stupid, fickle, hopeless thing… it wants to fix him. It wants me to wrap my arms around his sinful body and hold onto him tight while he tries to deal with everything life has thrown at him.

But his temper almost got you killed.

"Nico, you nee—"

"I know, Brianna," he says, crawling up my body and sitting astride my waist. "I know why I did what I did. I know what I saw on your phone."

My breath catches as I stare up at his dark, mesmerising eyes.

"Y-you—"

"I'm going to be an uncle," he confesses, his eyes glittering with what I can only assume is emotion. It's so fucking dark in here it's hard to really tell because it's such an unusual look on him.

Needing to see more, I reach out to turn the bedside light on, but I never make it.

His fingers wrap around my wrist and that arm, and the other, is pinned above my head in one of his giant hands.

"Nico," I breathe, bucking my hips as if it'll be enough to get him off me.

"I've seen the scan. I've… I've seen him."

Internally, I roll my eyes as he assumes just like Daemon and Alex that Calli's baby must be a boy. It only makes me want it to be a little princess even more.

"And you felt the need to have to come and tell me this right now because?" I prompt.

"I'm here just like I have been every night, because I can't stay away from you, Siren. And I'm here after discovering this because I owe you yet another apology."

"Right, well, that orgasm barely scratches the surface of what you owe me, but I appreciate the release, so thanks, I guess."

Pride washes through me for my ability to stand up for myself while I'm pinned beneath his tempting body.

I keep my eyes trained on his, scared that I'll cave if I so much as look down and catch sight of the outline of his hard cock pressing against the fabric of his sweats like I know it is.

"The orgasm wasn't my apology."

"So what is, then? Because watching me sleep like a creep certainly isn't i—" My words are cut off when his lips land on mine. His tongue plunges past my open lips, licking deep into my mouth in an attempt to make me give in to him.

Every muscle in my body locks up tight, and as he shifts his hips, allowing his erection to grind against my stomach, my restraint almost snaps.

"No," I say around his tongue. "Nico. No. We're not doing this." He pulls back, taking my no seriously for once.

His brows knit as disappointment and defeat floods his features.

"I wasn't lying, Nico. We're done. You know where the door is."

I grit my teeth so hard it hurts. But I have to do something; otherwise, his pathetic, sad puppy face is going to win. And he will not beat me.

"Brianna," he breathes, his voice cracked with emotion.

"You can't win your way back in with orgasms, Nico. No matter how good they are. You saw for yourself last night that I don't actually need you."

In a flash, his sadness morphs into anger. Relief slams

into me. I can deal with angry Nico. Emotional Nico, not so much.

"You're a fucking cock-tease, Siren."

"So what are you going to do? Try and force yourself past my lips again and then come all over my face when I refuse to open up for you like a good little whore?" I ask, my mind shooting back to Theo's bathroom.

"I should," he says, roughly grabbing one of my exposed breasts in his burning hand.

I swallow the moan of satisfaction that wants to rip from my lips as he begins plucking at my nipple. Electric shocks shoot straight to my clit, making my already slick pussy wetter.

I wasn't lying. That orgasm he gave me was needed.

Despite my better judgement, I've been craving his touch all week, hence how I ended up in the mess I did last night.

"Go, Nico. I don't want you here," I force out through clenched teeth.

That sadness washes through his face once more, dampening the anger.

He doesn't move, and for a few seconds, I think he's going to ignore me.

But then, in a rush, he releases my wrists and climbs from my body.

He stands there staring at me for a few moments, giving me the chance to do what I was desperate to only moments ago and drop my eyes down his body.

Sure as hell, his cock is rock hard and desperate to get in on the action. The thought of exposing him and sucking him into my mouth makes me salivate.

And when I drag my eyes back up to his, I know he knows it too.

Part of me expects him to reach out, drag me from the bed and force me to my knees to do exactly what we both want.

But he doesn't.

Instead, he does the complete opposite and walks straight out of my bedroom without another word and without looking back.

"Fuck," I hiss the second the door swings closed behind him.

I'm on my feet in less than a heartbeat and standing at the door, my fingers wrapped around the handle. But I freeze right before I push it down.

I can't chase him. It'll give him hope.

I made a stand and told him to leave.

I need to be firm with that decision.

Going after him will only confuse things that are already beyond fucked up.

So instead of pulling the door open and chasing after him like my body and heart scream for me to do, I release the handle and take a giant step back, following my head. And I follow her all the way to the bathroom to take a shower that will wash his scent from my skin.

I don't know what it is about the solitude of a shower, but the second I stand there beneath the insane waterfall raining down on me, I break.

Loud, ugly sobs rip from my throat as tears fill my eyes.

I'm not even sure why I'm crying. But I do, harder than I ever remember doing.

Sliding down the tiled wall, my arse hits the shower tray

and I pull my legs up to my chest and wrap my arms around them.

The bandage that's doing a really poor job of covering my shoulder and upper arm catches my eye, and it only makes me cry harder.

Picking at the loose edge, I pull it off, staring down at the puckered, red skin. My forever reminder of Nico. Of the level of anger he holds within him that can explode at any given moment.

Time blurs as I sit there, lost in my own head, my tears mingling with the water, swirling down the drain as if my pain, my frustration with this whole bullshit situation is nothing.

I don't hear any voices or the door open, so when a shadow falls over me, I shriek in fright.

"Bri?" Jodie says softly as she drops to her haunches and reaches out to place her hand on my uninjured arm.

"I'm okay," I say weakly.

"Don't lie to me." She gives me a stern look that makes a smile twitch at my lips.

"Do I need to send Toby up to his flat to beat his arse?"

I shake my head. For once, he hasn't actually done anything wrong.

It was me. I was the one who ripped my insides in two by sending him away.

"Are you done in here?" she asks, watching me through concerned eyes.

"Yeah," I whisper. No sooner has the word fallen from my lips that she stands, turning the shower off and reaching for one of Toby's massive, fluffy towels to wrap me in.

"Come on." She takes my hand and leads me through to the bedroom and pulls the vanity stool out. "Sit."

I do as I'm told, too emotionally spent to do anything else.

After cleaning my face with a wipe, she applies my moisturiser before setting about taming the mess that is my hair.

It was pretty fucked up after Nico's visit, and the shower, minus shampoo and conditioner, didn't really help matters.

She works through the knots gently, her silent support wrapping around me like a warm hug.

Once she's happy, she squeezes out the excess water and reaches for the hairdryer—something that I can't imagine was in here until she moved into Toby's bachelor pad.

She works meticulously, drying and straightening in the way she knows I like but never have time to do.

My eyes get heavier and heavier as she works, my need to curl back up in bed and pass out getting stronger by the second.

"Do you want to talk about it?" Jodie eventually asks when she's finished, placing the dryer and brush down.

"There's nothing really to tell. He remembered some stuff from Friday night and came to talk to me about it," I confess, not willing to go into details. Avoiding her intrigued stare, I stand and walk to the dresser for clean pyjamas.

"Didn't sound like there was much talking going on from our room," she teases. "Did he remember why he flew off the handle?" she asks once I'm in bed.

"Yeah."

"And you're still not going to tell me," she surmises, a little hurt flicking through her eyes.

"I can't, Jojo. It's not about me, or even Nico."

"It's Calli." It's not a question. It doesn't need to be—she said so herself on the drive back here from the hospital.

My lips open but quickly close again.

"As long as everyone is okay, she can keep all the secrets she likes."

"Everyone is good."

"You should sleep," she says, leaning over me and pressing a kiss to my head.

A lump crawls up my throat once more, stopping me from replying.

"You want me to stay?" she offers, shooting a look at the other side of my bed.

I shake my head. "I'm okay. I'm just tired."

"As you should be after that orgasm."

"Jodie," I chastise.

"What? Did you really expect me not to acknowledge just how loud you screamed? I knew for sure you weren't alone this time."

"Thanks for not telling me he was here last night and that you walked in on me getting myself off."

She holds her hands up in defence.

"I thought you were awake and fully aware of the situation."

"Well, I wasn't," I sulk, making her laugh.

"Oh, just get out and go and wake your man up with a blowie."

She sucks in a surprised breath but quickly recovers. "You know, that's not a bad idea. If you need me, just shout, yeah?"

"I'm okay. Go and enjoy him."

I watch as she walks around the bed and frowns when she comes to an abrupt halt in front of the door.

"What's wrong?"

As she bends down to pick something up, I sit up straighter, more than a little intrigued.

"It's…" She stands with a white envelope in her hand. "For you."

My brows pinch in confusion, but a little realisation dawns the second she holds it out for me. I know that handwriting.

"You should read it," Jodie encourages.

I take it from her with a trembling hand.

A letter from Nico was the last thing I was expecting.

Unless it's not, and a whole heap of sordid photographs are about to fall into my lap or something. That seems more likely.

I don't realise that Jodie has gone until the click of the door closing hits my ears.

I slump down in the bed, my eyes locked on my name that's scrawled in his handwriting across the front of his envelope.

My hand trembles and my heart pounds as I flip it over and rip it open.

I don't find photographs, just a folded piece of lined paper.

Unfolding it, I hold it out in front of me, my eyes immediately tearing up again with just the first line.

Siren,

My siren.

I had a meeting with a shrink tonight and amongst other things, she asked me what I wanted. What I really wanted.

I could only think of two things that were worthy of telling her.

1. I want to prove my right to step into my father's footsteps. Whether that is next week, next month, or in ten years, I want it.

2. You.

16

———

NICO

I lower my phone to my lap and blow out a breath. I've spent most of the night tossing and turning, pointlessly hoping that she'd read my letter and come to me.

I even left the front door unlocked so she wouldn't need to question whether her print would allow her entry. It would, but she doesn't know that.

She didn't.

She never came, and my phone never lit up with any kind of response.

She might not have read it. When I pushed the envelope under the door, there was a hair dryer running inside, so I knew she was awake. But that doesn't mean she saw it.

She could still be sleeping, blissfully unaware that I've left a piece of paper on her bedroom floor that I've bled all over. Not literally, that would be fucking weird, but metaphorically.

When I wrote that letter after Jade left on Monday night, I wasn't sure I'd ever actually be brave enough to give it to her. But then after she sent me away last night like I was nothing more than a glorified sex toy—there's something I never thought I'd be bothered by—it felt right.

She needs to know that things have changed for me. That my intentions with her have changed.

Okay, so I might not be getting down on one knee and offering her forever anytime soon, but also, I know that I've been lying to myself about what we are. About how much I enjoy spending time with her.

I've already lost too much. I'm only hurting myself by continuing down that self-destructive path, denying myself what I want. What I need.

The minutes tick by as I sit there replaying the events of the middle of the night in my head, from waking up remembering why I freaked out quite so epically on Friday night to being told by Brianna, again, that we were done.

I didn't want to believe it when she turned her back on me in the hospital on Monday night, and I still don't want to now. But it feels more final this time. Like she really meant it.

If only she could have sucked me off first...

No.

I chastise myself for that thought.

You're meant to be starting over, Nico. Treating her like she deserves.

My phone startles me when the alarm starts blaring, letting me know that I really need to get my arse out of bed if I want to make it to school on time today.

"Fuck it," I grunt, throwing the covers back and padding toward the bathroom.

Every step is hard work, and there's this new ache in my chest that I'm not used to. But I shove it all aside in an attempt to tick off one of those two things I wrote in that letter.

I will prove myself. One way or another, I will do it and step into my dad's shoes.

***

"You can wipe that smirk off your face," I mutter when I stalk into the common room an hour later to find a knowing grin on my boy's face.

Yeah, there was no way he wouldn't have heard what was going on in his guest room last night.

"Bro, the fucking walls were vibrating," he announces happily, earning us the attention of Alex and Seb, whose heads whip around faster than I'm sure they should.

"She let you back in her good books, man?" Seb asks while Alex's eyes narrow in concern.

"No, I wouldn't say that. Got back in her pussy though."

"She must have been feeling desperate," Seb teases.

"Prick," I grunt as I fall onto the sofa next to Toby.

"For someone who got laid, you're not exactly happy," Alex points out.

"I never said anything about getting laid," I mutter. "Only one of us saw heaven."

"Uh-oh," Seb laughs. "It was that kind of night. Dog house fucking sucks," he says knowingly. "Never known blue balls like it."

Thankfully, Theo emerges with his arm slung around

Emmie's shoulder and the two of them steal Alex and Seb's attention.

"What the fuck happened? I thought you were making up, then Jodie came back after you left, saying—" He cuts himself off abruptly and slams his lips shut.

"Saying what?" I ask, concern for my siren flooding my system.

"Nothing. She said nothing."

"Tobias," I growl, my fist curling on my lap. I'm more than happy to beat it out of him if I have to.

He rolls his eyes, frustrated at himself for saying anything.

"She was upset, okay? Jodie said she found her crying in the shower."

All the air rushes out of my lungs as I stare at him in disbelief.

"She was crying?" I ask, assuming I must have misheard him.

"Forget I said anything."

"Yeah, like that is going to happen."

Pushing back to my feet, I pull my phone from my pocket and walk back out of the common room.

Finding her contact, I hit call and put my phone to my ear as I lower my arse to a picnic bench away from the students who are crowded out here in the morning sun.

It rings and rings and rings. But eventually, instead of her sultry voice, I'm forced to listen to her automated voicemail.

She couldn't even do me a solid recording a personalised one so I could listen to her voice.

Way to sound like a pussy, dickhead.

"Fucking answer," I demand, trying again. I know she's staring at the screen, looking at my name staring back at her.

Hell, she might even have a photo of my cock as my contact. It certainly is my best feature, after all. I also know that she's tempted. Really fucking tempted to answer. To hear what I've got to say to her. Or at least that's what I keep telling myself as I ring again and again.

Fucking pussy.

I'm about to do it again, because I've apparently stooped to those levels today, when the bell rings out loudly in the building behind me.

Instead of hitting call once more, I pull up our messages.

> Nico: You can try and avoid me all you like, Siren. You know I'll get to you eventually.

I can't help but smirk as I think about how she's going to read that as a threat.

It isn't one, though.

It's a promise.

I'm not expecting to hear anything from her, so I'm hardly surprised when my phone remains silent during my classes.

I almost tried again at break, but I figured it would be pointless. If I'm going to get to her, then I need to be smarter.

Lingering at the end of the hallway in the building that houses the English department, I wait for Mrs. Hendrix to leave her office in favour of the restaurant.

All the staff here make use of the talented chefs that are employed to feed the masses, so I have no doubt that she'll be heading out any minute to get to the front of the queue. Hell knows I'd be doing the same if I didn't have other plans.

I don't have to wait long to be proved right, and because she works in the most exclusive school in the city, she makes it easy for me by not even locking her door. What's the point when every single kid in this place could buy the contents of it one hundred times over?

Double-checking that I'm not being watched, I slip down the hallway and then into her office.

The space is spotless, and my eyes land on the phone sitting on her desk in seconds.

Bingo.

Pulling up Brianna's number, I key it in and press the handset to my ear.

It rings a couple of times, just like before, but unlike all those times, the line crackles, the ringing stops, and her sultry voice fills the line.

"Hello?" I can only assume that she knows it's someone at Knight's Ridge calling her, but I doubt she's suspicious that it's me.

"I hope you know that your voice alone gets me hard."

"Fuck's sake," she hisses. "Didn't ignoring your calls tell you anything? I don't want to talk to you."

"Siren," I growl.

"I mean it, Nico. Nothing has changed."

I startle as the irritating dial tone rings in my ear.

She fucking hung up on me.

I sit there for a few seconds feeling utterly defeated. But it doesn't last all that long.

She might think she can keep me away, but she has to know that I'm better at finding her than she is hiding from me.

Pulling up our tracking app, I wait for it to load.

I'm expecting to find her sitting in Toby's flat. That's easy enough to get into, I have access after all, but there's a twisted part of me that wants something a little more challenging than that.

A smirk curls up at my lips when her and Jodie's phones finally load, showing me that they're in a shopping centre in east London.

Yeah, that's a little more like it.

My mouth waters as images of stalking around the shops, watching her being relaxed with her best friend fill my mind. Although not as much as all the ways I could announce my presence to her.

I can almost hear the shriek of shock that will pass her lips before I slam my hand over them, forcing her into a darkened corner.

"I should warn her that she's got a creepy arse stalker," a soft voice says from behind me, scaring the ever-loving shit out of me.

One second my arse is in the chair and the next, I'm reaching for the switchblade in my pocket and holding it out ready to hurt the prick who thought it was a good idea to sneak up on me.

But when my vision clears, I discover hurting the intruder would be a really bad idea.

"Rhea? The fuck are you doing?" I ask, flicking my blade closed and pocketing it once more.

"Could be asking the same of you, cuz," she teases, folding her arms across her chest. Her shirt is unbuttoned so low I get way too much cleavage than my fourteen-year-old cousin should ever be showing off.

"You forget how to dress correctly or something? You're fourteen, they need to be away where no motherfucker can see them," I state, nodding toward her breasts. When the fuck did she even grow them? I'm sure she was an eight-year-old running around in frilly dresses only a week ago.

"Fifteen, actually."

My mouth opens to say something, but she beats me to it.

"It was last week. Thanks for remembering, dickhead."

My eyes widen, but I don't really have a comeback for missing her birthday.

"Shit, I—"

"Fuck that, Nico." She waves me off. "You can make it up to me now."

"Oh yeah?" I ask, mimicking her stance and crossing my arms over my chest.

"Take me with you, wherever you're going." Her eyes hold mine, her fire burning brightly within their green depths. They're just like Theo's, only a little less cold and closed off. Although, not by much. Everything I've warned her older brother about stands. She is going to be a fucking nightmare.

"How do you know I'm going anywhere?"

"You were tracking someone. I'm pretty sure you're not content with watching whoever it was through your phone."

My teeth grind, because she's right.

"You want to go see her, I can see it in your eyes."

"Her?" I ask naïvely.

"I know you're fucking Miss Andrews, Nico. Don't insult me."

"Jesus," I mutter, scrubbing my hand down my face.

"And unless you want me to go out there shouting it from the rooftops, then you need to take me with you."

"You wouldn't." Honestly, it doesn't really matter if she does. No one is going to do fuck all about it. The boss will make sure of that. But even still, I don't actually want the rest of the staff here to know what Brianna is up to in her spare time, or not right now, as the case may be. I might have wanted to scare her into proving herself as loyal to the Cirillos, but I never would have tarnished her reputation by allowing every member of staff under this roof to be aware of the fact she's been fucking one of her students.

"You want to risk it?" Rhea asks, quirking her brow.

Silence falls around us as her challenge rings in my ears.

"Why are you even in here?" I ask, narrowing my eyes. It's no secret that Rhea isn't Knight's Ridge's most dedicated and courteous student.

"None of your business," she hisses, although a wicked smirk threatens. Whatever she did to earn herself lunchtime in Mrs. Hendrix's office, she's damn proud of.

I'm almost scared to find out.

"And how do you think Mrs. Hendrix will take your running off when you're meant to be here doing time for your misdemeanours?"

"I have no idea. But I figure that's your issue now. Family emergency seems like the easiest excuse, don't you think, cuz?"

"You're a fucking pain in the arse, Rhea Cirillo."

"And here I was thinking you had a soft spot for strong, independent women."

"Yeah, not my fucking cousin though, kid."

I march toward the door, aware that she's going to follow me.

But the longer we stand here arguing, the more likely we're going to be caught, or that Brianna and Jodie will get bored shopping and head somewhere else.

"Well, that was easier than I was expecting," Rhea muses behind me.

My teeth grind, but I don't stop her. It's not worth it.

"If you tell your brother about this, I'll—"

"Threaten me all you like, Nico. I have nothing to hide."

"Oh no. What about that hickey on your neck?"

I glance back just in time to see her hand lift to cover the very faint mark that should be hidden by her school shirt, should she be wearing it correctly. Which of course she's fucking not.

"I'll tell you all about it if you want to know," she says confidently as we blow out of the building, the hot summer sun burning my retinas.

"How many guys will I have to kill if you tell me?"

"Umm... two or three."

I stop dead on the spot.

"Tell me you're fucking joking, Rhe."

Her eyes hold mine firm for a few seconds as a vein in my temple pounds. But then she throws her head back and laughs.

"Fuck, you should see your face, cuz."

"Fucking hell," I mutter taking off once again. "Theo needs to lock you in his basement and not let you up until it's time to marry you off for babies."

Her light footsteps slap against the tarmac of the car park as she catches up to me.

"I mean... who might I find down there with me?"

"Not the fucking point, Rhea" I grit out.

"I do love a dangerous playmate. They make the games all that much more fun."

"You're lucky I've got issues of my own right now." Maybe I should be grateful that my sister got knocked up by Daemon. At least I know him and what he's capable of. Fuck knows who Rhea is hanging out with and allowing to suck on her neck like a fucking vampire.

"You're right, you do have issues," she confirms, as if I fucking need that shit from my fifteen-year-old cousin. "But if this little covert mission goes well, we might just fix one of them."

"I'm not entirely sure there is any fixing anything where Brianna is concerned," I confess, unable to explain why opening up to my kid cousin is easier than almost everyone else in my life. She's the last person I should be laying this shit on.

"Of course there is. She's fucking gone for you, cuz."

"She hates me."

"She thinks she hates you. From what I've heard, she loves the things you can offer her way too much to really hate you."

"Where've you heard that from?" I ask as we drop into my new car. She whistles in appreciation but doesn't say anything.

"Oh, I hear all kinds of things. But lucky for you, I'm a vault."

"That doesn't make me feel any better."

"Any news on when the Italians are going to strike?"

"How the fuck do you know that?" I bark, glancing over at her in shock.

All she does is shrug innocently as she pulls her phone from the inside pocket of her blazer.

"Now, now, Nico. I'm not spilling all my secrets. Smile," she says before leaning over the console and snapping a photo of us.

"Seriously?" I bark.

"Hell, yeah," she says happily before leaning closer and snapping a few more. "My followers will love it."

"Your followers?" I deadpan.

"Pfft. Alex would get it."

"Then fuck off and blackmail him into helping you skive off school."

"Maybe tomorrow. I'm looking forward to our little shopping trip now," she says, proving that she was watching me long enough to know exactly where we're heading. "I need some new bras. Mine are all too small. And you're just the guy for the job."

Fuck. My. Life.

17

BRIANNA

"Another, please," I say when the server comes over to take our empty glasses away.

After grilling me on what happened the night before, Jodie insisted we get out of the flat.

I wasn't overly excited about stepping out of the building and returning to real life. It seemed like a good idea when I was safely locked away in their guest room, but as I stood at the front door, I was questioning everything.

"You want to go back to school on Monday, remember?" she reminded me as we descended the stairs, proving that the brave face I was putting on wasn't fooling her for a second.

"Brianna," she warns once we're left alone in the bistro she selected for us to have brunch in. "You shouldn't be drinking on your painkillers."

"I stopped taking them," I confess.

"What? Why?"

"Because they make me drowsy and I hate it."

"Aren't you still in pain?" she asks, making the aches

throughout my body a little more persistent as she mentions them.

"Nothing another mimosa won't fix."

She glares at me. The look is so similar to the one Joanne has given the pair of us so many times in the past when we've done something stupid.

"It's fine, Jojo. I promised I'd stay with you tonight, then tomorrow, I'm going home. It's time." And I really need to put some distance between me and Nico.

"I don't like it," she sulks as two fresh drinks are placed in front of us.

Immediately, I lift mine to my lips and take a sip.

Jodie sighs, aware that she's not going to win, and slides her own drink closer.

My phone buzzes on the table and my stomach knots.

He's been calling and messaging all morning. But I'm yet to respond to any of them.

Sure, his letter hit home in more ways than I want to admit. But that doesn't mean I'm going to cave to him just because he spilled a few truths.

If that's what they even are.

I wouldn't put it past him to make up all kinds of bullshit in that letter just so I'll give him easy access to my pussy again.

"Nico?" Jodie asks when I pick my phone up and turn it over.

My heart sinks when I find a different name staring back at me.

"Nope. Brad."

"You really have them running around like lovesick fools, huh?"

"Neither of them love me, Jojo. They're just missing an easy lay."

"Brianna," she chastises. "You're more than that and they both know it."

"It doesn't matter what they think. I'm focusing on what's important from here on out. Me."

"I couldn't agree more with that, Bri. But do you really think that either of them will give up? How many calls and messages have you racked up from both of them since you woke up this morning?"

I mumble an unintelligible response, because I haven't counted, and I don't want to.

Granted, I've had a hell of a lot more from Nico than I have Brad. But still, I know he won't just give up. I'm not going to have it that easy.

He hasn't listened to a word I've said since the first night we hooked up and I told him it was a one-night-only thing; why should I expect him to listen to my unspoken words now?

"What does he want?" Jodie asks as I swipe the screen and read his message.

I turned all my read receipts off when I first put my phone back on the other day. I knew I was going to get messages, and I knew I wouldn't be able to ignore them. My curiosity and nosiness were going to get the better of me, so I knew I'd be better off stopping them from seeing if I read them or not.

"To see me."

"And?" she prompts.

"I'm not. Not yet, at least."

"Not yet?" she quips, raising a brow at me.

"I'm going to have to face him one day and tell him we're finally done. No more quick hook-ups and epic orgasms."

"Why do I get the feeling you're already mourning your loss?"

"He's good, but he's not worth the drama. Neither of them are."

She stares at me as if I'm about to follow that up with something. A laugh, maybe.

"I'm done, Jojo. Going forward, I'm all about the vibrating friends and the smuttiest books I can find."

"I give you a week."

"Wow, your support astounds me," I deadpan.

"I'm right and you know it. Now drink up. We're hitting the shops."

I groan. "I hoped you were joking about that."

"Nope. I need some new lingerie for my man. He keeps ripping everything I own."

"Nothing like distracting me from my vow of celibacy," I mutter, downing what's left of my cocktail and stuffing my phone into my handbag without replying to Brad.

"Aw, you can dress up for your vibrators. They'll totally appreciate it."

"Bitch," I cough. Jodie throws her head back on a laugh before walking to the bar to pay for our brunch.

When we step outside, I find an Uber waiting for us, and before long we're heading into the shopping centre.

She doesn't immediately make a beeline for her favourite lingerie store; instead, we start wandering in and out of all the shops.

It's just like old times. Only now, she can afford to buy anything she wants thanks to her boyfriend.

I've got a nice buzz going on after the mimosas, but it's not going to be enough when she starts sexy lingerie shopping.

"What do you think?" Jodie asks, holding a dress up against her body.

"Hot," I reply, barely looking at the dress in question.

"Bri," she sighs, her eyes softening with sympathy.

"No, don't give me that look. I'm fine and fully present."

Her brow quirks at my blatant lie.

"You need to talk to him."

"I'm not doing this again."

I take off across the shop, my eyes scanning the clothes on offer, but I don't really see any of it.

My phone buzzing in my handbag distracts me, and despite my better judgement, I reach in and pull it out.

I'm expecting to see Nico's name staring back at me. I did have a photo of him naked in my bed as his contact, but I removed that after vowing that we were done to stop any kind of temptation when he reached out for a booty call. But when I see Knight's Ridge College as the caller, I immediately swipe the screen, expecting Melissa to be on the other end. I emailed her to let her know that I was planning on coming back Monday, and she said we'd catch up before then.

"Hello?" I say the second I have my phone pressed to my ear.

There's a pause that's just long enough to make my heart begin to race before the inevitable happens.

"I hope you know that your voice alone gets me hard." His deep voice washes through me, hitting me right between the thighs. All the hairs on my arms and back of my neck stand up as my hands begin to tremble.

"Fuck's sake," I hiss in the hope only my anger is audible down the line. "Didn't ignoring your calls and texts tell you anything? I don't want to talk to you."

He's silent for a beat, and I can't help picturing his face dropping like it did last night when I sent him away.

But all that changes when he growls, "Siren."

Heat washes through my body and an unignorable ache starts up between my thighs.

Damn him. Damn him to the pits of hell.

Gritting my teeth, I force myself to remember all the reasons I keep sending him away and telling him we're done.

"I mean it, Nico. Nothing has changed," I snap, putting as much conviction into my tone as possible before I pull the phone from my ear and hang up.

My chest heaves, my breaths race past my lips as I stand there staring at my screen, waiting for him to try again. But my phone goes to sleep, proving me wrong.

"Are you okay?" Jodie asks, coming around the rack of clothes I'm standing by.

My eyes lift to hers and I straighten my spine.

"Yeah, everything is fine."

"Nico again?" she guesses correctly.

"Yeah, he's trying new tactics and using the school phone to confuse me."

"Cheeky. But I like his style. Come on, I can't find anything I like in here."

"What about the dress?"

"Meh. I can do better."

"Okay, but I want more drinks after the next one."

She shoots me a look but doesn't argue.

Thankfully, the next shop doesn't excite her much either, so we're lowering our arses to a bench in a cocktail bar before I know it, waiting on two manhattans to be delivered.

Three cocktails later, we emerge from the bar in fits of laughter.

With the alcohol flowing through my veins and my girl's arm looped through mine, I almost feel like my old self again.

As we round the corner, Jodie having already announced that we're heading to her new favourite lingerie shop next, a shiver runs down my spine.

Spinning around, I drag Jodie with me to search the space around us for a familiar face, or even an unfamiliar one who might be watching us.

Now I know we have security following us, it makes our reality that much more serious.

The guys think we're at risk enough to employ a detail each to keep us safe. That's either some serious shit, or they're taking their possessive tendencies to a whole new level.

I find both our tails fairly quickly, but it's not their attention that caused me to react like that.

Seeing nothing of concern, I push my worries aside, telling myself it's just the alcohol making me paranoid.

"What's wrong?" Jodie asks when I drag her around once more.

"Nothing. Please proceed."

Her eyes narrow as she looks at me.

"I knew I should have cut you off at two."

"Where's the fun in that? Let's go buy you some sexy outfits for your boy," I announce happily, allowing her to lead me toward the shop. A shop we never would have stepped foot in prior to her getting with Toby. It was well out of our price range. Well, for me, it still is.

I can't help but smile as I think about her new life. Trips to Primark are long over for her.

I trail behind her as she runs her fingers over the delicate lace and soft satin. She plucks her size from the racks and hooks them over her fingers, ready to go and try on.

"Oh my God, this one has your name all over it," she says, pulling a bra from the rail and spinning around to show me.

I can't help but laugh. "I don't think so, Jojo."

I don't need to look at the price tag to know that it's well out of my reach.

"My treat," she says, turning back to the rail and pulling my size out.

"No, Jodie. I'm not—"

"Just try it on. You're going to be bored waiting for me to get through this lot. You could snap some photos while you're in there to torture Nico with."

A growl rumbles in the back of my throat at her suggestion, but she shoves the garments into my arms and flounces off before I get a chance to say anything.

I catch up to her as she hits the nightwear section and snatches up a few more items.

Toby has no idea what's coming his way.

"Are you trying to break your boyfriend or something?" I ask lightly.

"Nope, just remind him how lucky he is to have me."

"I'm pretty sure he already knows," I mutter as another shiver rushes down my spine.

Spinning around, I scan the shop. But just like outside, I find no one. Other than a handful of other women and two shop assistants, there's no one in here.

"Come on, let's go try these on."

She heads in the direction of the fitting rooms before I get a chance to say a word. I follow behind like a good best friend with the lingerie set swinging from my fingers.

I don't really want to try it on—it'll mean standing in front of at least one full-length mirror with my battered shoulder on display.

Probably the exact reason why you should do this.

The fitting rooms are empty, just four lonely cubicles with their heavy curtains tied back, waiting for someone to use them.

Jodie selects one, and I choose the opposite in case she feels the need to share her wares—which she probably will.

It's been a long time since there was any shame between us. We have literally seen everything and talked about everything else. Usually, I'd love a trip like this—a slightly less expensive one maybe.

Unhooking the curtain, I allow it to fall closed behind me, hang the lingerie from the hook and drop my bag to the chair in the corner.

I stare at myself in the mirror, trying to dig some of my old self up from somewhere to find the courage I need.

I hate that it's even an issue. My stomach knots up as I chastise myself for being so pathetic. But I can't help it.

After sucking in a deep breath, I shrug off the cover-up I'm wearing over my fitted t-shirt dress that hides my upper arm. And without looking in the mirror, I strip down to nothing but my thong.

"Oh my God, Toby is going to blow his load when he sees this one," Jodie announces happily, dragging me back to reality.

"Lucky arsehole," I call back, although it's with a heavy heart.

He's going to look at her like she's the only woman in the world.

I want that. I crave that. Even more so now I've got this ugliness on my shoulder.

"He's not the only one," a deep, familiar voice growls from behind me.

My eyes shoot up, but before I manage to scream, a hot hand is wrapped around my mouth to stop me.

18

BRIANNA

"You don't need to be dressed in anything and I'm always dangerously close to blowing, Siren."

My wide eyes hold his in the mirror, my heart like a runaway train in my chest.

"You've been ignoring me," he breathes, running the tip of his nose along the shell of my ear.

I try to scream at him, to tell him to get the fuck off me, but it's pointless. Instead, I go for actions over words.

I start swinging my arms backward in the hope of hurting him enough to force him to let go.

But all the motherfucker does every time I land a less-than-impressive blow on him is chuckle. And before I know it, he's somehow managed to gather both my wrists up in one of his giant hands, stopping me from fighting.

I gasp when the entire front of my body is pressed against the cold glass mirror before me.

"Nico," I cry from behind his hand, making him laugh once more.

"All you had to do was talk to me, babe," he soothes in

my ear. "But I must confess that right now, I'm damn glad you didn't."

He leans closer, aligning every inch of his body against mine. It's impossible to miss just how hard he is as his erection presses against my arse.

Heat floods my core and my thighs tighten of their own volition. My nipples pucker against the mirror, begging for his warm touch instead.

"I just needed to know that you were okay."

My brows pinch. Why would he think I wasn't okay?

Panic hits me that he might not have left when I thought he did last night and heard me crying. But that's ridiculous, because Jodie would have seen him.

I'm so lost in my own head and the fire burning through my veins that I don't notice him move back a little until something hard wraps around my wrists.

My eyes drop to my waist just in time to see the end of his belt as he restrains me.

Holy fuck.

"Did you read my letter?" he asks. There's a little hesitancy in his voice, and I can't help but notice that he doesn't meet my eyes. Instead, his gaze is locked on my injured skin. Unease and vulnerability washes through me. But I refuse to cower, to appear weak before him.

I hold still until he has little choice but to look up.

Then I nod.

"I meant it. Every fucking word."

My heart slams against my ribs as I remember what he said. How serious he sounded about us having a future.

Releasing my now bound wrists, he skims his hand over my arse.

"Fuck, you're sexy," he groans, sliding his hand around to my stomach and then up to cup my breast.

A moan rumbles in the back of my throat when he pinches my nipple.

Jodie says something, but I don't make out a single word of it.

"She has no idea," Nico whispers in my ear. "No idea that you're in here being my dirty little slut."

Another whimper.

He pinches my nipple hard enough to make me suck in a sharp breath through my nose before his hand descends once more, his fingers disappearing beneath the lace of my thong.

I scream behind his hand. A part of me wants to believe that it's me trying to refuse his touch. But there's a bigger part of me that knows I'm really spurring him on.

I fucking love being at his mercy, and he knows it.

My entire body jolts when he finds my swollen clit.

"Damn, Siren. Your knickers are ruined already and I've barely touched you."

He knows how much I like the risk of being caught just as much as he does. It's why he's fucking here, trying to prove to me why I should give in and jump into what he's offering me with two feet.

It's tempting. Really fucking tempting.

But I'm not ready.

"Were you thinking about me before I slipped in here?" he asks, and I shake my head.

It's a lie and we both know it.

He's all I've been able to think about. Much to my own irritation.

"Not sure I believe that, Siren."

I cry out when he drops his fingers lower and spears two inside me, stretching me open for him.

"Fucking miss this pussy," he murmurs as if talking to himself.

My eyes hold his in the mirror before he drops his face to the crook of my neck, kissing a line down the sensitive skin, and he doesn't stop until his lips brush the first cut on my shoulder. Regret and apology glitter in his eyes as he continues staring into mine.

Goosebumps break out over my entire body as he continues finger fucking me like a pro.

My lungs scream for more oxygen than I'm able to suck in through just my nose alone. My head starts to spin, but it's not unwelcome as he curls his fingers, grazing my G-spot just so.

My eyes drop from his when he closes them for a beat, and they find the healing cut across the bridge of his nose.

That, and his bruising, look so much better than when I last saw him in the light. But it still looks painful as fuck. How the hell he ate me out last night without screaming in pain, fuck only knows. I'm not complaining though, because it certainly didn't hinder his performance.

He shifts slightly behind me, resulting in his hard cock landing in my hand. Something I can only assume wasn't an accident.

My fingers curl around his steel length the best they can with the fabric of his trousers covering him.

My mouth waters behind his hand for a taste of him.

"Fuck, you just gushed around my fingers, babe. Whatever you're thinking about, keep going," he encourages. "Fuck," he barks, a little louder than he should as I clamp down on his fingers, my release surging forward.

Latching back onto my neck, he sucks hard, ensuring that everyone outside of this enclosed space is going to know what I've been up to and that I'm owned by someone.

The thought shouldn't turn me on as much as it does.

"Yes, Siren. Come all over my fingers. Give me everything and remember how good we are."

The second his teeth graze the already sensitive skin of my throat, I detonate.

My entire body convulses between him at my back and the now slick mirror at my front.

My screams would fill the cubicle if it weren't for his hand as wave after wave of pleasure washes through me.

He doesn't stop fucking me until the last tremors of my release have faded, and as he pulls his fingers from my pussy, he lets his other hand fall from my mouth.

Hungrily, I suck in deep lungfuls of air as my entire body trembles from the release.

Lifting the hand that was inside me, Nico holds my eyes as he parts his lips and sucks on the two fingers he just used to get me off, licking my juices from his skin.

"Tastes like mine," he growls after pulling them free.

"Nic—"

I startle when his hand covers my mouth once more.

"No arguing, Brianna. You're mine. I know it. You know it. And it's about time the rest of the world did."

I narrow my eyes, silently telling him that he's crazy. But all he does is smile menacingly at me.

After long, torturous seconds, his eyes finally leave mine in favour of the lingerie hanging from the rail to my right.

"Buy it," he orders. "And whatever else you want."

Pulling his credit card from his pocket, he makes a show of tucking it under the waistband of my thong.

"Then I want photographs of you in all of it."

"You're fucking crazy, and I'm not a whore," I grit out the second he releases my mouth.

My shriek of shock cuts through the air as he twists me

around and slams me back against the mirror with his hand around my throat.

"You're my whore, Brianna. And if I want you to have sexy lingerie, then you will."

"I'm not yours," I manage to gasp out as he cuts off my air supply.

A menacing smile plays on his lips.

"Oh, but you are. And the sooner you realise that, the better."

"You're certifiable. Last week you were more than willing to throw me away like a piece of rubbish," I argue when he loosens his grip slightly.

"Stop lying to yourself, Brianna." He leans in, his nose brushing mine. "I don't fuck girls twice. Ever. Yet you... I can't fucking get enough of you. It might have taken a near-death experience to make me see it differently, or maybe it was the shrink. But whatever it was, I see it now.

"Me and you. We're inevitable, babe. Your cunt knows it. Now we just need the rest of you to get on board."

All the air rushes from my lungs.

"You're serious?"

"What? Did you think I was joking in my letter? That came right from here, Siren," he says, lifting his free hand and tapping his chest, right above his heart. "Now start listening to yours and give me what I need."

"Someone needs to send you back to the hospital to get your head checked."

He smiles again, and damn it if it doesn't make every muscle south of my waist clench.

His free hand slips from where it's resting possessively on my hip to release my wrists.

My arms fall to my side the second my restraints are gone, and I have to fight the need to lift them and rub them.

"I'll see you soon, Siren." He releases my throat and takes a step toward the curtain before he pauses and looks back over his shoulder. "Spend my money, babe. What's mine is yours, yeah?"

I don't realise I'm holding my breath until the curtain falls back into place and I'm left alone with only my memories of whatever the fuck just happened.

The second the curtain falls closed behind me, I'm met with a pair of dark, confused but equally heated eyes.

Oh yeah. She knows what I did, and she's jealous as fuck.

"What the fuck are you doing?" Jodie hisses.

I take a step closer, and her eyes drop from mine in favour of the belt in my hand.

"If you hurt—" she starts to warn, but I quickly cut her off.

"I didn't hurt her. Not in any way she doesn't want, anyway," I quip. "I just came to prove a few points."

Her chest heaves as she stares at me, a million and one things she wants to spit at me on the tip of her tongue.

"Go on, I can take it. I'm not good enough for your best friend. I should leave her alone. Trust me, I know them all."

Her mouth opens and closes before she finally decides on something to come back at me with.

"If you hurt her again in any way, I will kill you with my bare hands."

A smirk curls at one corner of my mouth. "As much as I'd love to see you try, Jojo," I tease, "it won't be necessary."

"You sound overly confident about that," she points out.

My stomach knots. There's no way I can make those kinds of promises. Firstly, I'm a fucking liability. I didn't need recent events to prove to me that I'm hot-headed and irrational when I'm angry. But also, I don't exactly live a life that lacks danger.

Stepping out of the flat could be a risk on any day, let alone when we're at war with the Italians.

Anyone connected to us, let alone ones we truly care about, are always in danger. They just need to decide whether being with us is worth the risk.

Stella and Emmie embraced it early on. Cirillo blood runs through their veins. Calli has always been desperate to break free of the restraints our mother insisted on; Dad and I just followed her demands because why fucking not? She's my little sister—she deserved to be protected from the ugliness of our lives. Jodie might have taken a little longer to jump on the bandwagon. But much like Stella and Emmie, she's a Cirillo girl. Even if none of us want to mention the man who had a hand in creating her ever again. She's one of us. Willing to go to war with us, for us.

But Brianna...

She's not like them. Well, not from the background report Theo pulled on her.

There was a part of me that had hoped we'd find out that she was connected somehow. I mean, she still could be. It wouldn't be too much of a stretch of the imagination to believe that while Joanne was having it off with Jonas, her little sister was also involved with the same crowd. After all, someone knocked her up at fourteen. Whoever her father is might not even know he's got a hot-as-fuck daughter flaunting herself around town.

"She's mine," I growl at Jodie, remembering that she said something.

"She doesn't agree with that statement."

"She will."

With that said, I take off, leaving both Jodie and the woman hiding behind the curtain behind.

"Absolutely fucking not," I snap, ripping the sheer lace lingerie from my cousin's sticky fingers.

"What? It's hot," she argues, trying to grab it back.

"When you're twenty-one, go for it. Right now, you should be wearing cotton ones with Peppa Pig on the front."

Her face turns purple with my comment.

"Fuck you, Nico. I'm not a child."

Spinning on her heels, she storms out of the shop, leaving me standing there as if I'm the child who just got scolded and abandoned.

Movement to my right catches my eye, and when I look up, I find Jodie still glaring at me with her arms crossed over her chest.

She looks fucking savage. Toby would be hard as fuck for her right now if he were here and dragging her into one of those fitting rooms, I have no doubt.

I roll my eyes at her and take off, reluctantly leaving Brianna behind in favour of searching for my defiant cousin.

Why did I think allowing her to tag along would be a good idea?

"Rhea, wait," I demand, wrapping my fingers around her upper arm and pulling her to a stop.

"What?" she spits, her face still tight with anger. "Going to try and book me into the soft play?"

I can't help the snort of laughter that escapes me.

"Come on, I'll buy you an ice cream."

Throwing my arm around her shoulder, I steer her in the other direction.

"Ice cream won't make up for it," she sulks.

In only a few seconds, we're standing in line.

I can't lie, there was a slight ulterior motive to offering her ice cream. From here, I'll be able to see the second Brianna and Jodie emerge; hopefully, Brianna will be swinging a bag full of sexy lingerie from her fingers, and then I'll get to see where they go next.

An afternoon stalking the woman, who refuses to be mine, around while she shops is a totally sane thing to do, right?

"I know what you're doing," Rhea murmurs once she's content with a salted caramel ice cream in the guy's fanciest cone. "You're so transparent."

"What would you know about what I'm doing?"

"You've stalked the woman you're screwing—and also tried to kill, I might add—to a shopping centre. Slipped into her fitting room to do things I really don't want to think about that resulted in you walking out looking like your trousers shrank while you were in there." I shift on the bench we've found, hiding behind some weird plant to keep us out of sight, trying to cover the fact I'm still rocking a semi while eating ice cream and sitting next to my kid cousin. "And now we're sitting out here pretending to be 007 or some shit waiting behind a bush for her to appear. And something tells me that when we do, you're going to want to follow."

My mouth opens and closes, but I quickly discover that I don't have a response, because everything she just said is correct. Painfully so.

"Oh, look out, here we go," Rhea teases as both Jodie and Brianna emerge. Brianna is without a shopping bag.

My teeth grind, my ice cream cone shattering under my grip.

"All right, caveman. Calm down," Rhea quips as I just about stop my ice cream from landing in my lap when the top half falls off.

Movement catches my eye from either end of the row of shops, and I relax a little as their security details trail behind them at a safe distance.

They both know they're there now, and I'm so fucking glad they haven't made a big thing about it. None of us would get anything done if we knew the girls were out in the open, a waiting target for the Italians.

"You're such a fucking sap," Rhea starts when we also begin to tail them, watching as they move around shop after shop. Brianna never buys anything, but I get close enough to clock the things that do catch her attention and send Rhea in to buy them after they've left.

"Hey look, they're headed to a jewellery store. Should I just pick up an engagement ring while I'm in there?" she asks almost an hour later.

Her suggestion makes my heart rate increase, but I don't offer a response or allow her to see any kind of reaction when she looks back at me.

"Should have locked you in the car," I mutter.

"Yeah, but then you wouldn't have all this Brianna bait," she teases, holding up the bags with a wide grin on her face.

I'm not stupid. I know that I'm more than likely to get a knee to the balls for doing this. But the pain of that isn't enough to stop me.

She deserves to be treated like a queen, and I'm going to do it in any way I can.

"Fuck," I hiss when my phone starts buzzing in my pocket as our targets head into a bar.

Brianna had been drinking before I found her, that much was obvious when I looked into her gorgeous blue eyes. But as much as I like the idea of her loosening up, I also hate the idea of her being near any other guys in that bar.

My need to follow and sit myself at their table to warn anyone off her is almost enough for me to ignore Theo's call.

But the reality of what he could be ringing me for is too much to deny, and I swipe the screen and lift my phone to my ear.

"What?" I bark.

"Empire. Now," he demands, his voice cold and chilling.

A shot of adrenaline rushes through my veins. My hand trembles against my ear as my stomach turns over.

"Tonight?" I ask cryptically.

"Yes."

He hangs up the second he's confirmed my suspicions.

"Fuck. We need to go," I say, grabbing Rhea's upper arm and dragging her away from the bar that was my biggest concern only seconds ago.

"Go?" Rhea blurts, her eyes widening in shock. "Go where?"

"Back to school, where you should be," I growl, grabbing her upper arm and dragging her along with me as I regretfully turn my back on Brianna and storm through the shopping centre like my arse is on fire.

"Oh no. I'm not going back to school now. Hendrix will throttle me."

"Then maybe you never should have left."

She chuckles behind me, barely able to keep up with my pace but not complaining. I guess she's choosing her battles. Although, I'd have thought by now that she would have realised she's not about to win any. "Because that's what you would have done," she scoffs.

"Fine," I concede. "I'll take you home."

"Fuck no. That's worse."

I grind my back teeth as we finally make it to the car park.

"Rhea," I growl. "I'm not taking you with me."

"Did you hear me ask? I don't want to get involved with your little games. Leave me at your building, I'll go hang out with Daemon as I doubt he'll be allowed out to play."

The need to demand she tells me where she gets all her information from burns through me. But I push it aside. Her snooping is the least of my worries right now.

"Fine," I sigh, not even bothering to point out just how unimpressed Daemon will be by this. After all, she's right. He's not going to be heading to this meeting in person. He's more likely to be on video link, and I'm sure he's capable of hiding that from her, if there's even any point. It seems she already knows everything. "But move fucking faster," I bark, picking up my pace even more as my car comes into view.

"Dad really spared no expense with this, huh?" she mutters when she drops into my passenger seat.

She's right. Of course. Damien replaced my written-off car with the newest model out, and it seems he's added every extra on offer.

I'm grateful. I am. But it also sends a huge wave of guilt washing through me every time I think about what I did that night.

"I deserve it," I state confidently, voicing the complete opposite of my thoughts.

"That's up for debate," Rhea scoffs.

"I'm sorry, did you want a ride or what?"

"Like you'd leave me here. I'm assuming you noticed we skipped out on my security detail."

My grip tightens on the wheel as my eyes lock on a blacked-out Range Rover behind us.

She might think she swerved her protection, but she's underestimating Damien's need to keep her safe.

"Don't fucking tempt me."

The engine roars before us and I floor it out of the space, catching the Range Rover pulling out behind us before I turn the corner, heading for our building.

I don't bother getting out to deliver my cousin to what I assume will be a pissed-off Daemon. As amusing as that meeting will be, I don't have time for it. Instead, I barely wait for her to disappear through the door in the underground garage that leads to the lifts before I take off again.

Nothing will happen to her; she's got eyes on her from all directions. She doesn't need me as well.

My heart is in my throat by the time I'm ascending through the Empire in the lift.

The need for retaliation burns through me, making my mouth water and my fingers ache to cause some pain. Ricardo Mariano has no idea what's heading his way. But he needs to be aware of one thing. It will be me who puts him in the ground. And it will be us who wins this motherfucking war.

I'm a fucking mess by the time I finally spill out of the lift. Thoughts of Dad and that night still have the power to consume me, to bring down a cloak of darkness like I've never experienced before. And being on the cusp of shedding some Italian blood only makes my need for vengeance stronger.

I barely notice the men who are working security as I march toward Damien's office, but the second I push the door open, inviting myself in, I sure as shit see the faces staring back at me.

Damien, Galen, Stefanos, and my boys—all bar Daemon—study me with understanding and the same need for revenge burning in their eyes.

No one speaks until the door falls closed behind me with a loud click.

"We've got this, bro," Theo finally says, breaking the silence.

"Come and take a seat, son," Damien says, gesturing to the empty chair beside his son, right in front of him.

It's only as I move toward it that I realise Alex, Seb and Toby are standing.

Toby's hand lands on my shoulder as I pass, and I feel his support right the way down to my toes.

"The Italians have taken the bait. They're currently planning to ambush our warehouse where they believe we're hiding Daemon and Anthony. Enzo has confirmed. We're just waiting on a time," Damien says, corroborating what Theo alluded to in his vague phone call.

I nod as my fist curls on my lap. But when I open my mouth, very different words fall out from the ones I was expecting.

"The girls need moving. If we've got this wrong again, they could be in danger."

A beat of silence fills the room as the tension turns heavier.

No one says anything, but I feel their agreement.

Finally, Damien nods.

"Agreed. Get it done. I'll send you an address to deliver them to. We're not losing anything this time. They've already taken more than we were willing to offer. This ends. Tonight."

20

BRIANNA

"You know, ignoring it doesn't mean that it didn't happen," Jodie says, and not for the first time, as we climb through the building toward her flat. She's been trying to get me to talk about what went down in that fitting room since I reluctantly pulled the curtain back to find her standing there with an amused yet curious expression on her face.

"It didn't happen," I state, point-blank refusing to accept that it did.

"Bri—"

"No," I argue as the doors open and we spill out onto her and Toby's floor. "Don't give me that tone. It was a lapse in judgement. He caught me off guard and I wasn't ready—"

"Or you miss him and were desperate for a piece."

"Whose side are you on here?" I spit.

"Yours. Always yours. I'm just trying to get you to talk. You've said nothing about that letter, not in detail, anyway. And now this. I'm worried."

Her words are like a kick in the gut. "You don't need to be," I whisper.

"I won't let you go back there, Bri. I won't."

"This isn't the same," I argue, knowing exactly what she's talking about.

When she and Joanne took me home from the hospital after Mum's overdose, I completely shut down. I refused to talk to them. To anyone. But what they don't understand was that it wasn't about not wanting to open up to them. I did. I was just so fucking scared that I'd be taken away again that it took me a long time to trust that they would stick by me.

This. Nico. It's entirely different.

I think.

I'm busy juggling takeout coffees and the few bags she allowed me to take off her after her epic spending spree as she presses her hand to the scanner to unlock her front door.

"About fucking time, bitches," a familiar voice shouts from deeper inside the flat.

We knew they were waiting on us.

Only minutes after Toby called Jodie to tell her they'd been called in, Stella was blowing up our phones, announcing that we were going to have a girls' night while the boys were out running around the city, trying to kill Italians.

My stomach knots just thinking about them all—Nico—being in danger, but I quickly stuff it down and focus on what's happening here instead.

"All right, pipe down," Jodie calls back as she kicks off her shoes.

"Coffee?" Stella spits when we finally spill into the living room. "We're having girls' night and you brought coffee?"

"Brianna has been on a mission to get shit-faced all

day. She needs it if she's going to keep going," Jodie teases.

"Speak for yourself," I mutter, dumping the cups down on the table and quickly plucking mine and Calli's from the tray. "But I know a good way to give these a kick. Here you go, baby C," I announce happily, delivering her decaf as I pass her in favour of the kitchen. Reaching up into the cupboard, I pull down a bottle of Toby's whisky and twist off the top.

"Bri," Jodie warns.

I don't react and certainly don't look up, because I know exactly what I'll find.

Concern.

I love her like the sister I never had. But I'm sick of that look. It's why I need to go home.

I need my own space to sulk about my stupid decisions and life choices.

"Trust me, Jojo. You'd be doing the same thing if the situation were reversed."

"Well, I guess if you get wasted, you might spill the details."

"What details?" Emmie asks, immediately taking the bait.

I shoot my best friend the best death glare I can dig up while all eyes in the room burn into my skin.

"There's nothing to spill. Just a momentary lapse in judgement."

"Just those few minutes or every time you've been close to him?" she asks.

"What the fuck, Jojo?" I hiss, my irritation levels growing. And her shrugging in response doesn't help.

"You need to stop this," she says finally.

"Stop what?" I slosh a very generous amount of alcohol

into my coffee, to the point it almost overspills on Toby's granite counter.

"Stop running away from the truth. From what you really feel."

"Oh? And what is it that I really feel? Seeing as you seem to be an expert."

"What's Nico done?" Calli asks, correctly guessing that this little spat involves him.

"It doesn't matter what he's done. Which, incidentally, was hot as fuck, by the way."

Calli groans as Stella and Emmie get even more interested.

"We're listening," Stella says, leaning over the back of the sofa.

"What matters is Brianna trying to live with her head buried under a rock."

"Being sensible isn't living under a rock."

"Getting fucked in a fitting room is not being sensible."

"I think that's open to opinions," Stella quips.

"You fucked Nico in a fitting room?" Emmie blurts, a wide, salacious grin across her face.

I let out a heavy sigh. "Technically, no."

"Did you or did you not get off?" Stella asks.

"Jesus," Calli mutters, clearly not requiring this level of detail. Thought she'd be used to it by now.

"I did. He didn't."

"He left with some serious blue balls. You can definitely expect a visit tonight."

"This isn't helping," I sulk.

"I disagree," Stella argues. "You should keep talking it out. We need to hear all this if we're going to help."

"Nocturnal visits are the best, aren't they?" Emmie muses.

I throw my hands up in despair before swallowing a large mouthful of coffee, the whisky burning all the way down my throat.

"I'm going to shower. I can still smell him."

With my coffee in hand, I take off through the room. Their eyes follow my every movement and I'm almost out of the room when Stella suggests, "Maybe you should send him a video. Show him the prize he might get after all his hard work tonight."

"You know, I don't think any of you are taking this seriously. It's more than sex. It's…" I trail off when I hear my own words.

"Exactly," Jodie announces. "That is exactly my point."

I cry out in frustration before shutting myself into her guest bedroom.

Lowering my arse to the bed, I take another sip of my coffee and will my heart to stop racing.

Jodie is pushing me for a reason. She only wants the best for me, and she knows that hiding from all of this and smothering how I really feel is only going to make things worse in the long run. But I don't know how to do anything else. The prospect of opening myself up to any kind of possibility other than what we've had in the past is nothing short of terrifying.

The second a soft knock sounds on the door, I know who it is.

"Come in," I call, and the door opens immediately, revealing who I expected.

"You okay?" Calli asks, softly closing the door behind her.

The pained sigh that passes my lips tells her everything she needs to hear. Lowering her arse next to mine, she reaches for my hand.

"Everything is going to be okay, you know. And it doesn't matter how long it takes you to process all of this and how you feel about Nico, or anything else."

"Thank you," I breathe, squeezing her hand.

"Jodie hates seeing you like this. She wants you to fix it all so she can see you smile again."

"I know."

Silence falls between us as I think of my best friend and everything she's done for me over the past few years.

Her intentions are never anything less than wanting the best for me. And there has been more than a few times that she's had little choice but to take the hard route and force me to deal with my shit.

"Nico knows about the baby," Calli finally confesses quietly.

"I know. He came to tell me."

"Was he... angry?"

I shake my head as I think back. "No. He was weirdly calm. Proud, I think."

I glance over just in time to see her swipe an escaped tear from her cheek.

"He crashed into our flat like a hurricane. I thought Daemon was going to shoot him when I dashed out of the bedroom behind him and found him with his gun raised."

"Not sure if I'm relieved or pissed off that he didn't," I confess.

"Same," Calli laughs.

"What did he do"

"Hugged me." My eyes widen as her words hit me. "He was... really sweet. Supportive. Everything I hoped he would be."

"Maybe last weekend helped knock some sense into

him, because it would have been a very different story if we made it here. He was like a caged bull."

"I hate that you were hurt, Bri. But I also think you're right. He needed that wake-up call. In more ways than one."

I nod, unable to find any words to respond with. She's right, of course. Nico was on a one-way track to a serious collision. I just wish... Hell, I don't even know what I wish.

"I should let you shower," Calli eventually says. "And then we're all going to enjoy ourselves and try not to worry about what the boys are out there doing."

Our eyes collide and I look deep into her blue ones, searching for the answer to all my questions.

"It's happening tonight, isn't it?"

All it takes is one single nod for the world to fall from beneath me.

Thoughts of Nico finally getting his chance at revenge. It fills me with as much relief as it does fear.

"Everything will be fine," Calli says again, but this time, there isn't as much certainty in her voice as when she said it previously. She's nervous too. Terrified, actually. She's already come too close to losing Daemon; I can't imagine that level of fear will ever leave her. Hell, she'll feel it every time he leaves this place to work. But unlike me right now, she isn't letting it rule her decisions. Instead, she's embraced it and jumped right into what she really wants.

If only it was as easy as she makes it look.

"By the end of the weekend, it'll all be over, and normal life will resume," I assure her, trying to be as strong as she is for me.

A laugh falls from her lips, making my brow pucker.

"Normal?" she asks. "I thought you, of all people, would understand that nothing is ever normal around here."

"Well, as normal as you ever experience. You and

Daemon could walk out of the building together as a couple. He could take you out on a date."

"Daemon on a date?" she blurts. "How hard did you hit your head, Bri?"

"Oh shush, that boy loves you something fierce, he would do anything for you."

Her eyes hold mine for a beat before she pushes to her feet with a soft smile playing on her face.

"He's not the only one," she whispers before excusing herself from my room and leaving my head spinning again.

***

By the time I emerge from the guest room freshly showered and in my pyjamas, it's obvious from the way Stella, Emmie, and Jodie are grinding it up to a classic Usher song that they're more than a few drinks in. I might have been somewhat hiding, but I didn't realise I was gone for that long.

"Bri, come dance with us," Jodie calls, a happy, lazy smile playing on her lips.

If I were anyone else, I would probably miss the concern darkening her eyes, but I don't. I see it, and I know it's one of the reasons she pushed me earlier. Every single woman in this room is terrified for their men right now. I guess that explains how fast the alcohol is flowing.

I help myself to two of the shots lined up on the coffee table and down them without a second thought before my face twists up in disgust.

"What the fuck is that? Lighter fluid?"

"Why do you think I'm avoiding it like the plague?" Calli asks with a twinkle of mischief in her eyes.

"It's good shit. Emmie special."

"If this is what you all drink in Lovell, then I can understand why most people down there are half brain-dead."

"Hey, that's my hometown. I take offence to that."

"It's no lie, though, is it?"

A wicked grin spreads across Emmie's face. "Nope. Far from it. And I can say with absolute certainty that you've barely experienced just how brain-dead some of them are. You should be thanking your lucky stars that you didn't have to teach there."

"You mean none of the students would have screwed me in the library?"

Emmie sprays Stella with one of the potent shots at my words and the two of them fall about laughing like lunatics.

"Would have probably been more like a gang bang."

"Huh. Maybe I underestimated the amount of fun I might have had there," I quip.

"It's the pits of hell. I wouldn't even send Sloane there."

"Fuck that bitch," Stella shouts. "Nothing matters but us enjoying ourselves right now. Everything's been too fucking stressful recently. We deserve this."

Unable to argue with her, I quickly down another shot of poison and climb up onto the coffee table.

After all, if you can't beat them, join them.

"Come on, baby C. Let's see those moves that bring Daemon to his knees." Reaching my hand out, I haul her up onto the table with me as the music that's already bouncing off the walls only gets louder.

"Who the hell is that?" Stella shouts a little while later when a pounding on the front door sounds out as a song comes to an end.

"Sorry, I left my magic glasses at home, so I can't see

through wood," Emmie quips as Jodie stumbles toward the door.

"Check the peephole," Calli shouts, the tone of her voice sending a chill through my entire body.

Stella pulls her phone from her bra and turns the volume down when the next song starts up, suddenly looking a lot more sober and alert than she was only a few minutes ago.

"It's okay," Jodie calls. "Just a gatecrasher."

Calli breathes a sigh of relief as I picture Isla joining us.

I've only met her a few times, but she seems cool. I mean, anyone who's managed to break down some of Daemon's walls must be pretty awesome.

But as Jodie returns, I quickly discover that it isn't Isla.

"Rhea?" I blurt, finding her standing there looking more than a little excited by what she's found while still wearing her Knight's Ridge uniform.

"I thought Daemon sent you home," Calli says.

"Pfft, as if I was going to go that easily," Rhea says with a defiant eye roll. "What are we drinking?" she asks hopefully, her gaze landing on the empty shot glasses. "You guys know it's still the afternoon, right?"

"One," Calli—the only sober and sensible one of us left—starts, "you're not drinking anything. You're fifteen, in case you've forgotten."

"Unlikely," she scoffs. "And two?"

"It's actually early evening, and we deserve to let go a bit, so stop judging."

"Who said anything about judging? I want to join. Life has been hella stressful recently."

All of us stare at her in shock.

"Why are you here?" I ask rather bluntly and rudely.

"Well," she says, dropping her school bag and kicking

off her shoes, "I was hanging out with my cousin at the shopping centre, but I got dumped back here to hang out with Daemon when my father summoned all his minions."

My chin drops at her words and the knowing glint in her eyes.

Jesus Christ, even Rhea knows what happened in that fitting room.

"Y-you were—"

"Yep, right outside the shop," she confirms with a smirk. "Poor Nico was like a bear with a sore head after that. You really left him high and dry, huh?"

"Rhea," Calli snaps.

"What? I'm fifteen, not five. I know exactly what was going down behind that curtain. I was pretty jealous, too," she confesses. "Ew, wait... that came out all kinds of wrong. I don't want my cousin. He's gross. I just meant—"

"Please, stop talking," Calli begs while Stella and Emmie barely hold back their laughter.

"You should have been hanging out with us before now," Stella announces happily.

"I don't disagree," Emmie says, "But Theo will kill us for corrupting his little sister."

Rhea scoffs. "A little late for that. Now, is anyone going to get me a drink? And do we have any weed on the go?"

21

NICO

"What the actual fuck?" Theo barks the second we pile into Toby's flat, where we know the girls are all hanging out.

We weren't expecting to find them partying... with Rhea right in the centre of their gyrating huddle.

"Oh hey, Bro. How's it going?" she asks innocently as everyone else, including his wife, pointedly ignores his approach.

Alex snorts a laugh beside me as Toby mutters, "Oh shit. I'm glad I'm not any of them right now."

"Turn the fucking music off, Doukas," he booms, correctly guessing who's in charge of this little party.

With a dramatic, you're-a-serious-fucking-party-pooper eye roll, Stella makes a show of pulling her phone from her bra and kills the music.

"You need some help there, princess?" Seb asks, surging forward for his girl.

All of them are drunk, that is more than obvious, and after studying Brianna for a few seconds while she looks anywhere but at me, my eyes find my sister.

"You'd better not be fucking drinking," I bark.

"What the fuck, arsehole? Who are you to tell Calli what she can or can't do?" Emmie slurs, clearly as far gone as Stella right now.

"We don't have time for this bullshit," Daemon barks, magically appearing at the most opportune moment. "We need to move. All of you, go and get fucking dressed," he orders, much to Theo's irritation.

"Who the fuck put you in charge?"

"Jesus Christ," Alex mutters. "D's right, we don't have time for this." Ripping his eyes from our fearless leader, he scans the girls. "You all need to sober up and pack a bag. You're having a night away."

"What?" Stella blurts before her eyes narrow suspiciously. "Why?"

"Consider it a treat on us."

Stella, Emmie, Calli, and Jodie all turn to us, standing shoulder to shoulder and looking fierce as fuck.

"Good fucking luck," I mutter, walking toward Alex so we can watch the show from the sidelines.

This whole thing might have been my influence, but like fuck am I getting in the middle of it.

"What's going on?" Emmie demands, placing her hands on her hips and staring her husband down like he doesn't possess the power to snap her neck without so much as breaking a sweat.

"We've booked you into one of the fanciest spa hotels in the city for the night."

"Why?" Emmie demands, refusing to back down.

"Oh no. We're not buying that shit. Tell us the truth," Stella demands.

Alex leans closer, his breath tickling my neck, before he whispers, "Is it wrong that they're making me hard?"

"Fucking hell, man."

"What? You can't tell me all that fierce hotness doesn't affect you."

My eyes float to Brianna, who remains on the periphery of this situation.

"I can honestly say that those four do nothing for me, no matter how fierce they get."

"Fuck me, man. She really has whipped you right up, hasn't she?"

My lips part to argue with that statement, despite the fact it's quite obviously true, when Stella's shrill voice cuts through the air.

"You can't just hide us away like some weak, incapable little women. Let us help. Let us fight for what's ours just as much as it is yours."

"Yeah, no. That's not fucking happening," Seb growls.

"Unbelievable. You know just as well as everyone here that I'm good for it."

"Don't I fucking know it," Seb mutters to himself.

"We need you to stick together. All of you. We need to know that you're all safe so that we can do our jobs, otherwise—"

"He's right, Stella," Jodie says, placing a calming hand on her shoulder. "They need you to protect us. Is Mum safe?" she adds.

"Yes," Toby assures her. "She's with a friend. Nothing to worry about."

"But—" Stella starts again.

"Baby, please," Seb all but begs.

Stella glances back at Emmie. She might not be joining in on this argument, but her need to shines bright in her eyes.

She wants it too, to stand beside us and fight. I fucking love it as much as I hate it.

The guys might be right in refusing to let them. It doesn't matter how skilled they are, the thought of putting them in the direct line of fire like that sends a cold chill racing down my spine.

"We need to know that we can come back to you when it's all over," I say, hoping to squash the argument once and for all.

Brianna's head immediately snaps in my direction, her eyes holding mine captive for a few minutes as something familiar crackles between us.

I need to know that I can come back to you.

I silently beg for her to be on our side, to help convince Stella that this is the right thing to do.

After a few seconds, she nods, and I just about manage to keep my sigh of relief locked inside.

"Let's go pack a bag. The longer we're standing here arguing, the more time we're wasting. The guys have a job to do, and so do we."

Finally, Stella stands down, but Seb doesn't let her move back as she takes a step away from him. Instead, he wraps his arm around her waist and hauls her back into his body, slamming his lips down on hers.

Before I know it, all the guys have swept their girls up into their arms and disappeared from the room with them, leaving me staring at Brianna, desperate to do the same.

"Right, well, that bag won't pack itself," she mutters, taking a couple of steps toward the bedrooms and dragging me from the trance I'd fallen into.

"Siren," I command, forcing her to stop.

When she doesn't do anything else, I move closer, eating up the space between us.

But the second she twists around to look over her shoulder, my movement falters.

"This doesn't change anything, Nico. I'll follow your orders because it's the right thing to do, but don't go getting any crazy ideas. I'm doing this for them, not you."

My lips part to respond, but she's faster, blowing out of the room as if those few seconds never happened.

"Oh, burn, cuz." Rhea's teasing voice flows through my ears, awakening the devil that lives inside me.

I spin around on the balls of my feet and rush over, getting right up in her face.

"Why the fuck are you still here?" I growl, my voice low and deadly.

"What?" she asks innocently. "I'm not allowed to hang out with my cousin and your girlfriend?"

That final word hits like a bat to my chest.

"She's not—"

"Leave it, man," Alex says, grabbing my upper arm and dragging me back from the defiant pain in the arse that is my cousin.

"She should be at home for Damien to worry about. Not us. We've already got enough on our plates."

"It's okay. She'll be fine with the girls. Let's just go get ready, yeah?"

He tugs on my arm once more, forcing me to stumble after him. I comply because I have little other choice, but not before my eyes lock on the hallway that leads to Toby's guest room.

"Later," Alex snaps. "Let's get this job done and then you can spend the rest of the night trying to win her over."

"Pfft, good luck with that," Rhea scoffs.

I tense, more than ready to turn around, but Alex's grip on me ensures I continue marching forward.

"Ignore the brat," he says loudly enough for Rhea to hear before he looks back at her and, I swear, fucking winks.

"Is Stella right?" I ask once we're out in the hallway and away from prying ears. "Should we allow her and Emmie to stand with us?"

"Are you fucking insane?" Alex asks, finally releasing me.

"No. You heard the boss as well as I did. We're low on numbers. Only those who we truly trust are in on this. We need all the help we can get."

"Are you suggesting we're not enough?"

"What? No. Never. I'm suggesting that we could have more backup."

While we're heading to the warehouse that Damien has baited the Italians to, along with Galen, Stefanos and a couple other of our loyal soldiers; Daemon, Ant and a few others are staying here. The risk of me being right and the Italians playing us once again was too high to leave our home—our girls—unprotected.

If they suspect we're lying and that Daemon and Ant are here, they'll swerve our decoy and head straight for this place to take back what they think belongs to them.

"I hope we've got this right," Alex muses. "Maybe more should stay—"

"We've got it right," I state confidently. "Plus, Daemon and Ant have it covered here. This place is locked down at the best of times. No Italian fuck is getting inside."

"Here's hoping. I'll see you in ten, yeah?"

I stand there motionless as he lets himself into his flat, leaving me standing alone in the hallway.

The need to go after Brianna burns through me, but Alex is right. There's time later for that.

Right now, I need to focus on tonight, on getting the revenge I've been craving since the moment my eyes landed on Dad's lifeless body.

The second I walk into my bedroom, pull my wardrobe open and stare at the black suits staring back at me, something settles within me. I forget about everything in my life apart from the task I've been set for tonight, and the only thing I can see is that motherfucker's smug face. The next time I stare into his eyes while my gun is pressed against his temple, he won't be so fucking happy with himself.

I dress on autopilot, my years of training taking over. The final thing I reach for in the wardrobe is my tie. Well, it's not my tie; it's Dad's. It's one of the few things I took from the house when Mum was too busy soaking up everyone's sympathy. It's stupid really, but wearing something of his as I go into battle makes me feel closer to him. Like he's here with us, urging us on. His cufflinks are the last thing I add to my uniform. They're silver with the Cirillo emblem engraved onto the flat square with shining gold gemstones.

I lower my arm after I've secured the second one and suck in a deep breath before looking up at myself in the mirror.

I stare deep into my eyes, trying to find anything that reminds me of him, something that can give me the extra strength I need right now.

"Give 'em hell, Son."

I hear his voice as if he's standing right behind me. They're words he said to me over and over again as I was growing up, as he was training me. But I've never needed to hear them quite as much as I do now.

"This is for you, Dad," I say before dipping my head and turning away from the mirror.

The others are going to be waiting, and I have no intention of letting anyone down tonight. Or ever again, if I can help it.

As I step out of my flat, Theo and Emmie also emerge from theirs. He's dressed like me, ready for battle. And while Emmie might also be head to toe in black, she hasn't attempted to cover the irritation written all over her face.

I get that they're pissed. I do. But also, there's no way in hell that any of them are going anywhere near any Italians tonight. My boys need their girls when this is all over. Hell, I need mine, too, but something tells me I'm going to have to keep dreaming there.

Disappointment sinks into the pit of my stomach as I think about all my boys being welcomed home after this to open arms and the promise of endless pleasure for what they've endured to keep them safe. Then there will be me, heading home alone to a cold, empty bed. Fucking great. The only bright side to that is that Alex will probably have the same experience, although, knowing him, he'll head out to find a willing woman to lose himself in. Something that I'd have thrown myself head first into in the past. But now, I couldn't think of anything worse.

Emmie offers me a terse smile as the two of them pass me, Theo carrying her bag. Something that has probably pissed her off even more. I can almost hear the argument they had over it only minutes ago.

The air is tense as fuck as we step into the lift and descend through the building, and it doesn't get better as we spill out and find the others waiting for us.

"Cars are waiting outside to take you to the hotel. No matter what happens, you do not leave until one of us comes to get you. You do not answer the door, you do not contact anyone. In fact, turn your phones off right now," Theo demands coldly.

Anyone outside of this group would think he doesn't care, but that is far from the truth. The set of his shoulders and the tightness of his jaw tells a very different story.

"We need to know that you're locked up safe. Do whatever you want within that room, but do not step a foot outside."

"Jeez, we got it, Dad," Emmie mutters.

He pins her with a look that would make others cower, but not Emmie Ramsey. The Cirillo and Reapers' blood that runs through her means she cowers to no one. Especially not her husband.

"I think you'll find it's Daddy to you, and you'll do as you're told."

"Fuck, I think I just came," Stella groans before a shriek of shock rips from her throat as Seb twists his fingers in her silver hair and drags her head back so she has no choice but to look at him.

"The cars are waiting," I state before they start going at it like animals. "Cal, be a good girl and lead the way."

My sister's brows lift in shock, but she keeps her mouth shut wisely. Daemon doesn't, although thankfully, whatever he says that makes her blush like a sailor is whispered so quietly I miss it.

After a few more seconds of PDA than any single and desperate guy needs to witness, the girls finally leave the building and slide into the two cars waiting for them.

The guys watch them with longing in their eyes. But the second the cars drive off and they all turn toward where Alex and I are impatiently waiting, their faces show nothing but pure determination.

"Daemon, go and get your team set up and in position," Theo demands. "The rest of you, let's fucking go. We've got blood to spill."

He takes off in the direction of the stairs that lead down to the underground garage, giving Seb, Alex, Toby and I little choice but to follow.

We're almost at his Maserati when my phone buzzes in my pocket.

Unable to ignore it, I pull it free and wake the screen up. The words that stare back at me make my breath catch and my chest constrict.

Siren: Give 'em hell, soldier.

22

BRIANNA

"You okay?" Jodie asks as I slip my phone back into my bag and rest my head back, staring up at the black ceiling above me.

"Yeah," I breathe.

"They know what they're doing. You have to trust them."

"I do. Everything will be fine," I say, thinking of Calli's words from my room earlier.

Lifting my head, I look around my best friend and find Calli's concerned blue eyes.

"You good?" I ask as she instinctively lifts her hand and rests it against her stomach.

She nods, her eyes filling with tears that I can only assume she's trying to fight.

"Umm... what Nico said earlier," Jodie starts as she follows my line of sight, "about you not drinking..."

"Fucking idiot," Calli mutters, much to my amusement.

"It's true... you're—"

"Yeah," Calli agrees. "The others don't know yet, though, so—"

"My lips are sealed," Jodie promises before she turns to me. "Can you believe this?" she asks excitedly before her face drops with realisation. "You knew."

"I did."

Her lips part to say something, but a heavy sigh passes them instead, and she slumps down in her seat a little.

"I guess that all makes a lot of sense," she muses.

"My brother is an idiot."

"Can't argue there, Cal," Jodie confesses. "But he's so much more than that."

"Yeah, that too."

Silence falls around us as we're driven across the city.

We have no idea where we're going, and I can only assume there is a reason for that, so I just sit back and trust that the guys know what they're doing. The women in these two cars are the most important in their lives. They wouldn't risk them for anything.

Jodie and Calli eventually pick their previous conversation back up when Jodie's curiosity over Calli's pregnancy gets the better of her and she begins asking all the standard questions. But I don't join in; I'm too lost in my own head, which is filled with images of Nico dressed up like the brutal soldier that he is.

The sight of him standing beside Theo as they stepped out of that lift made my heart stop, I'm fucking sure of it.

Dangerous. Formidable. Gorgeous.

And all mine, if I want him.

Although, wanting him isn't really in question here. I've wanted him since the first night I laid eyes on him. Who wouldn't? He's hot as hell. But embarking on regular hookups and allowing it to turn into something more is my sticking point.

I've never had a boyfriend. I've never wanted any man

to be a permanent fixture in my life. I don't want to fall into the trap of relying on one, and I certainly don't want anyone to rely on me for anything.

But if that is true, then why am I yearning for something more?

For something that terrifies me as much as it exhilarates me?

"Jesus," I mutter a few seconds after we've turned off the main road in favour of a secluded track that eventually reveals a huge manor house.

The sun is setting behind the Victorian building. Well, honestly, castle would be a better description of the place. It's like something I'm more likely to see while I'm quickly skipping past an episode of *Antiques Roadshow* than in real life.

It has turrets and pillars and everything.

"What is this place?" I ask, my nose practically pressed against the glass of the blacked-out window before me.

"No idea. It's beautiful, though," Jodie muses.

"Look, they have a wedding on," Calli points out.

Both Jodie and I turn toward her side of the car just in time to catch a bride and groom disappearing through the trees that line the grounds, a photographer hot on their tails.

"Her dress is stunning," Jodie breathes as the long lace train disappears.

"I bet those photographs will be incredible."

"That'll be you soon," Jodie says to Calli, who laughs.

"I'm in no rush," she says softly.

"What you've got growing in your belly says otherwise," Jodie teases.

"I've got everything I could possibly want right now." A sad smile curls Calli's lips. While she might be telling the truth, I know her pain from losing her parents is still raw. Just like her brother. "Plus, I don't want to be a beached whale in a white dress."

"Firstly, that's not possible. You'll be beautiful no matter how big you get. And secondly, nothing could ever put Daemon off making you his permanently."

"I am his permanently," she argues. "We don't need a certificate and rings to prove it."

"You make it sound so easy." I don't realise the words actually leave my lips until they both turn to me.

"I thought you of all people would be aware that it's been anything but easy, Bri," Calli says. "It's been all kinds of painful and traumatic getting to where we are now. And something tells me that we've got more coming our way."

"No, don't say that," Jodie says sadly. "This is all going to work out. The guys are going to put an end to all this and we can move on."

"I have every confidence they will, yes. But then what? This might be the end of the war with the Italians, but what comes next? This kind of thing will always be our lives. We're always going to be waiting for the next war, the next loss, the hit."

"Christ. Maybe I should run while I have the chance," I say.

"You should," Jodie agrees, shocking the shit out of me. "But you won't. This is where you belong and you know it."

"With you, yes."

She chuckles and shakes her head. "Not just me, Bri.

All of us. Remember when you were a kid and you used to fall asleep at night wishing for a family?"

I frown, hating her bringing up that depressing shit when we've got enough on our plates right now.

I sense Calli lean forward to look at me as I stare out of the window beside me once more. The right side of my face burns with her attention, her curiosity, but I refuse to turn and look into her eyes.

"This is it, Bri. It might not be what that little girl thought a family was all those years ago, but it's one all the same."

My eyes burn with tears as I nod in agreement.

"Those boys are out there fighting for all of us. It's scary, and terrifying, and I'm freaking the fuck out right now. But it's what they've got to do to protect their family, and we've got to do whatever we can to support them. And if that means we lock ourselves in there and wait it out, then that's what we'll do. We stick together."

"No matter what," Calli adds. "And when they're back, he's going to need you, Bri. Whether they've succeeded or failed at getting to Ricardo, he's going to need you in a way that scares him just as much as it does you."

"Jesus," I mutter, giving up on trying to contain my tears and instead swiping them from my cheeks.

"Come on, let's go check this place out," Jodie encourages. "I could certainly think of worse places to wait."

As Calli pushes the door open, movement outside my window catches my attention and I find Stella, Emmie and Rhea waiting for us.

"I totally made the right choice skipping school today," Rhea tells me happily, all of them thankfully ignoring the fact I'm teetering on the edge of an emotional breakdown.

"Do your parents know where you are?"

"All right, calm down, Miss Andrews. Jeez."

"The guys have sorted it," Emmie assures me. "We just need to keep her out of trouble."

Stella snorts a laugh.

"What? I'm an angel."

"So are we," Stella says with a wide, menacing smile.

"Christ, all of you are going to stay out of trouble," Calli warns, pulling rank as the sensible one. I guess she is closest in line to leadership here. Or is that Rhea? Fuck if I know.

Our drivers grab our bags from the cars and they trail behind us like good little puppies so we can check-in.

The second Calli and Emmie walk through the huge doors, the two women behind the desk rise to their feet.

"Good afternoon, ladies. We're glad to have you with us. Everything has already been organised for you. If you would like to follow, I'll take you up to your suite."

I share a look with Jodie as one of them slips from behind the huge mahogany desk they were sitting at and gestures for us to follow her.

I have no idea if they know who we are. From the situation we're in, I'd suggest not. But it's clear they think we're some kind of royalty.

We step into the most insane lift I've ever experienced in my life. And while I try to ignore my reflection, knowing that my face is going to be red and puffy from crying, and the fact I couldn't look like I belong here less in my pyjamas, it's impossible not to see myself. The walls are mirrored and even the gold decoration is so shiny our reflections are more than obvious.

We ride right to the top of the building before the doors open and we spill out onto thick, luxury purple carpet and follow the sharply suited woman to a massive set of intricately carved doors.

Our drivers diligently follow us with our bags, having refused to hand them over to the porter in the lobby.

"Here you go, ladies. If you need anything, just press one on the phone and we'll be able to assist you."

She holds the door open and I hang back with Jodie as the others rush into the room to check it out.

"Who could have predicted how our lives were gonna turn out, huh?" she asks beside me as we follow behind.

"Holy shit," I gasp, my eyes darting around the colossal room. It's bigger than most people's houses.

"This is our most exclusive suite. Six bedrooms lead from both the main room and that hallway," the receptionist says.

"Shouldn't the happy couple be in here?" Jodie asks, echoing my thoughts.

"It was out of their budget."

"How much is this place?"

"If you need to ask, you can't afford it," Jodie mutters, much to the woman's amusement.

"There are very few who can," she says in agreement. "Make the most of it. Everything you could need or want will be catered for during your stay. And we are under strict instructions regarding your safety, so please, relax, knowing that we've got everything covered." She glances back at our drivers, also our security details, as if to tell them that their services aren't required, although I can't imagine they'd go against Damien's order and abandon us here. Even if their skills could be used elsewhere tonight.

"Thank you. We really appreciate it."

She excuses herself, and Jodie and I share another look of pure disbelief before taking in the room in more detail.

"This is fucking insane," Rhea's excited voice comes from down the hallway. "All six of us could fit in this bath with room to spare."

Our eyes collide again, and both of us burst out laughing as our thoughts follow the same filthy line.

"If Rhea wasn't here, I might even suggest it. Stella and Emmie would be in. Not sure about Calli," I quip as we follow the voice to discover just how big this tub really is. "The boys would lose their shit when they found us."

We find Rhea fully dressed and relaxed as if nothing is wrong in our world in exactly what she said. A massive fucking bathtub.

"Christ, the fun that could be had in that," Stella says when a door on the other side of the room opens and she emerges into the elegant white and copper room.

"It's really something," Jodie mutters.

"Anyone wanna grab me that bottle of bubbles we passed in the living room?" Rhea asks.

There's a beat of silence before we all look at each other, an unspoken agreement passing between us, and without a word, we all turn on our heels and race from the room.

"Hey," Rhea complains. "What did I say? Where are you going?"

Emmie reaches the ice bucket that contains two bottles of champagne while Stella collects up the six glasses.

"Wait, this one is non-alcoholic," Emmie says, screwing her face up like the label physically offends her.

"You're shitting me," Rhea sulks, having climbed out of the tub to follow us. "We're at war and I can't even have a little alcohol? They were all getting wasted and fucked every weekend when they were my age. It's fucking bullshit."

"It's not for you," Calli blurts. "It's for me."

Rhea's lip peels back, not understanding why anyone would want a non-alcoholic drink. Although, in this situation, I can't help but want to agree with her.

"Why the hell would—"

"No," Stella gasps, her eyes widening as she steps closer with the champagne flutes still in her hands. "Are you—"

"Pregnant?" Emmie finishes for her.

Calli swallows nervously before she holds her head high.

"Yep. Ten weeks."

"Ho-ly shit, Cal."

"Does Daemon know?" Stella asks, still in as much shock as if someone told her that she's the one who's pregnant.

Calli throws her head back and laughs.

"Of course he knows. It was only you guys I was hiding it from."

"Oh, nice," Emmie teases.

"You're really pregnant?" Rhea asks. "Like, growing an actual person?" Her eyes drop to Calli's flat stomach in horror.

"Yep, a real person. I've got my money on a girl, but Daemon, Alex and Nico are convinced it's a boy."

"Of course they are," Emmie scoffs.

"Definitely a girl," Stella agrees, not looking at all put out by Calli's confession about both of their brothers already knowing.

"Well, I guess that deserves a toast," Emmie says, finally ripping the foil from the bottle in her hand and popping the cork.

She fills five glasses, one much smaller than the rest, which gets handed to Rhea. She looks thrilled until she sees the contents compared to ours, and then Emmie opens the bottle for Calli and pours her a glass too.

The six of us find ourselves seats on the unbelievably comfortable sofas surrounding a coffee table that's bigger than most dining tables, and we fall into easy conversation, mostly surrounding Calli's pregnancy, but also drifting to Nico and what happened last weekend.

It's nice. It's easy. But as time passes and the champagne goes down, the tension surrounding us becomes heavier and heavier.

Everyone's concerns are growing, and we're all utterly helpless to do anything about it.

I know this isn't their first rodeo. They've experienced this before, but honestly, I don't know how they do it. My nerves are shot. Every noise that comes from outside the suite startles me and my eyes jump to the door like they're about to crash through it.

But it never happens, and as night falls, all we can do is sit there, trying to distract each other while we continue drinking as if it'll help drown out the concern and unease of what's happening right now in another part of the city.

23

NICO

"Well, this is… an anti-climax," I sulk to Theo as we sit in the dark, waiting for these motherfuckers to show their faces.

We were early, wanting to make sure we were in position long before the Italians' expected arrival time, but shit. This is fucking boring.

Theo glares at me. He's in full-on soldier mode—hell, I am too, but his comes with a heap load more patience than mine. Especially tonight.

"It's going to happen," he assures me. "Enzo said the intel was vague. That his brother was talking in riddles to stop this leak from getting out. But they will be here."

"You know, if this goes wrong, then they're going to know they've got a leak. This might be our only shot."

"We'll get it done," he promises before pulling his phone out and staring at the screen, the light illuminating his face like a beacon in the dark.

"Still nothing," he sighs, making me wonder if he's doing as well with this waiting game as he makes out.

It might have been my dad we lost that night, but I

know he feels his loss almost as deeply as I do. He wasn't just his uncle, he was almost as important as his own father. He wants this justice just as fiercely.

"Anything from Daemon?"

"Nope, still clear over there too."

"If they already found out that this is a set-up, then we could all be fucked."

"They haven't. Only the most trustworthy of soldiers know about this mission. It would not have got back."

"How do we know they're trustworthy, though? Someone has been spilling our intel despite everyone being looked into and monitored. There's no reason to believe that—"

Theo's phone buzzes and he quickly lifts it once more.

"Movement," he states, making my heart jump into my throat.

"Yeah?" I ask, hope filling my veins that tonight really is going to be the night.

"Get ready," he says, getting to his feet and pulling his gun from his waistband.

We're inside the warehouse that we've tipped the Italians off about. The plan is simple, understated, and hopefully perfect.

We want them to break in, making them believe they're about to find their two lost prisoners, only our guys are going to follow them in, silently taking out their entourage. And when they get to the deepest part of the building, all they're going to find when they get here is us with our guns pointed at their heads.

We discussed other options. Many were keen to ambush them on the way in, take them all out in one fell swoop, but we quickly agreed that wouldn't be the best way to handle this. Firstly, I don't want Ricardo to die from a distance. I want to look him deep in the eyes as I put an end to his miserable existence. And second, Enzo is going to be with them. He's a part of Ricardo's inner circle, just like his brother, who we've all slated to take the reins over there once the power-hungry oldest Mariano sibling is out of the equation. And after everything Ant and Enzo have done for us... well, even our dark and twisted hearts couldn't cast them aside in favour of our need for vengeance.

Jumping to my feet, I follow Theo's move and have my gun in hand, ready for action as we stand there shoulder to shoulder.

Nothing but silence and the sound of our increased heart rates can be heard as we wait.

"Are your comms on?" Theo asks after tapping his ear.

"No, there's nothing," I confess, pulling the small device from my ear to inspect it.

"Shit," Theo hisses. "We must be out of range."

"I thought these were the shit?"

"Yeah, well. Clearly fucking not."

Ripping his own device out, he throws it across the room in frustration. It collides with the wall before bouncing across the floor.

Anger and frustration come off him in waves.

"We're ready for this, man. Chill," I say.

His eyes find mine, and I swallow as I find them full of emotion that he's usually able to lock down.

"I want this for you, cuz. I don't want anything to fuck this up."

"We don't need comms. We'll hear them coming and we'll make them our little bitches."

He nods once, blinking away that unusual show of his true feelings, pulling his stone-cold mask back on.

With our stares locked on the closed door before us, we wait. And wait. And wait.

Without any communication from those who can see what's going on, we can only assume that they're searching what they think is an abandoned warehouse. Well, abandoned bar the prisoners they're hunting for.

If they're smart, they might realise it's a set-up when they discover there is no one on guard. But other than putting someone in the firing line, we'd be risking the life of someone too important if they were to put them out there to be found first.

A loud bang somewhere beyond the door is our first clue that they're getting close. The second is their loud yet muffled voices.

Oh yeah, they're fucking pissed.

Good. It'll only make the end of this so much sweeter.

Adrenaline shoots through my veins when the sound of footsteps hits my ears.

We have no idea how many are out there. We could be evenly matched, or we could be well outnumbered.

Honestly, it doesn't matter. Theo and I have enough hate for these cunts between us to take their entire family down. Or at least, that's what I like to tell myself.

We move into position on either side of the door, fingers on triggers and ready for some action as the footsteps get louder.

We look at each other, a silent agreement passing between us before they come to a stop on the other side.

"This is the final room, Boss," a heavily accented voice says.

"They're not here," he states confidently. "Motherfuckers have been playing us."

My heart drops at the thought of them turning around and walking away.

"They're waiting for us."

My eyes collide with Theo's a beat before something rolls beneath the door.

The flashbang immediately lights up the room, stealing my vision and making my ears ring like a motherfucker. I don't know anything else has happened until the gun is wrenched from my hand and a fist collides with my cheek.

My head snaps back as pain spreads across my face and shoots down my neck.

My body acts on instinct, fighting back against whoever is on me, and despite being practically fucking blind for longer than necessary, I manage to land a few solid punches, all the while praying our guys are about to spill through the door and help us out.

Even after my vision clears, I don't get a good look at the man who's trying to end me with his fist like his own life depends on it. I mean, to be fair, it does. The second I can get my hands on my gun, I'm going to blow his brain to kingdom fucking come.

"Motherfucking cunt," is the first thing I hear when my hearing comes back to me before I watch Theo charge at the guy he's been fighting with.

It takes a second, but I boom, "Stop," when I see the tattoos that cover the hands raised in preparation for Theo's strike.

Theo immediately follows orders, even if they do come from me, although he doesn't avert his gaze from the hooded figure before him.

And to prove I'm right, no more punches are landed.

"You can take them off, cunts," I scoff, lifting my hand

to wipe the blood trickling from my split lip. "They've gone."

I don't know for sure that there were more than two of them when they entered, but my sixth sense says there were and that they've fled like fucking pussies.

Proving me right, both Matteo and Enzo rip off the masks covering their bloody and bruised faces, right as Alex, Toby and Seb come racing through the door.

"What the fuck is going on?" they bark, finding the four of us fighting for breath and covered in blood. Not that the four of them look that much better, to be fair.

"They've gone," Toby confesses, holding my eyes and allowing me to see the regret within his.

"Motherfucker," I bellow, slamming my already busted-up knuckles into the wall. "Where?" I shout, getting right up in Matteo's face.

We knew that Ant and Enzo were firmly on our side with this fight, and we suspected that Matteo might also be, but Enzo never openly confirmed that.

It seems we might just have been right, though.

He shakes his head.

"No," I bark, slamming my palms into his chest and making him back up. "There is more to this. Where have they gone?"

He swallows as Theo steps into my line of vision.

The second our eyes collide, the answer becomes more than obvious.

Daemon.

"Let's go," I demand, already spinning on my heels in preparation to run to where Theo abandoned his car.

Footsteps pound the dusty concrete floor behind me as I force my legs to move as fast as they'll go.

My body screams in pain from Enzo's attack as I fly

down the long corridor lined with what used to be offices back in the day.

I spill out in the dark night, my eyes scanning the area and focusing on the spots that are flooded with light.

"Oh fuck," I breathe.

"We weren't out here having a fucking party," Seb scoffs, coming to a stop beside me and surveying the chaos they left behind when they came for us.

Stefanos, Galen and the others that were out here waiting in case we needed backup are busy dragging bloody Italian bodies into a pile ready for our clean-up crew to sort out when they arrive.

"We're a few down," Stefanos says proudly.

"Yeah, not the fucking one we want, though," I mutter.

"What the fuck happened?" Theo barks.

"Gave us the slip when he discovered it was a set-up." Galen confesses.

"Yeah, but it's where they are now that's the issue." I scoff.

"Daemon?" Stefanos asks, concern replacing that previous pride.

"Only one way to find out."

Abandoning the bodies, he commands everyone to follow us as we race through the trees in favour of the cars.

Ripping Theo's passenger door open, I drop into the seat as the others follow suit.

"Dude, you're bleeding," Alex says, making me turn around to see who he's talking about.

"So are you, arsehole," Seb barks back, his eyes dropping to the mess of Alex's face. But my gaze is quickly averted to where Seb is clutching his upper arm. And just like Alex said, blood is seeping over his fingers.

"Were you fucking shot?"

"It's fine. Just a graze."

"Bro, you should—" Theo starts.

"Just fucking drive, Boss. We've got a job to finish."

Theo jams his finger into the start button, bringing his beast of an engine to life before he floors the accelerator, and we fly away from the warehouse.

No words are said as we race across the city, multiple black cars right behind us.

We have no idea what we're about to drive into the middle of, but I'm pretty sure we're all preparing for the worst.

And thank fuck we are, because as we turn the final corner, we discover that the smoke billowing up into the sky before us isn't just some random house fire.

It's the Italians trying to bring our Family to its knees.

24

BRIANNA

"I'm fucking starving," Stella complains, clutching her stomach as if it's about to eat itself.

"It's been like three-quarters of an hour; the room service will be here soon."

"In a place this expensive, it should have been here thirty minutes ago."

"Money doesn't make things cook faster," Calli rationalises while Stella sulks.

It's been hours since we saw or heard from the guys, and the anxiety levels of our group are growing by the second. And as much as Stella's whining about her stomach might be annoying, I get it. She needs a distraction. Hell, so do I.

We stopped drinking after draining a second bottle of champagne. We might have craved a buzz, but none of us wanted to be so wasted that we weren't with it when the guys return. If the guys return. My stomach convulses at that thought alone and I chastise myself for even considering it.

They will come back, and they will be fine. There is no other option.

"Maybe if you didn't order so much then it would have been here by now."

"Blob is hungry."

"Ugh, don't pull that cute pregnancy shit with me right now, Cirillo," Stella warns teasingly.

"Seriously, do you guys have to?" Emmie asks, clearly more pissed off by their banter than I am.

Silence falls around us.

Rhea is asleep on the end of the other sofa. Despite claiming that she could hold her alcohol, she got very giggly after only a few sips of champagne. And lucky for her, it seemed to be enough to help her forget about the reason we're all here in the first place and she passed out like a freaking baby.

"She looks cute," Jodie muses, clearly seeing who is holding my attention.

"Don't tell her that when she's awake, she's likely to shank you," Emmie mutters.

"Takes one to know one. And anyway, she's not from the ghetto, so she'll have a better weapon."

"Fuck you, Stel. I hope you starve to death."

"Enough, children."

"Sorry, Miss Andrews," they all sing like pre-schoolers, making me roll my eyes.

"Can we just... get on? Turning on each other isn't going to make any of this better."

"We're good. Stella's just vile when she's hungry," Calli assures me.

"Hadn't noticed."

Reaching for the TV remote, I flick the channel over as the film none of us are actually watching comes to an end in favour of finding something else we can all ignore.

"Fucking finally," Stella shouts when a knock rattles the suite's door.

She's on her feet and racing toward her food before I've even registered the words.

From my position on the sofa, I can see the door and how she elegantly ploughs into the wall beside it.

Laughter is about to spill from my lips until Calli jumps to her feet beside me, shouting, "Stella, no," just as the woman in question twists the handle and pulls the door open ready to retrieve her coveted room service.

Everything happens so fucking fast I wonder if I'm actually hallucinating. But instead of her twisting around with a tray in her hands, or even a trolley, she's flipped around and slammed back with a gloved hand around her throat.

Her grunt of pain as the back of her head cracks against the wall pierces through me as Calli screams, she, Emmie and Jodie running full speed toward the guy choking Stella out.

My head screams at me to move, to go and do something, anything that might help, but my body is frozen in position, my blood turning to ice as another man dressed head to toe in black prowls into the room.

Thankfully, Stella isn't as high as she previously appeared, or the attack sobered her immediately, because just as Calli reaches the other guy, she finds her fight, kicks the arsehole right in the nuts and manages to twist out of his hold.

I'm too distracted by her skills to notice what the other guy is doing until a blood-curdling scream rips through the suite and I look over just in time to watch Calli slide down the wall and curl up in a ball on the floor.

"You're going to fucking regret that," Emmie screams,

throwing herself into a fistfight with a man who's at least double her size.

Stella's attacker recovers from his busted balls and follows her deeper into the suite.

I want to scream, 'wrong fucking way', but I'm incapable of anything as I watch the carnage.

"No matter what happens, you do not leave until one of us comes to get you. You do not answer the door, you do not contact anyone."

Theo's deadly serious warning from earlier comes back to me.

They're going to fucking kill us. If these two dudes don't get their first.

Movement on the other sofa catches my eye, and I watch Rhea slink off around the opposite side to where Emmie is handing the man his arse and crawl over to Calli, who's trembling on the floor.

Jodie is distracted, following Stella and her attacker deeper into the suite with a dark look in her eyes that I've never seen before. A flash of light from her waist catches my attention and when I drop my eyes, I find she's got her fingers wrapped around a flip knife.

What the actual fuck?

I know that the girls and Toby have been training her, but I think I might have underestimated just how easily she's embraced the mafia blood that runs through her veins.

"You fucking cunt," Emmie screams as her attacker manages to get the upper hand and trips her, forcing her onto her back.

Not that it stops her for long, and thankfully, the move distracts him enough for Rhea to be able to drag Calli from the floor.

But before they get very far, another dark figure fills the

doorway. He stands there for a beat, assessing the carnage before him. I can only imagine that he wasn't expecting to walk into a war zone being commanded by brutal female Cirillo Family members.

His eyes widen as he watches Emmie once again get the better of his buddy before he remembers what he's meant to be doing and locks his gaze on Rhea and Calli's retreating backs.

Lifting his hands, he cracks his knuckles and pulls a length of rope from his pocket, snapping it together menacingly.

His foot leaves the floor, and he begins stalking after them.

They're both totally oblivious that they're being stalked by some deranged killer, and I know that if I don't do something, then I'm going to be forced to sit here while he achieves what I can only assume he was sent here for.

A savage roar rips through the room that I had no clue I was capable of until it hits my ears.

I lurch forward, needing to do something to stop him from getting his hands on either of them.

My fingers wrap around the empty champagne bottle still littering the coffee table, and I bring the neck of it down on the corner, shattering the glass and leaving me with a jagged edge.

I launch myself across the coffee table and onto the other sofa as the guy closes in on Rhea, standing slightly behind Calli. Just as he lifts his arm to reach for her, I bring my own arm up and plunge the sharp edge of the bottle right into the motherfucker's neck.

He stills instantly as blood sprays from him, coating me in a heartbeat.

My stomach revolts as what I just did hits me.

In shock, the guy reaches back and stupidly pulls the bottle free. If I thought I was covered in his blood before, it's nothing compared to what happens the second the glass leaves his body.

Fuck knows what I hit, but a river of fucking blood pours from the hole in the side of his neck.

He tries covering it with his hand, but it does nothing to stem the bleed. And after only a few seconds, he stumbles forward before colliding with the wall, covering it in blood before collapsing in a heap on the floor. And it's only then that Rhea and Calli notice just how close to death they both came.

"Brianna," Jodie screams. "Go and lock the door. NOW."

I spin around in a complete daze but knowing that I need to follow her order just as Stella thrusts her own sparkling pink knife toward the guy still battling to overpower her.

The blade slices through his stomach as if it's butter. Bile rushes up my throat as more blood is spilled around me and the guy roars in agony, staring at Stella's manic grin in pure disbelief. I guess no one filled him in on the details of this job. Poor fucker probably thought he was in for an easy night being sent to what... abduct, kill, maybe, six helpless young women? Oh, how naïve.

"Now," she starts, "are you going to admit defeat, or would you like me to continue?"

He stares at her from his bent-over position and his lips part to respond, but he doesn't get a chance because Stella pulls her arm back and punches him so hard in the temple that he falls motionless and crashes to the floor.

"Em, you good?" she asks casually, shaking her hand out and checking in on her friends as Emmie and Jodie work together to restrain the other guy. Unlike his friends, he's still alive and conscious, and he looks all kinds of confused as Emmie and Jodie tie him up as if he's about to be roasted over an open fire.

"Door, Bri," Jodie reminds me, her head nodding to where it's still wide open.

Rushing over, I slam it shut and twist the lock.

Spinning around, I take in the carnage before me that I never noticed on my journey over here.

The room is destroyed. Pictures and artwork that were previously hanging on the walls are now shattered and twisted on the floor. Furniture is broken, the walls are covered in blood, and there are ornaments, glasses, lamps, and anything else that had been carefully placed throughout the living area now scattered everywhere.

"Holy shit," I breathe, the weight of everything I witnessed over the last... however long pressing down on me.

A terrified scream rips from my lips when someone knocks on the door behind me.

"Room service."

Emmie, Jodie, and Stella all pause at the sound of the female voice, but none of them make a move to answer it. In fact, this time, Stella is firmly against it.

"We've changed our minds. You can eat it," she bellows. "Thank you."

"Bri, come help us," Emmie says, ensuring I don't register what the woman on the other side of the door says in response.

"Shit, yeah."

The four of us work together to dump all three of the dudes into the epic bathtub before running the cold tap, leaving them shivering. Well, the two of them that are still alive.

"Shit, Calli," I breathe when we shut the bathroom door behind us.

Rushing over, we all crowd around her as Rhea remains pinned to her side, holding her as she sobs.

"Calli, talk to us. Are you okay? Did he hurt you? Are you—"

"I'm okay," she forces quietly.

"The baby—" Stella starts.

"N-nothing hurts. Nothing feels... different. I think... I think I'm okay."

"Fuck. We need to get you checked out," Emmie hisses.

"No, we can't. We need to wait. We've already screwed up."

Lifting her eyes from her lap, Calli scans the room, taking in the carnage around us.

"This is all my fault," Stella admits, dropping her head in defeat.

"No, it's not. We should have been safe here. The only person to blame is whoever is feeding back information to the Italians about what we're doing."

"What if they knew about the set-up? What if they—"

"No," Jodie barks. "Don't go there. Don't even think it."

"I'm scared," Rhea confesses.

Sitting on her other side, Emmie pulls her in for a hug while I climb onto the sofa beside Calli.

Stella and Jodie drag the coffee table closer, moving it away from the glass I left on the floor, and sit so their knees are touching ours. Reaching out my hand, I grab Jodie's. She does the same to Stella, who then reaches for Emmie.

"You were fucking fearless," I say to no one in particular. Because while Stella and Emmie might have some seriously impressive skills, all of them deserve praise for what we just lived through.

"It's not about being brave," Stella reasons. "It's about fighting for your family, for those you love."

Her words make my chest ache as I'm reminded of what Jodie said to me in the car just a few hours ago.

Calli sobs once more and it breaks me. The tears that were already filling my eyes finally overspill, cascading down my cheeks and landing on my blood-soaked pyjamas.

"I really need to shower."

"You really shouldn't," Emmie states.

"I'm covered in blood. Why the hell wouldn't I?"

Emmie and Stella share a knowing look.

"She's right," Stella agrees. "I know someone who will get a serious kick out of helping you wash it off."

"What time is it?" Rhea asks, not lifting her head from Emmie's shoulder.

"Almost one."

"Where are they?" Jodie asks.

Without having an answer, we fall into silence, each of us doing our best to support the others and not fall apart under the pressure this night has forced on us.

And that's exactly how we're discovered not long later when the door to our suite swings open, revealing some familiar faces who look like they've been through even more than we have.

25

NICO

My adrenaline finally begins to run out as the lift climbs through the building of the hotel we secured the girls in for the night.

But as I look around at each of my boys, I don't see the same exhaustion on their faces. Behind the blood and dirt, their eyes are still alert and their jaws are set as if this night, this fight, isn't over.

Well, I guess it's not. We're no closer to Ricardo fucking Mariano than we were this time yesterday. In fact, we're further away.

The motherfucker hadn't run back to our building to try and flush Ant and Daemon out by force; instead, he left his foot soldiers to do the dirty work for him while he hid like a pussy.

"We'll get him, Nic," Toby assures me, his bloody hand wrapping around my shoulder in support.

"You need to get him out of your head, because there's a woman in there waiting for you to take her to heaven," Alex adds, trying to lighten the mood a little.

"Doubtful," I mutter. "She probably won't even look at

me," I confess, sounding like a fucking pussy as I think about her reaction, or lack thereof, when I walked into Toby's flat with the guys earlier.

"Dude, you need to get over this 'oh boohoo me, my girl doesn't want me bullshit'," Seb announces, pissing me the fuck off. "If we all had that attitude then we'd all be single right now. You want her, fight for her. Make her see that she can't possibly live a life without you or your dick."

"I thought I was."

"How? Name me one thing you've done to prove to her that you're the one."

My lips part but no words come out. "I... uh... I..."

"Case in point."

"I wrote her a letter," I blurt like an idiot. "Told her how I felt, what I wanted, and she's just... ignored it. Tried pushing me further away."

"And you've let her," he counters. "She's scared, Nico. Scared you're joking. Terrified that the player she first met can't possibly be serious about her."

"Jesus, who made you the expert?"

"It doesn't take an expert to see what's right in front of your face," he points out. "Go in there and show her with actions, not just words on a scrap of fucking paper."

The lift dings, putting an end to his possibly useful advice, and the second the doors open we all spill out into the pristine hallway.

It's empty.

"Where the fuck are our guys?" I bark.

We left the girl's security details here with the sole job of keeping them safe.

There was no sign of them as we walked in. To be fair, there was no sign of anyone, but then it is the middle of the night.

This isn't one of our hotels, but it's one the girls should be safe in. If something were to happen here, then it's not just the Cirillos the Marianos need to be looking over their shoulder for but someone much, much worse.

Heeding that advice, I surge forward, getting to the door a beat before Theo and Seb. I don't look up at them for fear of the expression on their faces making my fears seem founded.

Everything is fine. It has to be.

My fist slams down on the solid wood hard enough to wake the living dead a beat before Theo helpfully pulls out a master key and pushes it into the lock. Of fucking course.

I can barely contain my eye roll as he unlocks it with ease, happily shouting, "Honey, I'm home," and pushing into the suite.

For just a couple of seconds, everything that's been rioting inside me all night settles. The prospect of seeing her, of pulling her into my arms, breathing her in, proving to myself that no matter how fucked up everything might be outside of this room, she's here and she's safe.

But then, I look up and everything comes crashing down around me once more.

The room is destroyed. Furniture is trashed, things are shattered and there's—

Vomit crawls up my throat at the sight of blood... everywhere.

"What happened?" Seb demands a beat before Daemon surges from the back of our group.

"Calli, what's wrong?"

He's breaking through the girls huddle in seconds and pulling my sister into his arms.

"Are you okay? Are you hurt? I'm taking you to the

hospital," he states, not giving her enough time to respond to the first two as his panic takes over.

I get it. I more than fucking get it.

I just catch her whisper, "I'm okay," before Stella confesses, "It's my fault."

"Why doesn't that fucking surprise me?" Seb mutters as all of us crowd around the girls.

"We need to get you both checked out, baby," Daemon coos, sounding like an entirely different person from the one we know caused nothing short of an Italian massacre tonight.

"She's fine, D. Stop freaking out. There isn't a mark on her," Theo argues as my eyes lock on Brianna.

She's covered in blood. And not just a little bit.

My heart jumps into my chest, my pulse hammering so fast it makes blood rush past my ears.

"It's not mine," she assures me quietly, reading my thoughts as if they're her own.

I don't know whether I'm more relieved of that fact or that she's no longer ignoring me.

I stalk close to both her and Calli, my concern for both of them swallowing every other thought I had in my head before entering this room.

"Daemon's right," Brianna says, ripping her eyes from mine and turning to Calli. "You hit that wall pretty hard. You should—"

"What's going on?" Theo demands, standing before Calli and Daemon with his hands on his hips and a fierce expression on his face.

Calli blinks up at him, trying to force the tears away while Daemon stares down at her like she's the most precious thing in the world.

"I'm pregnant," she whispers, causing Theo's entire body to lock up in shock.

His lips open and close, but no words come out.

I'm pretty sure it's the first time I've ever seen him stunned into silence.

"Y-you're—"

He looks at me with wide eyes, as if he's expecting me to freak out.

Internally, I am, but for the same reason Daemon is. I'm over the initial shock of his life-changing news now.

"And you have nothing to say about this?" Theo asks.

"Yeah, I do. Daemon needs to get her to the hospital right fucking now."

"I'll take them," Alex offers, seeing as both Seb and Toby now have their hands full with their girls.

"I've got this, Bro. You help out here. We won't be long," Daemon assures him.

Before Calli has had a chance to process those words, she's wrapped up in Daemon's arms and guided out of the room.

It's on the tip of my tongue to tell him to stop, that he should be hiding. But I know it's pointless. His priority is Calli, exactly as it should be, and nothing will stop him right now.

"And you're just going to stand there?" Theo snaps at me as they disappear.

"No, I'm not."

Surging forward, I sweep Brianna off her feet, forcing a squeal of shock from her lips before I carry her down the hallway toward what I hope will be a bedroom, followed by a bathroom.

"Wait," Stella calls before I pass the first door. "We've got something you need to deal with."

"Or somethings," Emmie adds.

"What?" both Seb and Theo bark at their women.

Stella jumps up, rushing toward where I'm standing with Brianna, who surprisingly isn't fighting me for once.

"We've got some toys for you to play with."

She throws the door open, allowing me, Seb and Theo full sight of what they've done.

"Jesus," I mutter as Brianna tucks her face into the crook of my neck so she doesn't have to see.

"Only one of them is dead. Isn't that right, Bri?" Stella says proudly.

"Fucking hell," Seb mutters.

"We'll call the boss, organise getting this place cleaned up."

"It's a Cirillo hotel, right?" Stella asks innocently.

"No," Theo states. "And the people who own it won't be all that impressed."

I glance over just in time to see her swallow nervously.

"A," Theo calls, "get your ass over here. Got a job for you."

"Me? You too fucking busy or something?" Alex sulks.

"I will be in about two minutes, yeah. Sort this out, call the crew. I'll talk to my father when I'm done."

"Done? Done with wha—"

Alex cuts his own words off as Theo marches over to Emmie, throws her over his shoulder and races away with her.

"Right. I see."

Seb quickly follows his lead. "So you say this was all your fault, Princess?" he mutters. "I guess that means you need punishing for your actions."

"Jesus fucking Christ, are you all going to go and—"

"See you later, man," I add continuing on my previous mission to get Brianna alone.

"You can keep Rhea company," I call over my shoulder.

"Motherfuckers," he spits right before I march into a room and swing the door closed behind us.

Brianna doesn't so much as flinch as I walk her into the bathroom.

"Babe," I whisper, lowering her to the counter between the double basins.

She shakes her head and clings on to me. The move makes my heart hurt in the best possible way, but I can't focus on that right now. She needs me, and I fully intend on being everything and more than she thinks she requires.

"Trust me, I really don't want you to let go either. But I need to get you in the shower. You're—"

"He was going to hurt Calli and Rhea," she blurts, her voice choked with emotion.

My entire body freezes at the thought of anyone laying a hand on my sister and cousin.

"I-I... I just reacted. Stella and Emmie... they w-w-were —" a pained sob cuts off her words, and I finally manage to pull her face from my neck.

Cupping her blood-stained cheeks in my palms, I stare down into her eyes.

"You did so good, babe. So fucking good," I assure her.

Tears spill over, dropping down and running over my own dirty fingers.

"Stella... she opened the door," she tries to explain quietly.

"It's okay, Siren. It's over."

At my words, her eyes brighten a little, and for the first time since we walked in, I actually feel like she's seeing me.

"You're hurt," she breathes, brushing her thumb gently

over my aching cheek. If I haven't already got glowing bruises on it, then I've no doubt I will have by morning. That fucker Enzo has got some serious power behind him. I guess I should just be grateful that he steered clear of my nose.

"I'm okay," I promise her. "I've done worse to myself recently," I confess, referencing last weekend. "Your shoulder?"

"I'm fine."

I nod as relief rushes through me. If one of those men had hurt her, hurt what's mine, then I'm not sure I'd be able to hold myself back from going out there to finish the job the girls started.

Leaning forward, I rest my brow against hers, letting my hands drop to her shoulders, hating that her entire body is trembling. Her tear-filled eyes hold mine for a beat before her lids lower, cutting off our connection.

"Don't hide from me, Bri. Not tonight," I beg. "I-I need you, and I think... I think you might just need me too."

Silence falls between us, and I have no choice but to try and prepare myself for her rejection.

But thankfully, when her eyes open again, I don't find that she's shut down and ready to send me away. It's the opposite, and I breathe a massive sigh of relief before she says, "Wash it off me, Nico. I need it gone."

"You got it, babe. Arms up."

Releasing her, I wrap my fingers around the hem of her t-shirt and drag it up her body. Her crop top goes next, before I lift her from the counter and shove her cotton pyjama bottoms and knickers to her ankles, leaving her deliciously naked for me.

Naked and covered in our enemy's blood.

I keep my thoughts about how fucking hot that is to

myself for now. Something tells me she wouldn't appreciate the sentiment.

So instead of saying anything, I let my eyes do the work for me, running them up her mouth-watering body, taking in the curve of her hips, the dip of her waist, the fullness of her breasts and her hard, rosy nipples. My cock aches behind my trousers, my desperation for her causing precum to bead at the tip.

It's not until my eyes climb to her shoulder that she reacts and tries to hide away from me.

"No," I bark, making her flinch. "Every single inch of you is beautiful, Brianna Andrews. Never, ever hide anything from me. Especially the reminder of just how fucking close I came to losing you."

"It's ugly," she confesses weakly, dropping her eyes to the floor.

"Bullshit," I spit, reaching out and taking her chin between my fingers, forcing her to look up at me. "The only ugly thing here is me, my temper, my darkness."

She starts to shake her head, but I have no desire to hear whatever she might have to say in response to that, whether it be the truth or an attempt to argue with me. So I do the only thing I can think of to stop her coming back at me, and I slam my lips down on hers.

She remains motionless for a few seconds as I kiss her and my heart rate kicks up as I consider the fact that she might have changed her mind about asking me to wash the blood off her.

But the second I growl, "Give in, Siren," her resolve shatters, her lips part, and her tongue hungrily seeks out mine.

A deep groan of satisfaction rumbles in my throat as her taste explodes in my mouth.

I step forward, needing to feel her curves against the hardness of my body, and she gasps when I press her back against the counter.

"Nico," she moans when I pull back a little to catch my breath, and fuck if I don't almost come in my pants.

"Undress me, Siren. I need to feel you against me. Nothing between us," I demand before reclaiming her lips.

26

BRIANNA

My hands move of their own accord, tucking under the lapels of Nico's jacket and pushing it from his shoulders.

Thanks to the eye-wateringly expensive fabric, the second he lowers his arms, it slides free, pooling at his feet.

I pull his tie free next before making quick work of the buttons running down the front of his body.

His face is fucked up, his knuckles are busted, and every inch of skin not covered in his expensive suit is speckled with blood and dirt, but it doesn't deter me from taking what I need. It does the opposite, in fact.

Knowing what him and the others have potentially done tonight should turn me off. But then I think about what I've done and quickly push it aside.

I've spent all my adult life reading books about men who go out there and fight for what they believe in— whether it be right or wrong—and then come home and claim their women like cavemen and right now, I am fucking here for it. Anything that will stop the memory of me slamming the neck of that bottle into that guy's throat that has been constantly on repeat in my head since the moment it happened.

His shirt hits the floor, exposing his sculpted torso for me. Or at least it would, if I actually opened my eyes to look. But I can't. I'm too lost in his kiss, in the escape from the nightmare that tonight turned into that he silently promises me.

Our kiss falters when my fingers brush the skin above his waistband and he flinches, sucking in a sharp breath.

"Don't stop," he begs.

His voice sounds totally different from when he first brought me in here. It's softer, more... vulnerable. My heart tumbles the second it hits my ears.

"I need you, babe. So fucking bad."

Ripping his fly open, I shove his trousers and boxers over his hips. His hard cock immediately springs free, pressing against my stomach.

I reach for him as he begins toeing his shoes off and trying to kick his clothing free.

The second my fingers wrap around his shaft, he stills, barking out a loud, "Fuck."

He stares at me with wide, dark, desperate eyes, and I just stand there holding him with my chest heaving, my entire body aching for him.

Without saying a word, silent promises pass between us, ones that I don't want to accept but equally lap up at the same time.

Right now, I need them, and I'm not in any kind of position to question anything.

Needing to do something, I slide my hand down his cock, simultaneously sweeping my thumb over the tip, coating him in his own wetness.

"No, Bri. Stop," he commands. His voice is so stern, so demanding, that I have no choice but to follow.

My heart sinks and my fingers instantly release him.

"I-I'm sorry, I thought—"

"Fuck that, Brianna," he scolds, wrapping his hands around the backs of my thighs, lifting me from my feet and giving me little choice but to enclose my legs around his waist.

I gasp when his length brushes against my more-than-ready pussy.

"Fuck, that feels—"

"Take me," I beg as he walks us into the massive walk-in shower. I thought the one in his bedroom was impressive, but this... this is the size of most people's entire bathrooms.

I shudder as he presses my back against the cold tiles.

"Brace yourself."

A scream rips from my lips as ice-cold water rains down on both of us.

"You fucking cu—" My insult is swallowed by his lips as he resumes the kiss he broke only a few minutes ago.

Clenching my thigh muscles, I attempt to climb him like a tree to get into a better position, but he holds me too tight to have any success.

"I didn't bring you in here to fuck you like an animal, Brianna," he growls in my ear after kissing along the line of my jaw.

"Liar," I hiss, making him chuckle.

"It's true," he whispers. "I told myself when we were in the lift that I was going to come in here and prove to you that everything I said I wanted in that letter is true. That I was going to show you by any means necessary that I'm serious, that you're the only one for me. When I look into my future, you are the only one I see.

"But then I walked inside and saw you covered in blood, and I'm sure my entire life flashed before my eyes.

"Then I discovered the truth, and fuck, I didn't think it was possible to want you any more than I already did. But... you killed for us, Bri. You're one of us; no matter what, I'm never letting you get away now. Ever.

"You're mine. You can fight, scream, kick, and punch all you like. But I'll take it all. Because you're it for me, Brianna Andrews. Every defiant, sexy, corrupt inch of you.

"And as much as I might want to take you right now, I won't, because I owe you more than that."

"Fuck that, Nico."

"I'm serious. You're my fucking queen, and you deserve to be treated as such."

My heart pounds like a fucking bass drum in my chest as he pins me to the wall with just his hips, reaching out to grab the shower gel and sponge.

"Before I worship you until you have no choice but to forgive me and accept everything I'm telling you as fact, I'm going to wash every bit of that motherfucker from your skin, because the only person's blood you should ever wear is mine."

There are so many fucking things wrong with that statement, but I don't have a clue what they are in that moment as he makes the sponge erupt with bubbles and brings it to my neck.

He works in silence as he diligently cleans every inch of me, just like he promised.

My skin erupts in goosebumps with every brush of the sponge and every caress of his hands.

My chest heaves as I watch him care for me, and by the time he drops to his knees before me, I can barely breathe through the emotion that clogs my throat and the desire that floods my body.

The sponge glides down one thigh while his hand mirrors the move on the other until he gets down to my ankles.

Sitting back on his haunches, he lifts one of my feet onto his thigh, dropping the sponge to the floor before leaning forward and pressing a kiss to the inside of my knee.

My core clenches at the sight of his lips on my skin.

But that reaction is nothing compared to when he looks up at me.

His hair hangs over his brow, and water droplets fall from the tips, running down his face as his dark eyes stare up into mine.

"I'm yours, Brianna. And I'll spend as long as it takes on my knees worshipping you until you understand how serious I am."

I suck in a shuddering breath as I finally lower the walls that have enclosed my heart since I was a child.

It's a risk. A huge fucking risk, one I have every confidence I'm going to regret. But I'm powerless but to let it happen.

My tongue sneaks out, licking up the shower water that's lingering on them as I fight to find some words in response.

Unable to dig up anything near as life-changing as he has in the past few minutes, I fall back on something I pray is going to work.

"So prove it. Make me yours."

His eyes flash with heat before his palm presses against my inner thigh, spreading me wide for him and leaving me barely balancing on one leg as he dives for me.

"Oh shit," I scream as he licks up the length of my pussy before focusing on my clit.

My fingers find their home in his hair, dragging him closer, demanding more of his talented tongue.

"Mine, Brianna. You're mine," he growls against me, the vibrations of his deep voice hitting me exactly where he wants them too.

"Yes," I cry, my back arching, my eyes begging to be closed so I can purely focus on the pleasure saturating my body.

But I fight them, because I want to see him.

I want to see him on his knees for me, confessing his true feelings, forgetting about all the bullshit and alpha bravado, and just being honest.

And, fuck, there's something about watching that playboy persona shatter right before my eyes. It's not something I'm willing to miss.

"Nico," I scream as his other hand slides up my trembling leg before he tucks two thick fingers inside me.

He increases the pressure on my clit as his fingers find my G-spot, and I almost instantly shatter for him.

My leg gives out, but even as he works me through my release, he somehow manages not to let me fall on my arse —something I really need to remember to thank him for later.

No sooner has my release subsided than my feet are placed back on the tiles beneath me and he's pushing to his full height again.

He looms over me, standing a full head taller than me.

"Fuck, you're so beautiful," he murmurs before his lips find mine.

My own taste explodes on my tongue as he kisses me like he did that very first time. It's full of promises, of hope, of filthy debauchery. Only this time, it's not just for one night but—dare I say it?—forever.

"You fucking ruin me, Siren. You bring me to my knees and make me want to be a better man. A worthy man."

"Nico," I groan as he wraps my leg around his waist, teasing me with what I need most right now.

The head of his cock circles my swollen clit, sending aftershocks from my orgasm shooting around my body and causing my pussy to contract, desperate to feel him stretching me open once more.

"Please, Nico. I need—"

"Told myself I wouldn't fuck you again until you forgave me. Until you believed me," he confesses.

"Please," I whimper.

"I haven't even got myself off since we were in that bathroom."

"I don't want you to punish yourself," I breathe.

"Yes, you do," he argues. "I deserve it and you know it."

"And do I deserve for you to hold out on me now?" I ask, hoping it'll hit the mark.

His eyes flash with surprise, although I'm sure there's a little pride in there too.

"I killed a man tonight, Nico. I killed him for this family." I don't need to explain what family I mean; he knows full well I don't mean their gang but the group of people who surround us. Those who have come to mean everything to me over the past few months. The family I always wished I had. "And I'd do it again, because you're everything to me."

His throat ripples and his Adam's apple bobs as he swallows thickly.

I might have said that as if I'm talking about everyone, but he knows just as well as I do that I'm talking about him.

Leaning forward, I brush my lips against his, although I don't allow him to deepen the kiss when he tries to return it.

"And I might be the stupidest bitch on the planet, but —" I suck in a breath, dragging some strength in with it. "I forgive you."

"Fuck," he breathes before finally thrusting forward while simultaneously stealing my lips.

My feet leave the floor as he wraps both my legs around his waist, using nothing more than his powerful thrusts to keep me up as he fucks me so deep, it makes my head spin.

The water pounds down on us as we lose ourselves in each other, remembering just how mind-blowing it is when we collide.

My body burns up as he fucks me with precision and restraint that he rarely shows.

Ripping my lips from his, I suck in greedy lungfuls of air as I watch him watch me.

"Let go, Nico. Give me everything."

His brows shoot up in surprise.

"I don't want to hurt you."

I can't help but bark out a laugh.

"Bit late to be worried about that, don't you think?"

"Fuck, Siren." Remorse floods his eyes, and I instantly regret my words.

"Just me and you, Nico. Nothing else exists. Now, show me why that's the best place in the world to be."

At my challenge, he drags me from the wall and carries me back into the bedroom, both of us dripping all over the luxurious carpet before he comes to a stop at the end of the massive bed.

"You asked for it," he warns before launching me onto the mattress.

I bounce once, but any further movements are halted as he lands on top of me.

Giving me little choice but to spread my legs wide, he looms over me, grabbing both of my wrists and dragging my arms above my head, restraining them there with one of his giant hands.

"You're gonna want to hold on, babe," he warns, getting himself into position between my thighs, pressing the head of his cock against my entrance once more.

My muscles contract, desperately trying to suck him back inside me.

"My desperate little whore," he mutters, watching me writhe beneath him.

Digging my heels into his lower back, I try to force him forward.

"Fuck me, Nico. I need YOU," I scream as he does as he's told for once and thrusts back inside me.

"Oh fuck," I gasp as he sets a punishing rhythm that even has the heavy oak bed frame crashing back against the wall. "Fuck. NICO."

He consumes me, utterly fucking consumes me as he fills me so completely, finally ruining me for anyone else.

He stares down at me with such reverence and… love? It makes my chest ache in the most incredible way.

"I'm not going to let you down again, Bri. I fucking promise you."

I barely hear it over the banging and creaking of the bed, but each word hits me right in the heart. And it may be naïve and fickle and fucking stupid, but I believe every single one of them.

"Fucking missed this pussy, Siren. Fucking addicted."

Holding himself up with the hand he has wrapped around my wrists, he drops the other down my body to play with my clit as his movements become jerky and erratic, his release approaching.

"Yes," I cry the second he presses his thumb exactly where I need him.

"Come for me, Siren. And make it loud enough that every motherfucker in this building knows you've just given yourself to me."

He thrusts once more and I go off like a rocket, screaming out his name just like he commanded.

"Fuck. Fuck. Brianna. Fuck." Just before he falls, there's a loud crack, then a bang, and the world falls from beneath us. Or at least a foot or two of it.

"NICO," I squeal, but if he's noticed, then he's paying it no mind as his release finally claims him, and he throws his head back and roars out as his cock jerks violently inside me.

I'm enraptured by the sight of him losing control as he pumps me full of his cum, staking his claim once and for all.

When he's spent, he falls forward, crushing me into the wonky mattress as he fights to catch his breath, his cock barely softening inside me.

I lie there, my own chest heaving, my head spinning with thoughts of what this night has held. But the one thing that's missing is any kind of regret. I did what I had to do tonight. Both in the living room of this suite and right here with Nico.

I guess everyone was right. The two of us? We're inevitable.

—

27

NICO

Okay, I'll admit it. Snuggling with Brianna is my new favourite thing.

The moment I came back to myself and discovered that we were almost upside down on the bed, I obviously made the most of the situation and flipped her onto her front, fucking her like a savage as all the blood rushed to her head.

It was more than worth it because when she came, fuck me, I thought she was going to make my cock pop right off my body with how tight her cunt contracted around it.

Sex with my siren has always been off the charts. But sex with her after she's agreed to be mine? Pure fucking ecstasy.

After that round, and with my cum running out of her cunt and my bright red handprint glowing on her arse, we once again collapsed on the destroyed bed. Neither of us said anything about our legs being higher than our heads. We were too blissed out to care.

Gripping her thigh, I slide my hand down her soft skin, getting closer to temptation than I probably should. There's no way she isn't sore after how roughly I've taken her in the last...

"Nico," she purrs, the roughness of her voice making my cock stand to attention once more.

The second she opens her eyes, I stare deep into them, searching for any sign that she might regret what she told me in the shower.

I don't deserve her forgiveness. I know that much. But it doesn't mean that I'm not going to be a selfish motherfucker and take it regardless.

Not finding anything that makes me think she's about to do a U-turn on me, I rip my eyes from hers in favour of her injured shoulder.

"Don't," she whispers, attempting to twist away from me so I can't see it.

Sliding my hand higher, I grab her luscious arse and roll her closer, stopping her from retreating.

"You don't hide from me, Siren. Ever. You're beautiful, every inch of you."

"It's ugly," she says, disgust with herself evident in her voice.

"Impossible."

Leaning forward, I press my lips to one of the worst cuts, peppering it with kisses.

"I'll never be able to express how much it kills me that I caused this. I was stupid, reckless."

"You were lost, Nico. Grief, it's—" Her words are cut off when I blow out a heavy sigh and rest my brow on her shoulder.

"Not a good enough excuse. I could have lost you too that night. That terrifies me, Siren. I wouldn't survive that. I know I wouldn't."

"I'm just a girl, Nico."

I drag my head up and find her eyes once more.

"No. You're not just anything, Brianna. You're everything. Every-fucking-thing." I lean closer and drop a chaste kiss to her lips. "And." Kiss. "All." Kiss. "Mine." Kiss.

Her fingers wrap around the back of my head and she holds me in place on that final brush of our lips, giving me little choice but to deepen the kiss.

"I don't belong to anyone, Nico. If anything, I own you," she says fiercely when we come up for air.

"Ain't that the fucking truth," I mutter before rolling her onto her back, more than ready to embark on a slower, gentler round three.

Until someone starts pounding on the bedroom door.

"Time's up, fuckers. Get your cock out of Brianna, Nico. We've got to move," Toby barks in amusement.

"Fuck off, Tobes," I shout back.

"No can do. Boss wants us to move out. This location has been compromised."

"Fuck's sake," I groan, already mourning the loss of Brianna's pussy and I'm not even in it yet.

But then the girl in question makes it all better with four little words.

"Take me home, Nico."

"Fuck, babe. Do you have any idea what you do to me?"

She smiles coyly up at me before wiggling her hips and letting my hard cock graze her pussy.

"I have an idea."

"You're trouble."

"You've only just figured that out?"

"NICO," Toby bellows. "Five seconds to move or I'm coming in."

"Feel free," I call back, rolling off of Brianna and sitting on the edge of the mattress. "You can see the state of this bed."

Looking over my shoulder, I wink at Brianna as she giggles like a schoolgirl.

"Never broke a bed before," she confesses.

"And I thought you were an expert in the bedroom," I tease.

Her brows shoot up in shock. "Is that your way of diverting from the fact you have broken a bed before? Because if it is, I'm more than happy to tell you all about my experiences with other men. In detail."

"Time's up," Toby announces a beat before he swings the door open.

"What the fuck, man?" I snap quickly, grabbing a pillow to cover Bri up.

"What? I've seen her tits plenty of times. I'm not about to suggest a trade. Jesus." His eyes shift from mine, but instead of them moving to my girl, he ignores her in favour of the bed. "Fuck me, you really did break it. How? Those legs are almost as thick as tree trunks."

"I'm just that good," I confess, shamelessly pushing to my feet and walking naked toward my pile of clothes to grab my boxers.

"Here," Toby says, throwing a pair of sweats and a t-shirt at me. "Daemon grabbed us some shit."

"Are they back? Are Calli and the baby okay?" I ask in a rush, guilt knotting up my stomach that I allowed myself to get so lost in Brianna that I forgot about my sister and nephew.

"Our future queen and I are fine," a soft female voice shouts from somewhere behind Toby.

"Thank fuck," I breathe quietly.

"We're heading home. Clean-up has been in, Boss has

dealt with the cops, and the motherfuckers in the bathtub will be on their way to the basement for playtime any minute."

"Playtime?" Brianna echoes behind me.

"I'll let Nico tell you about that. Good work on the dead guy, though, Bri. He had no chance of surviving that."

I glance over at my girl just in time to see the blood drain from her face.

"We'll be out in a minute."

Toby drops the overnight bag Brianna packed earlier just inside the room before he closes the door and leaves us to it.

"He's right, Siren. You did so good."

"I killed someone," she says, her voice void of any kind of emotion.

"To save our family. It wasn't premeditated or unnecessary. If you didn't do that, any of you could be in that position now, or they could have taken all of you, treated you like they did Daemon and Ant." I swear her previously pale face turns a little green at my suggestion.

"I'm so fucking proud of you. The guys are too."

"It was Stella and Emmie really. They're brutal," she says, deflecting the praise.

"Yeah, they are a little terrifying when it comes to protecting those they love. I'm sure plenty would say the same thing about us. But I don't think that's a bad thing."

"I never had that," she confesses. "Growing up, no one would have fought like that for me. It's... weird."

"Well, it's time you started getting used to it because all of us will fight to the death to protect you."

She shakes her head. "I don't want that."

"Tough. You have it anyway. Come on," I say, dropping her bag to the end of the bed that's still standing. "Time to head home." Her lips part to argue, but I cut her off before she gets a chance to say the words that I know are right on the tip of her tongue. "Don't even think about it, Siren. After what's happened tonight, I'm not letting you out of my sight."

"I'm sure I can cope with that," she concedes. "And I'm pretty tired."

"Something tells me you're going to be even more exhausted before I finally let you sleep tonight."

"Big promises for an injured man, Nico."

Her eyes drop down my body, pausing on each angry bruise that darkens my skin.

"Have I shown any sign of not being capable of giving you what you need yet?"

"You're insane."

"Certifiable, babe. It's fun."

Once we're both dressed, we take one more fond look at the broken bed before pulling the door open and walking out of the room that forever changed our lives.

I don't care if she wakes up in the morning sober and regrets all of this. There's no way in hell I'm letting her go back on it. Ever.

This is it now. No more bullshit or drama.

Nico Cirillo is officially off the market. Not that I was ever really on it, but whatever.

Only a couple of minutes later, Bri and I walk out of that room dressed in sweats and t-shirts, hand in hand, to a sea of smug faces.

"Oh, you can all fuck right off," I scoff, immediately dragging my girl toward the suite door.

"Wait," Bri says, tugging on my arm and turning back to my sister. "Is everything really okay?" she asks.

Stepping up behind her, I wrap my arms around her

waist and rest my chin on her un-injured shoulder. It feels like the most natural thing in the world, and I can't help but wonder why I haven't been doing it all this time.

What the hell was I so scared of?

"Yeah, everything is good."

"So what now?" Bri asks, looking at Theo and then back at me as if we hold all the answers to our current situation.

"I'm not comfortable discussing it here. If..." Theo shakes his head. He doesn't need to say any more; we all know. The evidence of what happened here is all around us. "We can clock off."

"What time is it?" I ask, looking around at the exhausted faces before me.

"Almost four a.m."

My eyes widen as I discover just how much time I lost in Brianna's body in that bedroom.

"We'll go back and debrief, then you can all crash," Theo explains.

"Are you all okay?" Bri asks, looking around at the girls.

Stella hops to her feet like this is just any other day.

"You don't need to worry about us, girl. Those pricks never stood a chance."

Bri shakes her head, her body jolting with her soft laughter.

"Rhea, you good?"

She nods sleepily.

"Come on, you can crash at my place and I'll take you back home tomorrow," Theo offers, pulling his sister to her feet and tucking her under his arm protectively. "Ready?" he asks everyone.

"Yeah, get me the hell out of this place," Emmie agrees, finding his other side.

He passes us on his way to the door, pausing to release both girls in favour of pulling his gun from his waistband.

Without instruction, Emmie takes Rhea's hand and follows him out.

Bri and I follow and then the rest fall into line behind us.

We're all on full alert as we descend through the building and walk out through the deserted foyer and to where our cars are waiting.

"What happened to our security?" Bri asks as we climb into the back of Theo's car.

"We're not one hundred percent right now, but I wouldn't put too much money on seeing them again," I confess.

"Dad's already working to pull the security footage to find out how the Italians got in without being stopped. Hopefully, it'll give us some answers."

The second we're all in, Theo takes off. Alex, Daemon and Calli, and then Toby and Jodie follow in their cars.

By the time we get back across town, both Bri and Rhea are asleep on my shoulders.

"Aw, look at you," Emmie says, twisting around in the passenger seat. "Who knew you'd be such a big softie."

"Fuck off," I grunt, "there isn't anything soft about me."

"Oh, I don't know," Bri says sleepily, dragging her hand up my thigh and giving my junk a squeeze.

"Barf," Rhea mutters as Theo opens her door to let her out.

"You want to go straight to my place so you can sleep?" I offer Bri, aware that I'm not going to get out of sitting down with the guys to discuss everything.

"Nope. I'll be where you are."

A smile curls at my lips, happiness like I've never felt

before blooming inside me. I ignore the little voice in the back of my head that says she's just feeling vulnerable after making her first kill and doesn't want to be alone. I remember it well.

"I'll get him to make it quick," I say as she opens the door and climbs out.

"It's okay. This is important. We've got all the time in the world."

"You really mean that?" I ask, hating how pathetic and desperate I sound. Apparently, tonight has turned me into a fucking sap.

Fingers crossed a few more hours in her pussy and a good sleep will sort me the fuck out. I have no desire to turn into a pussy-whipped prick like that lot.

28

BRIANNA

After two hours of discussing every single thing that happened tonight on video link with Damien, Galen, Stefanos, and Enzo and his brother, Nico finally wrapped his arm around my shoulders ready to lead me to his flat, and hopefully his bed.

I'm utterly fucking exhausted. Both physically and emotionally.

Hearing everything that the guys had been through tonight, how close this place came to being taken over by Italians, was terrifying. But then when Stella and Emmie started retelling the events of our night, I discovered that what we lived through wasn't much better.

I have learned a few things though, things I never wanted or needed to know, like who actually owns that manor house we were in, and the fact that more staff than necessary lost their lives tonight when the Italians made the dumb-arse move to attack it in the hope of getting to us.

I have no idea what they were thinking. None of the guys do, which isn't exactly reassuring. They can only assume that Ricardo Mariano's ego has just inflated so much that he thinks he can take anyone on and win. That's something that almost everyone else in the city seems to be disagreeing with.

Turns out, it wasn't just the most trusted members of the Family who were out fighting tonight in order to take the twisted fuck down. Much to Emmie's surprise, her uncle, dad, and her old friends from the Lovell estate were all trusted to get involved.

That move in itself, and the fact we were all allowed to be present for these discussions, really just proved how serious the situation with the leak is.

Damien and the guys can't trust their own men right now.

Someone leaked our location, and as far as we were all concerned, only we knew. It seems their issues might be closer than they initially thought.

"Back here tomorrow night," Theo commands when we all start moving.

"You got it, Boss." Seb salutes like a moron before sweeping Stella off her feet and throwing her over his shoulder. "We'll be busy until then anyway. You know my girl going all bad-arse gets me horny as fuck."

I don't feel Nico move until his fingers twist in my hair and my head is dragged back so I have no choice but to look up at him.

"He's not fucking wrong, babe. Pretty sure I'll never forget the sight of you covered in our enemy's blood. Gets me so fucking hard," he growls, and just in case I thought he was lying, he presses his length against my hip to prove his point.

Despite my exhaustion, a growl of desire rumbles deep in my throat as a bite of pain shoots down my spine from his possessive hold of me.

"Fuck my actual life," Alex barks suddenly, dragging us from our lust-filled haze in favour of him. "Are you all seriously about to fuck off to... well, fuck? Again?"

I glance at the other couples around the room.

"Yeah, pretty sure that's how it's about to go."

"What about me?" he pouts like a cute little puppy dog.

"Umm..."

"One of you will let me join, right?"

"Fuck off, man," Theo barks.

"What? I don't even have to touch anyone but myself. But it's no fun alone."

"See you later, man. Enjoy that right hand," Seb announces, marching out of the room with Stella still over his shoulder.

"Bro?" he asks, looking at Daemon hopefully.

"Nice try. You had your chance to steal my girl, and you fucked it. She's all mine now."

Toby and Jodie quickly follow suit and leave Theo's penthouse.

"Fuck this bullshit," Alex hisses, correctly assuming that Nico and I aren't about to invite him to play—or at least, I hope Nico is on the same page as me with this.

"Where are you going?" Emmie asks, much to Theo's horror.

"Hellcat," he growls.

"Chill out, *Daddy*," she taunts. "I'm not about to suggest anything." She rolls her eyes in exasperation.

Alex shakes his head at the two of them.

"I'm going to find someone who's more fun than you motherfuckers." He blows out of the flat dramatically, slamming the door behind him.

"Right, well. Have a good night, cuz," Nico mutters

before steering me out of the room and in the direction all the others went in.

My legs barely keep up as he practically runs to the other end of the hallway to his own front door, and the second we're inside and alone, he slams me back against the wall and crashes his lips down on mine as if he can't wait another moment to taste me.

It's everything.

I match his desperation as I kiss him back fiercely. Our teeth clash and our tongues collide as we devour each other.

"Fuck. That was longer than it needed to be. All I could think about was kissing you, eating you, fucking you, hearing you scream," he confesses.

Dragging me from the wall, he begins pulling at my clothes, abandoning them behind us as we move toward his bedroom.

By the time we get there, both of us are bare and more than ready for what comes next.

The second my back hits the sheets, my legs are spread and he's inside me. No prep, no fuss, just a desperate man taking exactly what he needs, and I am here for it.

"Fuck, yes," I cry as he bottoms out inside me, my entire body shooting up the bed with his powerful thrusts.

Unlike the previous bed we destroyed, Nico's is a little more sturdy. The thing doesn't so much as rattle as he rails me like his life depends on it.

"Come for me, Siren. I need to feel you strangling the life out of my cock."

"NICO," I scream, my nails raking across the already scratched-up skin of his back as he drives me higher and higher.

"Fuck, yes. Fuck, NICO."

"FUCKING YES," he bellows, following me right over the edge, filling me to the brim once again.

His arms give out and he collapses on top of me. It's hot, sticky, and sweaty, but neither of us do anything about it. He doesn't even pull out of me before we both pass out.

When I come to again, the bright summer sun is streaming in through the open curtains, the heat of it making my body burn up right along with the dead weight pinning me to the bed.

Looking down, I find Nico fast asleep and curled around me like a fucking snake.

If it weren't for my desperate need to pee, I might just lie back and enjoy this rare peaceful moment with him. But as it is, if I don't move, we're both going to be getting the kind of bath neither of us wants.

"Nico," I whisper-hiss, hoping to wake him enough that he'll release me. But the great oaf doesn't so much as flinch. "Nico," I say a little louder.

Nothing.

"You really were sent to test me, huh?" I mutter, attempting to unwrap his limbs from my body.

It takes a bit of effort, but eventually, I manage to slide out from beneath him.

And he still doesn't wake up.

I walk to his bathroom with a sappy smile on my face, ensuring I spin around before I close the door to take in the sight of Nico lying on his front, his bare arse fully on show as he hugs a pillow.

My need for the bathroom stops me from running to find my phone to snap a photo, but he can bet his playboy reputation on the fact I'll be getting that image for my spank bank the second I emerge.

"Oh, yes," I breathe as relief floods my system.

As I sit there, I look around Nico's tidy bathroom, thinking of other times I've been here and appreciating just how different everything feels this time.

For the first time... possibly in my life, I'm not planning my escape.

I might have spent the night with Nico before—Brad, even... shudder—but I've always woken with an escape plan, my need to put space between me and my bedmate the single most important thing in those few moments.

But right now, leaving is the last thing on my mind.

I'd have thought this moment would be terrifying, but after everything that happened yesterday, I'm mostly just relaxed about walking out of this room and crawling back into bed with him.

This time last week, I was doing everything I could think of to remove him from my life. I knew it was pointless, even if I refused to acknowledge the fact. It's amazing how fast things can change. Especially when you live a life like Nico and the other guys do.

Any of them—any of us—could have died last night. One wrong move and our little family could be missing vital parts today.

Sobering thoughts of how last night could have ended are enough to stop me trying to get back into bed. I know that if I do, I'll just end up lying there, replaying it all in my head over and over until I drive myself insane.

So instead of sneaking back out, I turn the shower on, borrow Nico's toothbrush and set about getting ready for a day of hopefully doing nothing.

He's still passed out, gloriously naked when I return

from the bathroom with a towel wrapped around my still-damp body.

Ignoring my overnight bag, I pull Nico's wardrobe open instead and steal one of his t-shirts. I grab a pair of knickers, but I don't put them on. Instead, I twist the lace around his exposed fingers and go in search of my phone.

Once I'm happy I've got his delicious arse from every angle possible, I tiptoe out of the room and close the door behind me.

I walk around every room in his penthouse, taking in every ounce of Nico that I can.

I might have been here a few times now, but I've never seen behind most of the doors. I might have had full access to his body, but his life, his home, was always different.

Back then, I would never have dreamt of snooping. But things are different now, or at least to me, they feel different.

Suddenly, I don't feel like a part that doesn't fit in his home. Like a piece of furniture that doesn't belong.

How quickly everything has changed makes my head spin. But then, I guess two near-death experiences in a week will do that to you.

Both of us were so lucky to walk away from that collision last weekend, but even more so last night.

I close the door to his office, a room I didn't even know he had, and make my way back to the kitchen.

I find a coffee pod and drop it into his machine before hunting the cupboards for a mug.

I bark out a laugh when one with a cartoon dinosaur catches my eyes.

Written around the cute little character is 'don't be a cuntasauras'.

Definitely something Alex bought.

My thoughts linger to the only single member of the group, and I can't help but wonder what he got up to last night. There's a good chance he just went downstairs to his flat, grabbed a tub of Vaseline and got jiggy alone. But if he did push through the exhaustion of the night, where would he have gone? A club? For some reason, I can't see it.

Shaking thoughts of him from my head, I grab my steaming mug and my phone from the counter before opening Nico's floor-to-ceiling glass wall and getting comfortable on his outside sofa in the shade.

The heat of the summer day wraps around me like a warm hug, making me wish I was abroad somewhere dressed in only a bikini and about to hit the beach.

Heaven.

I take a sip of my coffee and just relax.

Everyone is okay and we're safe here.

If I learned anything last night, it's that this building is one of the most protected in the city. I guess it shouldn't be a surprise, really. The next generation of the Cirillo Family lives here. Something tells me that they're protected even more fiercely than the current leaders. They're the future; they hold all the power.

It blows my mind to think of what the future holds for these guys. On one hand, they're just normal teenage boys. Okay, so insanely wealthy and good-looking teenage boys. But on the other, they're these important, formidable mafia soldiers. Some days, it's really hard to marry the two together. But then there are times like last night when they all walked into that hotel suite covered in blood and dirt like they'd been to war, and it becomes so much easier to understand it all.

They're like me, only way more dangerous.

I can be Brianna the party girl who will hook up with

any guy who gives me the right kind of look at the same time as being the sensible teacher who stands in front of a room full of impressionable teenagers and tries to teach them how to be decent human beings.

Two entirely different personalities can co-exist.

My phone buzzes beside me, dragging me from my thoughts, and the second I find Jodie's name waiting for me, I unlock it and read her message.

> Best Bitch: Morning! How's your head and vag? Spinning and sore?

I snort out a very unattractive laugh.

> Bri: Couldn't say it better myself. Can you talk?

> Best Bitch: Give me five and I'll call you.

Lowering my phone, I lose myself in my own head once more as I sip my coffee, and before I know it, my phone is ringing with an incoming video call from my girl.

"Hey," I say after swiping the screen and holding it in front of me.

"Hey, how are you?"

"Aside from spinning and sore?" I ask lightly.

"Yeah, last night was—"

"Intense?" I interrupt.

"That's one way to describe it."

She slumps down, allowing me to see where she is.

"Jodie Walker, are you still naked in the bed your man fucked you in last night?" I ask, faux horrified.

"Hell yeah, I am. I'm also wondering why you're not in the exact same place with a Cirillo between your thighs."

I can't help but giggle like a girl at her suggestion.

"Bri," she breathes, getting all soft and gooey at my show of affection for the man I've been trying to convince everyone I don't want for months.

"He's still sleeping. Think I wore him out."

She scoffs at my suggestion. "Doubtful. I've seen that boy in action. He could go all night."

"And I can confirm that that is true."

"Lucky bitch," she teases.

"Oh yeah, because you've got anything to complain about with your kinky man."

"You won't be hearing any complaints from me," she says with a wide grin.

"Liked the new lingerie, huh?"

Christ, buying that yesterday morning seems like a lifetime ago now.

"Didn't even get it out of the bag."

I whistle in appreciation.

"Seriously though, Bri. Are you doing okay?"

She doesn't need to say any more for me to know she's talking about the guy whose carotid arteries I severed with a bottle last night.

A shudder rips through me at the memory of his warm blood spraying over my face. My stomach rolls, bile racing up my throat, but I manage to get a grip of myself before I'm forced to run to Nico's fancy master bathroom.

"It... It was necessary."

She nods, but I don't miss the way she studies me closely.

"I'm okay, I promise."

"Okay. But if that changes, I'm right here."

"I know," I say softly, more grateful for her support than I think she understands.

I'm not naïve, I know that what I did last night will

come back to haunt me. But right now, I'm focusing on the other big change in my life—the more positive one than the one where I turned into a murderer.

That bile sloshes around in my stomach again.

"So, how's your favourite sex pest?" Jodie asks, changing the subject.

"He's... Nico," I say with a laugh as way of explanation.

"So, is this it? Are you actually together or—"

"Yeah," a deep voice growls from behind me. "We're together. Done deal. Isn't that right, babe?"

His shadow falls over me, but I don't turn to look at him before Jodie squeals, "Nico Cirillo, put your cock away right this second."

At her words, I twist around faster. Exactly as I was expecting, he's standing there bold as brass and as naked as the day he was born, with his already erect cock in his hand, something I appreciate the hell out of. My best friend, though, not so much.

"Aw, Jojo, don't be sad," he teases. "I know Toby's is small, but he can totally make up for it with effort and a sex toy or two."

I bark out a laugh while Jodie fumes on the other end.

"Yeah, I'm gonna go. You enjoy that, Bri. And call me if you need me."

My phone is snatched out of my hand before I get a chance to say goodbye.

"Hey," I complain, watching as Nico blows Jodie a kiss and cuts the call.

He throws it onto the other end of the sofa and stares down at me with heated, slightly unsure eyes.

"You'd gone," he says, those two words fully explaining that unusual look.

"I needed to pee," I explain. "Then I came for coffee

and… I wanted you to rest." I shrug, feeling weirdly shy under his intense stare.

"Is what you said to Jodie true?" he asks cryptically, forcing me to wrack my brain for what we talked about. It's easier said than done while he's slowly stroking his cock right in front of me.

"Umm… which part?" I ask, shamelessly watching him.

"About you being okay."

"Oh, not about you being a sex pest?" I ask, suddenly remembering something he must have overheard.

"We already know that's true," he teases, bringing his mouth-watering body closer.

Uncurling my legs from beneath me, I place my feet on the floor, more than ready to go to him.

"Brianna," he warns, forcing me to rip my eyes from his cock in favour of his face.

It's his fault. If he wanted to have a serious conversation, he really should have come out here fully dressed. Or pulled on a pair of boxers at minimum.

"I'm okay," I whisper, feeling the intensity of his stare right down to my soul.

"Don't lie to me. If—"

"I'm not, I promise. I'm not thinking about it. But when I do, if I need to talk, I'll talk."

He nods once, accepting my words. "I've been there, remember? I know how it feels to do what you did last night."

"Maybe we can compare notes one day."

"Yeah, maybe," he muses. "So, if you're not thinking about that, what are you thinking about?"

I let my eyes trail back down his body, taking in every sculpted muscle, indent and ridge of his impressive chest and stomach until I trace his V lines to his hard cock.

"You really need to ask?"

"Filthy little whore," he murmurs.

"No point in changing things now," I mutter.

"Get on your knees, Siren. I want to watch you suck me dry while the city moves around us."

I glance through the glass balcony, seeing the tiny cars moving on the road stories beneath us. There are people down there. Hundreds, thousands of them. But none of them can make us out up here. Not that it would matter, even if they could. Fear of being watched is unlikely to stop me from getting a taste of my man right now.

Sliding from the cushion, I press my knees against the warm tiled floor and run my palms up his solid thighs before leaning forward to lap up the precum that's leaking from his slit.

29

NICO

Panic.

Pure unfiltered, heart-stopping panic.

That's the only way I can describe the bone-chilling feeling when I woke and found myself in bed alone.

It was ridiculous. Pathetic. Weak and needy. But fuck, I couldn't stop myself.

My first thought was that she'd snuck out like she's so prone to doing and that everything that happened yesterday wasn't real. It was just some incredible and totally fucked-up dream.

But then I sprang from the bed, my body hurting in a way that only pointed toward my memory being real, and I flew out of the bedroom like the hounds of hell were snapping at my heels.

I was more than prepared to go running out of the building stark bollock naked to hunt her down and drag her back kicking and screaming if necessary.

She'd made me a promise the night before. A promise I fully intend on making her stick to.

She told me she was mine. And that's how it's going to fucking be.

My heart rate doesn't slow and my muscles don't relax despite the signs that surrounded me that she was still here.

I didn't even notice her knickers balled up in my fist while I slept like a toddler with a fucking blankie, or her bag that was still on my bedroom floor.

It isn't until I hear her voice that everything settles and the red haze of panic that had descended over me fades.

And the second that happens, I feel like a pussy.

So what if she left? I could have handled it, right?

I'm a fucking man.

I torture and kill people for a living. One woman should not have the power to bring me to my knees when fully grown scary motherfuckers barely make me break a sweat.

She's not just one woman, though.

She's my woman.

Every day since waking up in that hospital bed, I've understood that to be a fact more and more. And I'm also beginning to understand that those feelings aren't new. In fact, I'm pretty sure they've been there all along. I just refused to embrace them in favour of smothering them with the bullshit lies I told myself.

I stand next to the kitchen island watching the back of her head, listening to her talk. I can't hear what she's saying from here. I don't need to know. She's here, and that's all that matters.

Well, it is for a few minutes, because my need to see the front of her, to find out who she's talking to instead of being in bed with me gets the better of me.

With my eyes not leaving her, I stalk closer until I begin making out words. It becomes instantly obvious who she's talking to. And I guess I shouldn't really be surprised.

"Seriously though, Bri. Are you doing okay?" Jodie asks, concern for her best friend more than obvious in her tone.

Brianna pauses and I still, needing to hear the answer to this question as much as Jodie does.

Making your first kill is a big deal when you've trained almost all your life to do it. I can't even imagine how she must be feeling right now.

"It... It was necessary," she reasons. But I quickly discover that that's not enough for Jodie, because she follows it up with, "I'm okay, I promise."

"Okay. But if that changes, I'm right here."

"I know," Brianna says softly.

As grateful as I am that Brianna has Jodie's support—something that I'm sure will be priceless in the coming months and years as they both navigate living as part of the Cirillo Family—I want her to be confiding in me, allowing me to support her through this.

"So, how is your favourite sex pest?" Jodie asks, changing the subject and dragging me from my previous thoughts.

Now we're talking. I can totally get on board with eavesdropping a bit of girl talk about how good I am in bed.

"He's... Nico," Brianna says with a laugh, killing all my fantasies. I was hoping she might fall into a very long and in-depth description of just how magical my cock is.

"So, is this it? Are you actually together or—" Unable to remain out of sight, and just in case she's about to give the wrong fucking answer, I make my presence known.

"Yeah," I announce, stepping out onto my balcony behind where Brianna is sitting.

Okay, so I probably should have put some clothes on, but fuck it. Jodie has seen it all before, and it's not like I have plans to wear anything here while it's just the two of us. As far as I see it, we've got time to make up for and clothing will only waste it. "We're together. Done deal. Isn't that right, babe?"

The rest of the conversation passes me by. My only focus is her, and of course my aching cock.

I have no idea how long I've been asleep or how many hours it's been since I was inside her. Whatever it is is too long.

The second she drops to her knees and wraps her sinful lips around my length, I feel like the king of the fucking world.

"Yes, Siren," I bark when she leans forward, taking me right to the back of her throat.

My fingers twist in her messy, curly hair, and I hold her down on my length for a few seconds.

"Look at you," I groan, pushing her lower once more. "Such a good little whore taking all of me."

A whimper rumbles in her throat that I feel all the way down the length of my cock.

"You like that, don't you? You like knowing you're a good girl for sucking my dick."

She whimpers again, taking me deeper this time.

"Fuck, I bet your cunt is dripping for me right now."

Releasing her head for a beat, I reach for the shirt she's wearing and drag it over her head, forcing her to release my cock for a few seconds as the fabric passes her face.

"That's more like it. Now, where were you?" I ask, holding myself out for her.

Eagerly, she gets back into position and begins licking around the head of my cock, making it jerk for more.

Releasing my fingers in favour of her hair, I let her do her thing, watching as she licks down my shaft, teasing me mercifully before finally taking me in her mouth once more.

"That's it, babe. You suck me so fucking good. Touch yourself, show me how wet you are. Show me how much you love pleasing me."

Without missing a beat, she spreads her knees, her hand dipping between her thighs.

Her attention on my dick falters for a beat as her fingers collide with her sensitive flesh.

"Push your fingers inside your pretty cunt, Siren. Then let me taste you."

She gasps around my length as she does as she's told before lifting her arm and offering her hand up to me.

Grabbing her wrist, I bring her fingers to my lips, painting them with the juices on her fingertips before I suck them deep into my mouth, licking at them with my tongue as her taste explodes.

She mimics my actions with my cock, licking up the vein that runs on the underside, making my balls ache with my need to blow.

"As soon as I'm done, I'm going to push you up against the railing and eat you until everyone in this city knows who you belong to, Siren," I promise as I release her fingers.

She ups the ante, her need for her own release spurring her on as she deepthroats me like a pro.

"So fucking beautiful. And all fucking mine," I announce a few seconds before my release slams into me and I spill hot ropes of cum down her throat. "Don't swallow," I demand before pulling out of her, ensuring I leave the last of it on her tongue. "Show me."

The second my cock slips from her mouth, she parts her lips.

"Fuck, yeah," I grunt, my cock already revving back up for more action.

Dipping my finger into her mouth, I scoop up some of my cum before painting her lips with it.

"Mine," I growl. "All. Fucking. Mine."

She nods, her body trembling with need as she fights to sit still and not try to find the friction she needs.

"Swallow," I finally command.

Her lips slam closed, following orders as I reach for her, lifting her to her feet and pushing her up against the glass that stops us from falling to our death.

The chrome railing presses against her soft stomach, allowing me to bend her over and expose what I need.

"What do you know... perfect height."

"Nico," she whimpers desperately.

"Never had anyone out here before, Siren. Do you reckon your screams will echo?"

"Only one way to find out."

"Yeah. You're right."

"NICO," she screams when my palm collides with her round arse cheek before I drop to my knees.

"Nope. Gonna need to be louder, Siren."

***

After eating her and then railing her until she was hoarse from screaming my name so loudly, I carried Brianna into the flat and refused to put her down until we were once again in the shower getting rained on by ice-cold water.

We cleaned up, fucked again, washed again, and then headed out in the search of food. And then, while we waited for the delivery to arrive, we fucked again.

Other than a brief catch-up with Theo and the others on Saturday night, that is basically how we spend our weekend.

Clothes are banned and orgasms are a necessity.

I want it to last forever. A world with just the two of us where everything outside the four walls of my flat ceases to exist. But when Brianna vanishes into my bedroom on Sunday evening for longer than I'm willing to lose her for, it all comes to an abrupt end.

"What are you doing?" I ask, watching in horror as she covers up her delicious curves with a pair of sweats and an oversized t-shirt.

She chuckles, but as cute as it might be, it gets my back up.

"You're not leaving," I state firmly.

"Nico," she sighs, turning to look at me as she drags her hair up into a ponytail. "You can't keep me locked up here as your sex slave forever."

"Watch me." I step farther into the room, more than ready to use my naked body to convince her of all the reasons to stay.

"I've got a job, Nico. A life. One I'd like to return to."

"You don't have to. I've already got more than you could ever possibly—"

She barks out a laugh of disbelief. "Are you actually serious right now?"

"Uh—"

"I don't want to be your trophy housewife, Nico. I won't ever be the kind of woman you can pacify with money. I won't bend to your will or anyone else's. I am my own person, I—"

"Whoa," I say, holding my hands up in defence. "Calm down. I was just saying that if—"

"Well, don't. I don't want your money, your handouts, or your connections. I want to go home and get prepared to return to my job tomorrow."

I swallow nervously, more than aware of what that job is.

"I might have agreed to this. But that doesn't mean it's all going to be on your terms."

"I never said it had to be. I just don't want you to feel like you need to rush back after all this if you're not ready. Money no longer needs to be the driving force for anything you do in life."

"I don't want your money."

"Well, that's tough, because you can have as much of it as you like."

And I damn well fucking mean it.

Now I've made my decision about what I want in life, I'm willing to open up everything for her.

What's mine is hers. Now and always.

30

BRIANNA

I stare at Nico in disbelief.

His U-turn on what he wants in life gives me bloody whiplash.

The need to argue burns red hot in my stomach, fury at the fact he thinks I'll drop to my knees once more and accept all the handouts he's offering me bubbles in my veins. But I fight them both.

He's not saying these things to be vindictive or controlling. I can see in his eyes that he's saying them because he genuinely wants to help.

I won't accept it, though.

It doesn't matter if he decides he wants to put a ring on it and give me his name; I still won't accept his fortune.

I earn what I spend. I work for what I have.

Okay, so should I ever move in with him, I might need to bend my rules slightly. But that's an issue for the future. Right now, I have no reason to think we'll make it to the end of the week.

All of this, all these promises of the future, of no financial burdens when I've spent almost all my life counting the pennies... They're too much. This... all of this is too much.

"I need to go home, Nico. I need to get prepped for tomorrow and I—" I swallow nervously, knowing this is going to hurt him. "I need some space."

His brow furrows, his eyes darkening with confusion.

I fucking hate it, but I know what I need and I'm going to make it happen no matter what.

I will not lose my head after only a few hours. The orgasms have been insane, but they haven't entirely addled my brain.

"I'll take you to get what you need and then we can—"

"Nico, you're not hearing me," I say, stepping up to him and cupping his rough cheeks in my hands. "I've spent my life looking after myself, not allowing anyone close enough to have any impact on my decisions. This..." I say, gesturing between the two of us, "is going to take some adjusting to."

He seems to have jumped head first into this, but I can't forget all the reasons I act as a lone ranger quite so easily.

The last time I truly relied on someone...

I shudder thinking of all the situations Mum left me in all those years ago.

"One step at a time, yeah?"

Grabbing my phone from the bed, I open up the Uber app.

"No," he booms, snatching my phone away from me.

"Excuse me?" I fume. "You did not just do that."

"You're not getting a fucking Uber. Anyone could be waiting outside this building for someone to emerge."

"I have a new security detail, don't I?" I ask, referring back to the meeting we had with Theo yesterday evening when he and Damien laid out the plan going forward.

"Yes, but—"

"He can take me home, then you can sleep well tonight knowing I'm safe."

"I won't be sleeping at all unless you're right beside me."

"Who would have guessed that you'd be the one with attachment issues." Honestly, after the amount of therapy I've had thanks to mummy dearest, I'd have thought that would have been me.

"It's not—I don't—Brianna," he breathes, sounding utterly exasperated, "I'm just trying to protect you. If something were to happen, I'd never forgive myself."

"Nothing is going to happen to me. I'll be safe in my flat, and then tomorrow I'll drive myself to school with security no doubt following me. My phone is tracked, right? You'll be able to see where I am."

"I still think we should go and get your stuff and—"

"No." I stand firm. "If it makes you feel better, you can take me back, but I won't be returning here today. I need a night in my own place. It's been... too long," I say, having lost track of just how long I've been gone.

Dropping my phone to the bed once more, he wraps his hand around the back of my neck and drags me into his body.

"I thought it was meant to get easier now," he confesses quietly.

"Whatever gave you the impression that life with me would be easy?" I tease, wishing I could be the kind of person who could make his life simpler instead of fighting him at every turn. But honestly, what would be the fun in that?

"Stay here with me tomorrow night," he begs.

"Do you think that's appropriate, Mr. Cirillo? You have a double English lit lesson tomorrow, remember?"

"Fuck appropriate. I'm sure there are plenty of things you can teach me."

I cringe internally, regretting bringing up this student-teacher banter. It's wrong. So fucking wrong, and yet, it's not going to stop me.

"Mrs. Hendrix knows, Brianna. Middleton won't care because he can't afford to go against Damien. And, I promise to behave."

"Boring," I mutter.

"Or I won't," he teases with a knee-weakening smile. "I guess you'll just have to wait and find out."

I shake my head at him, attempting to step back so he can take me home.

"Just one more thing," he says, dragging me back and slamming his lips down on mine for another earth-shattering kiss.

By the time he grabs my packed bag and throws it over his shoulder so we can leave, I'm seriously questioning my choices. Would it be such a bad thing if I turned up at school tomorrow totally unprepared?

Yes. Yes, it would.

With my head held high and my decision to head home my only focus, I walk through Nico's front door and head toward the lift.

The drive home is somewhat tense. He's not happy about this, that much is obvious, but thankfully he doesn't try to argue with me, or attempt to change my mind again.

My stomach knots painfully as I question my own decision once again when he pulls up outside my building.

It's weird. This place has been my home for quite some time now, but sitting out here, I don't get the same sense of contentment, the feeling of coming home that I'm used to.

Nico kills the engine and I make the mistake of looking over at him.

My demand for him to turn around again dances on the tip of my tongue, but my refusal to bow down, my stubbornness to follow through on my own plan wins out.

"I'll walk you up, then you need to message me before you leave in the morning, and then again when you get to school."

My lips part to tease his over-the-top demands, but then I look into his eyes and see his genuine concern and my words are swallowed by guilt.

His concerns are warranted. And it's selfish of me to demand this. But it's what I need. I've been smothered almost since the moment I woke up in that hospital. I told Jodie I was going home before school tomorrow, and I fully intend on seeing that through.

"I will," I agree, pushing his passenger door open and climbing out.

The familiar scent of home hits me as I swing my front door open and look around.

It looks exactly the same as I remember. The glass I left on the coffee table is still there, along with the pile of dishes in the sink.

"You want some help tidying up?" Nico asks, taking in the chaos I usually live in.

"No, it's okay. I'm sure you've got better things to be doing."

He wants to argue, I can practically see it on the tip of his tongue. But thankfully, he never gets the chance to voice it, because his phone rings.

Pulling it from his pocket, he stares down at the screen.

"I need to take this," he says reluctantly.

"I'll be okay here. I'll keep my phone on. Everything will be fine."

"I still don't like it," he confesses.

"I know, but it's how it is. Go and spend the night strategizing with the guys. I'm just going to be working and having an early night for tomorrow."

"Call me in the morning, yeah?"

"You got it, big man."

A cocky smirk twitches at his lips at my nickname.

"Come here. I'm not leaving without a reminder of why you agreed to this at the forefront of your mind."

"You think it would be possible to forget about you?" I say quickly before he steals my lips once more.

His phone rings again before he finally stumbles back, studying me through hooded, hungry eyes.

"Go," I urge. "I've got things to be doing."

With one final chaste kiss on my lips, he turns and walks away.

His fingers are twisted around the handle before a thought hits me and I call his name. He freezes before turning back with a smug grin.

Ignoring it, I rush toward the dresser beside him and pull the top drawer open.

"I know you don't like this, but here."

Pulling two keys free, I pass them over.

He stares down at them, confusion written all over his face.

They're for the building. For this flat," I add in case he hadn't figured that out.

"Shit, I—"

"For emergencies. For peace of mind."

"Not for letting myself in in the middle of the night and fucking you senseless?"

"I guess that would depend on your definition of an emergency."

His phone rings again, and he lifts his other hand to look at the screen once more.

"Go, before I get whoever it is to drag you out of here themselves."

He kisses me again and then finally leaves.

I close the door behind him and lock it up tight. But at the last minute, I pull the bolt loose again, assuming that he's not going to make it much past sundown before he reappears with some bullshit emergency.

With a laugh, I take off across my flat, making quick work of tidying up. Then, I throw myself in the shower to freshen up, and get to work.

I don't have all that much prep to be prepared for the morning. With fuck all else to do while I was stuck at Jodie's this past week, I got myself up to date, so before long, I find myself in bed with my Kindle and a hot chocolate, losing myself in the steamy age-gap romance I was in the middle of before my life got all dramatic.

Unsurprisingly, I'm soon struggling to keep my eyes open, the words all blurring and swirling around the screen in front of me.

Putting it on my bedside table, I pad through to my bathroom to brush my teeth and pee before heading back to bed. Although, something startles me when I'm almost at my bedroom door, and I can't help but laugh as the front door opens behind me.

"I knew you wouldn't be able to stay away."

Ignoring Alex's phone calls, I focus on the other name that's lit up my phone in the last ten minutes. But I don't bother calling her back. I might want to hear her voice, but I need more than that.

She's the only one I trust to give me sensible advice when it comes to Brianna anyway, so instead of turning around and heading back to my flat again, I go in the opposite direction toward the building I called home for eighteen years.

I have avoided this place since Dad died. There are too many painful reminders of him in every inch of the house, and I couldn't bear to see it, to feel it.

But facing it seems a little bit more possible today.

Although, I start to question that when I pull into the driveway and find Mum's car parked up.

I was hoping that she'd at least do me the favour of being out. Seems like my luck has run out.

Parking up, I swerve the front door and instead head around the back of the building.

Just as I suspected, the woman I'm here to see is

standing in the kitchen doing something fancy with some pastry, singing to herself happily as she does.

I feel lighter just watching her. It's a feeling that I'm sure most others get from watching their mothers do something similar. I guess I should be grateful that while my mother is a shit show of epic proportions, I still have a caring maternal figure who's been looking out for both me and Calli for years.

"Nico," she breathes, a shocked yet genuine smile lighting up her face. "How are you? You look... in pain." She winces as she takes in the fresh bruising that covers my face. "Has something happened?"

"You know I can't say anything."

She holds her hands up. "I know, I know. I just worry about you. How's Calli?"

I can't help but laugh. "Just Calli or Calli and her little secret?

Jocelyn's eyes widen.

"I'm happy for her," I say honestly.

"Me too. I've never seen her smile like she does with him."

My heart melts as Jocelyn's love for my little sister shines bright in her eyes.

"Oh, here," she says, suddenly coming back to herself. "I was ringing to see if I could drop these over."

"Nice of you to call," I tease.

"A little birdie told me that you had a flatmate this weekend."

An easy sigh falls from my lips. "Is there anything my little sister doesn't tell you?"

"I'm sure there's enough. So, talk to me, young man. Am I going to have to be buying a hat soon?"

I spend an hour talking everything out with Jocelyn. I don't know whether my sessions with Jade have helped to open me up, but being honest about how I feel about Brianna seems to come easier. To be fair, it could just be the fact that I've finally admitted to myself how I feel.

I have no idea if Mum knows I'm here. I didn't exactly hide my car or make my arrival a secret, but still, she hasn't made any kind of effort to poke her head into the kitchen and say hello. Not that I can say I'm surprised. She seems to have resigned from her role as a mother, and honestly, if that's how she really feels, then I'd rather she just stuck to it.

"She was up in her room getting ready for something," Jocelyn says, able to freakily read my thoughts.

"Who is?" I ask, attempting to brush the whole situation under the carpet.

"Why don't you go and try to talk to her?"

"Nah, you're okay. The chance of me killing her is a little too high for my liking."

"You think I don't know that?" Jocelyn teases.

"Is that what it'll take to steal you away from her?"

Jocelyn doesn't comment on that statement. She doesn't need to. Whatever has kept her here this long won't be severed until her remaining employer has gone.

There's a bang somewhere deeper in the house that rocks through me.

"Oh, maybe she will grace you with her presence," Jocelyn says somewhat hopefully.

"I'd rather she didn't."

I'm happy to ignore her existence just as much as she does mine, but then a male voice floats down to us and my curiosity is more than piqued.

Without saying a word, I slide off the barstool and move toward the entry hall.

The first thing I see is Mum's back. As usual, she's wearing a dress that looks like it's been painted onto her body. Her hair is immaculate, and I can only imagine that her face matches. She's always the image of perfection. A cover-up for the broken, ugly woman hiding beneath the surface.

A suited man stands on the other side of her, and while I can't see his face, I more than recognise his voice. Although, I can't actually make out the words he's murmuring to her.

"Where's Iris?" I ask, making my presence known as I march deeper into the room as the two of them quickly put a little more space between them.

"Oh, Nico," Mum breathes fakely, smoothing a steady hand down the front of her dress. "It's so good to see you. I didn't know you were here."

"No, you do seem to be somewhat distracted," I say, my gaze holding Christos, Jerome's father.

"I'm just helping Christos organise something for Iris's birthday in a few weeks," Mum tries to explain.

"Sure you were," I mutter, looking between the two of them.

To be fair to him, Christos has the decency to look a little embarrassed. Mum, on the other hand, is as cold and closed off as I've become used to.

"Right well, I only stopped by to see Jocelyn. But I'd be careful if I were you," I say, keeping my gaze trained on Christos. "The grass isn't always greener."

Spinning on my heels, I march back toward the kitchen.

Surprisingly, Jocelyn isn't watching from the shadows.

"Is he here often?" I hiss, blowing through the room like a storm.

"No," she says honestly. "He and Iris are only ever here as a couple."

"Well, something is going on there."

Her lips part to say something, but I quickly cut her off.

"Thank you for these," I say, grabbing the container of white chocolate and raspberry cookies she's baked—Brianna's favourite, apparently—and taking off toward the door. "I'll see you soon. The job offer stands, as always."

Without waiting for a response, I march around the house and to my car.

Christos's car is parked next to mine, making me question my confidence of something going on between them.

There's no way he'd have missed my car. Surely, he wouldn't have come inside if there was something untoward going on.

Shaking my head, I fall into my driver's seat and put my car into reverse.

The sun has almost set, the heat of the day finally ebbing away. Not that Bri and I experienced much of it, seeing as we've spent almost all our waking hours today rolling around in my bed.

With my head spinning with thoughts of Brianna along with Mum and Christos, I aimlessly drive around town.

I should go home. It's late and I have revision to do ready for tomorrow, but the thought of going home and walking into my flat without her doesn't sit right with me.

It hardly surprises me when I eventually end up driving down her street. My eyes scan the building as I approach, searching out her windows.

I pull into a space on the side of the road and keep

watching, waiting for some kind of sign that she's awake. That she's okay.

I haven't heard from her, but equally, I haven't messaged her either.

The song playing quietly through my speakers changes more than a few times as I sit here, waiting for a shadow to fill the window, but it never does.

"Come on, babe. Just show me you're there and that you're safe."

Her phone GPS says she is, and I have no reason to believe anything else. But still, something has me killing my engine and pushing my door open.

With the keys she gave me earlier in my clutches, I unlock the main front door and jog up the stairs.

I shouldn't do it, I know that. She gave me this key for emergencies, and this is hardly one of those. But my need for her knows no bounds, and I stop overthinking my decision as I push the key into her lock and swing the door open.

Everything is tidy, her sweet scent filling the air. But it's cold in a way I can't explain. I walk deeper into the flat, searching for her. But before I find her, a note on the kitchen counter catches my eye.

Her phone is pinning it to the dark wood, and when I look down at it, my world falls out from beneath me.

Nico,

I'm sorry.

Nico and Brianna's story concludes in Corrupt Union!

ABOUT THE AUTHOR

Tracy Lorraine is a *USA Today* and *Wall Street Journal* bestselling new adult and contemporary romance author. Tracy has recently turned thirty and lives in a cute Cotswold village in England with her husband, baby girl and lovable but slightly crazy dog. Having always been a bookaholic with her head stuck in her Kindle, Tracy decided to try her hand at a story idea she dreamt up and hasn't looked back since.

Be the first to find out about new releases and offers. Sign up to my newsletter here.

If you want to know what I'm up to and see teasers and snippets of what I'm working on, then you need to be in my Facebook group. Join Tracy's Angels here.

Keep up to date with Tracy's books at
www.tracylorraine.com

ALSO BY TRACY LORRAINE

Falling Series

Falling for Ryan: Part One #1

Falling for Ryan: Part Two #2

Falling for Jax #3

Falling for Daniel (A Falling Series Novella)

Falling for Ruben #4

Falling for Fin #5

Falling for Lucas #6

Falling for Caleb #7

Falling for Declan #8

Falling For Liam #9

Forbidden Series

Falling for the Forbidden #1

Losing the Forbidden #2

Fighting for the Forbidden #3

Craving Redemption #4

Demanding Redemption #5

Avoiding Temptation #6

Chasing Temptation #7

Rebel Ink Series

Hate You #1

Trick You #2

Defy You #3

Play You #4

Inked (A Rebel Ink/Driven Crossover)

Rosewood High Series

Thorn #1

Paine #2

Savage #3

Fierce #4

Hunter #5

Faze (#6 Prequel)

Fury #6

Legend #7

Maddison Kings University Series

TMYM: Prequel

TRYS #1

TDYW #2

TBYS #3

TVYC #4

TDYD #5

TDYR #6

TRYD #7

Knight's Ridge Empire Series

Wicked Summer Knight: Prequel (Stella & Seb)

Wicked Knight #1 (Stella & Seb)

Wicked Princess #2 (Stella & Seb)

Wicked Empire #3 (Stella & Seb)

Deviant Knight #4 (Emmie & Theo)

Deviant Princess #5 (Emmie & Theo

Deviant Reign #6 (Emmie & Theo)

One Reckless Knight (Jodie & Toby)

Reckless Knight #7 (Jodie & Toby)

Reckless Princess #8 (Jodie & Toby)

Reckless Dynasty #9 (Jodie & Toby)

Dark Halloween Knight (Calli & Batman)

Dark Knight #10 (Calli & Batman)

Dark Princess #11 (Calli & Batman)

Dark Legacy #12 (Calli & Batman)

Corrupt Valentine Knight (Nico & Siren)

Ruined Series

Ruined Plans #1

Ruined by Lies #2

Ruined Promises #3

Never Forget Series

Never Forget Him #1

Never Forget Us #2

THE REVENGE YOU SEEK
SNEAK PEEK

Chapter One

Letty

I sit on my bed, staring down at the fabric in my hands.

This wasn't how it was supposed to happen.

This wasn't part of my plan.

I let out a sigh, squeezing my eyes tight, willing the tears away.

I've cried enough. I thought I'd have run out by now.

A commotion on the other side of the door has me looking up in a panic, but just like yesterday, no one comes knocking.

I think I proved that I don't want to hang with my new roommates the first time someone knocked and asked if I wanted to go for breakfast with them.

I don't.

I don't even want to be here.

I just want to hide.

And that thought makes it all a million times worse.

I'm not a hider. I'm a fighter. I'm a fucking Hunter.

But this is what I've been reduced to.

This pathetic, weak mess.

And all because of *him*.

He shouldn't have this power over me. But even now, he does.

The dorm falls silent once again, and I pray that they've all headed off for their first class of the semester so I can slip out unnoticed.

I know it's ridiculous. I know I should just go out there with my head held high and dig up the confidence I know I do possess.

But I can't.

I figure that I'll just get through today—my first day—and everything will be alright.

I can somewhat pick up where I left off, almost as if the last eighteen months never happened.

Wishful thinking.

I glance down at the hoodie in my hands once more.

Mom bought them for Zayn, my younger brother, and me.

The navy fabric is soft between my fingers, but the text staring back at me doesn't feel right.

Maddison Kings University.

A knot twists my stomach and I swear my whole body sags with my new reality.

I was at my dream school. I beat the odds and I got into Columbia. And everything was good. No, everything was fucking fantastic.

Until it wasn't.

Now here I am. Sitting in a dorm at what was always my backup plan school having to start over.

Throwing the hoodie onto my bed, I angrily push to my feet.

I'm fed up with myself.

I should be better than this, stronger than this.

But I'm just... I'm broken.

And as much as I want to see the positives in this situation. I'm struggling.

Shoving my feet into my Vans, I swing my purse over my shoulder and scoop up the couple of books on my desk for the two classes I have today.

My heart drops when I step out into the communal kitchen and find a slim blonde-haired girl hunched over a mug and a textbook.

The scent of coffee fills my nose and my mouth waters.

My shoes squeak against the floor and she immediately looks up.

"Sorry, I didn't mean to disrupt you."

"Are you kidding?" she says excitedly, her southern accent making a smile twitch at my lips.

Her smile lights up her pretty face and for some reason, something settles inside me.

I knew hiding was wrong. It's just been my coping method for... quite a while.

"We wondered when our new roommate was going to show her face. The guys have been having bets on you being an alien or something."

A laugh falls from my lips. "No, no alien. Just..." I sigh, not really knowing what to say.

"You transferred in, right? From Columbia?"

"Ugh... yeah. How'd you know—"

"Girl, I know everything." She winks at me, but it

doesn't make me feel any better. "West and Brax are on the team, they spent the summer with your brother."

A rush of air passes my lips in relief. Although I'm not overly thrilled that my brother has been gossiping about me.

"So, what classes do you have today?" she asks when I stand there gaping at her.

"Umm... American lit and psychology."

"I've got psych later too. Professor Collins?"

"Uh..." I drag my schedule from my purse and stare down at it. "Y-yes."

"Awesome. We can sit together."

"S-sure," I stutter, sounding unsure, but the smile I give her is totally genuine. "I'm Letty, by the way." Although I'm pretty sure she already knows that.

"Ella."

"Okay, I'll... uh... see you later."

"Sure. Have a great morning."

She smiles at me and I wonder why I was so scared to come out and meet my new roommates.

I'd wanted Mom to organize an apartment for me so that I could be alone, but—probably wisely—she refused. She knew that I'd use it to hide in and the point of me restarting college is to try to put everything behind me and start fresh.

After swiping an apple from the bowl in the middle of the table, I hug my books tighter to my chest and head out, ready to embark on my new life.

The morning sun burns my eyes and the scent of freshly cut grass fills my nose as I step out of our building. The summer heat hits my skin, and it makes everything feel that little bit better.

So what if I'm starting over. I managed to transfer the

credits I earned from Columbia, and MKU is a good school. I'll still get a good degree and be able to make something of my life.

Things could be worse.

It could be this time last year...

I shake the thought from my head and force my feet to keep moving.

I pass students meeting up with their friends for the start of the new semester as they excitedly tell them all about their summers and the incredible things they did, or they compare schedules.

My lungs grow tight as I drag in the air I need. I think of the friends I left behind in Columbia. We didn't have all that much time together, but we'd bonded before my life imploded on me.

Glancing around, I find myself searching for familiar faces. I know there are plenty of people here who know me. A couple of my closest friends came here after high school.

Mom tried to convince me to reach out over the summer, but my anxiety kept me from doing so. I don't want anyone to look at me like I'm a failure. That I got into one of the best schools in the country, fucked it up and ended up crawling back to Rosewood. I'm not sure what's worse, them assuming I couldn't cope or the truth.

Focusing on where I'm going, I put my head down and ignore the excited chatter around me as I head for the coffee shop, desperately in need of my daily fix before I even consider walking into a lecture.

I find the Westerfield Building where my first class of the day is and thank the girl who holds the heavy door open for me before following her toward the elevator.

"Holy fucking shit," a voice booms as I turn the corner, following the signs to the room on my schedule.

Before I know what's happening, my coffee is falling from my hand and my feet are leaving the floor.

"What the—" The second I get a look at the guy standing behind the one who has me in his arms, I know exactly who I've just walked into.

Forgetting about the coffee that's now a puddle on the floor, I release my books and wrap my arms around my old friend.

His familiar woodsy scent flows through me, and suddenly, I feel like me again. Like the past two years haven't existed.

"What the hell are you doing here?" Luca asks, a huge smile on his face when he pulls back and studies me.

His brows draw together when he runs his eyes down my body, and I know why. I've been working on it over the summer, but I know I'm still way skinnier than I ever have been in my life.

"I transferred," I admit, forcing the words out past the lump in my throat.

His smile widens more before he pulls me into his body again.

"It's so good to see you."

I relax into his hold, squeezing him tight, absorbing his strength. And that's one thing that Luca Dunn has in spades. He's a rock, always has been and I didn't realize how much I needed that right now.

Mom was right. I should have reached out.

"You too," I whisper honestly, trying to keep the tears at bay that are threatening just from seeing him—them.

"Hey, it's good to see you," Leon says, slightly more subdued than his twin brother as he hands me my discarded books.

"Thank you."

I look between the two of them, noticing all the things that have changed since I last saw them in person. I keep up with them on Instagram and TikTok, sure, but nothing is quite like standing before the two of them.

Both of them are bigger than I ever remember, showing just how hard their coach is working them now they're both first string for the Panthers. And if it's possible, they're both hotter than they were in high school, which is really saying something because they'd turn even the most confident of girls into quivering wrecks with one look back then. I can only imagine the kind of rep they have around here.

The sound of a door opening behind us and the shuffling of feet cuts off our little reunion.

"You in Professor Whitman's American lit class?" Luca asks, his eyes dropping from mine to the book in my hands.

"Yeah. Are you?"

"We are. Walk you to class?" A smirk appears on his lips that I remember all too well. A flutter of the butterflies he used to give me threaten to take flight as he watches me intently.

Luca was one of my best friends in high school, and I spent almost all our time together with the biggest crush on him. It seems that maybe the teenage girl inside me still thinks that he could be it for me.

"I'd love you to."

"Come on then, Princess," Leon says and my entire body jolts at hearing that pet name for me. He's never called me that before and I really hope he's not about to start now.

Clearly not noticing my reaction, he once again takes my books from me and threads his arm through mine as the pair of them lead me into the lecture hall.

I glance at both of them, a smile pulling at my lips and hope building inside me.

Maybe this was where I was meant to be this whole time.

Maybe Columbia and I were never meant to be.

More than a few heads turn our way as we climb the stairs to find some free seats. Mostly it's the females in the huge space and I can't help but inwardly laugh at their reaction.

I get it.

The Dunn twins are two of the Kings around here and I'm currently sandwiched between them. It's a place that nearly every female in this college, hell, this state, would kill to be in.

"Dude, shift the fuck over," Luca barks at another guy when he pulls to a stop a few rows from the back.

The guy who's got dark hair and even darker eyes immediately picks up his bag, books, and pen and moves over a space.

"This is Colt," Luca explains, nodding to the guy who's studying me with interest.

"Hey," I squeak, feeling a little intimidated.

"Hey." His low, deep voice licks over me. "Ow, what the fuck, man?" he barks, rubbing at the back of his head where Luca just slapped him.

"Letty's off-limits. Get your fucking eyes off her."

"Dude, I was just saying hi."

"Yeah, and we all know what that usually leads to," Leon growls behind me.

The three of us take our seats and just about manage to pull our books out before our professor begins explaining the syllabus for the semester.

"Sorry about the coffee," Luca whispers after a few minutes. "Here." He places a bottle of water on my desk. "I know it's not exactly a replacement, but it's the best I can do."

The reminder of the mess I left out in the hallway hits me.

"I should go and—"

"Chill," he says, placing his hand on my thigh. His touch instantly relaxes me as much as it sends a shock through my body. "I'll get you a replacement after class. Might even treat you to a cupcake."

I smile up at him, swooning at the fact he remembers my favorite treat.

Why did I ever think coming here was a bad idea?

Chapter Two
Letty

My hand aches by the time Professor Whitman finishes talking. It feels like a lifetime ago that I spent this long taking notes.

"You okay?" Luca asks me with a laugh as I stretch out my fingers.

"Yeah, it's been a while."

"I'm sure these boys can assist you with that, beautiful," bursts from Colt's lips, earning him another slap to the head.

"Ignore him. He's been hit in the head with a ball one too many times," Leon says from beside me but I'm too enthralled with the way Luca is looking at me right now to reply.

Our friendship wasn't a conventional one back in high school. He was the star quarterback, and I wasn't a cheerleader or ever really that sporty. But we were paired up as lab partners during my first week at Rosewood High and we kinda never separated.

I watched as he took the team to new heights, as he met with college scouts, I even went to a few places with him so he didn't have to go alone.

He was the one who allowed me to cry on his shoulder as I struggled to come to terms with the loss of another who left a huge hole in my heart and he never, not once, overstepped the mark while I clung to him and soaked up his support.

I was also there while he hooked up with every member of the cheer squad along with any other girl who looked at him just so. Each one stung a little more than the last as my poor teenage heart was getting battered left, right, and center.

With each day, week, month that passed, I craved him more but he never, not once, looked at me that way.

I was even his prom date, yet he ended up spending the night with someone else.

It hurt, of course it did. But it wasn't his fault and I refuse to hold it against him.

Maybe I should have told him. Been honest with him about my feelings and what I wanted. But I was so terrified I'd lose my best friend that I never confessed, and I took that secret all the way to Columbia with me.

As I stare at him now, those familiar butterflies still set flight in my belly, but they're not as strong as I remember. I'm not sure if that's because my feelings for him have lessened over time, or if I'm just so numb and broken right now that I don't feel anything but pain.

It really could go either way.

I smile at him, so grateful to have run into him this morning.

He always knew when I needed him and even without knowing of my presence here, there he was like some guardian fucking angel.

If guardian angels had sexy dark bed hair, mesmerizing green eyes and a body built for sin then yeah, that's what he is.

I laugh to myself, yeah, maybe that irritating crush has gone nowhere.

"What have you got next?" Leon asks, dragging my attention away from his twin.

Leon has always been the quieter, broodier one of the duo. He's as devastatingly handsome and as popular with the female population but he doesn't wear his heart on his sleeve like Luca. Leon takes a little time to warm to people, to let them in. It was hard work getting there, but I soon realized that once he dropped his walls a little for me, it was hella worth it.

He's more serious, more contemplative, he's deeper. I always suspected that there was a reason they were so different. I know twins don't have to be the same and like the same things, but there was always something niggling at me that there was a very good reason that Leon closed himself down. From listening to their mom talk over the years, they were so identical in their mannerisms, likes, and dislikes when they were growing up, that it seems hard to believe they became so different.

"Psychology but not for an hour. I'm—"

"I'm taking her for coffee," Luca butts in. A flicker of anger passes through Leon's eyes but it's gone so fast that I begin to wonder if I imagined it.

"I could use another coffee before econ," Leon chips in.

"Great. Let's go," Luca forces out through clenched teeth.

He wanted me alone. Interesting.

The reason I never told him about my mega crush is the fact he friend-zoned me in our first few weeks of friendship by telling me how refreshing it was to have a girl wanting to be his friend and not using it as a ploy to get more.

We were only sophomores at the time but even then, Luca was up to all sorts and the girls around us were all more than willing to bend to his needs.

From that moment on, I couldn't tell him how I really felt. It was bad enough I even felt it when he thought our friendship was just that.

I smile at both of them, hoping to shatter the sudden tension between the twins.

"Be careful with these two," Colt announces from behind us as we make our way out of the lecture hall with all the others. "The stories I've heard."

"Colt," Luca warns, turning to face him and walking backward for a few steps.

"Don't worry," I shoot over my shoulder. "I know how to handle the Dunn twins." I wink at him as he howls with laughter.

"You two are in so much trouble," he muses as he turns left out of the room and we go right.

Leon takes my books from me once more and Luca threads his fingers through mine. I still for a beat. While the move isn't unusual, Luca has always been very affectionate. It only takes a second for his warmth to race up my arm and to settle the last bit of unease that's still knotting my stomach.

"Two Americanos and a skinny vanilla latte with an extra shot. Three cupcakes with the sprinkles on top."

I swoon at the fact Luca remembers my order. "How'd you—"

He turns to me, his wide smile and the sparkle in his eyes making my words trail off. The familiarity of his face, the feeling of comfort and safety he brings me causes a lump to form in my throat.

"I didn't forget anything about my best girl." He throws his arm around my shoulder and pulls me close.

Burying my nose in his hard chest, I breathe him in. His woodsy scent mixes with his laundry detergent and it settles me in a way I didn't know I needed.

Leon's stare burns into my back as I snuggle with his brother and I force myself to pull away so he doesn't feel like the third wheel.

"Dunn," the server calls, and Leon rushes ahead to grab our order while Luca leads me to a booth at the back of the coffee shop.

As we walk past each table, I become more and more aware of the attention on the twins. I know their reps, they've had their football god status since before I moved to Rosewood and met them in high school, but I had forgotten just how hero-worshiped they were, and this right now is off the charts.

Girls openly stare, their eyes shamelessly dropping down the guys' bodies as they mentally strip them naked. Guys jealousy shines through their expressions, especially those who are here with their girlfriends who are now paying them zero attention. Then there are the girls whose attention is firmly on me. I can almost read their thoughts— hell, I heard enough of them back in high school.

What do they see in her?

She's not even that pretty.

They're too good for her.

The only difference here from high school is that no one knows I'm just trailer park trash seeing as I moved from the hellhole that is Harrow Creek before meeting the boys.

Tipping my chin up, I straighten my spine and plaster on as much confidence as I can find.

They can all think what they like about me, they can come up with whatever bitchy comments they want. It's no skin off my back.

"Good to see you've lost your appeal," I mutter, dropping into the bench opposite both of them and wrapping my hands around my warm mug when Leon passes it over.

"We walk around practically unnoticed," Luca deadpans.

"You thought high school was bad," Leon mutters, he was always the one who hated the attention whereas Luca used it to his advantage to get whatever he wanted. "It was nothing."

"So I see. So, how's things? Catch me up on everything," I say, needing to dive into their celebrity status lifestyles rather than thinking about my train wreck of a life.

"Really?" Luca asks, raising a brow and causing my stomach to drop into my feet. "I think the bigger question is how come you're here and why we had no idea about it?"

Releasing my mug, I wrap my arms around myself and drop my eyes to the table.

"T-things just didn't work out at Columbia," I mutter, really not wanting to talk about it.

"The last time we talked, you said it was everything you expected it to be and more. What happened?"

Kane fucking Legend happened.

I shake that thought from my head like I do every time he pops up.

He's had his time ruining my life. It's over.

"I just..." I sigh. "I lost my way a bit, ended up dropping out and finally had to fess up and come clean to Mom."

Leon laughs sadly. "I bet that went down well."

The Dunn twins are well aware of what it's like to live with a pushy parent. One of the things that bonded the three of us over the years.

"Like a lead balloon. Even worse because I dropped out months before I finally showed my face."

"Why hide?" Leon's brows draw together as Luca stares at me with concern darkening his eyes.

"I had some health issues. It's nothing."

"Shit, are you okay?"

Fucking hell, Letty. Stop making this worse for yourself.

"Yeah, yeah. Everything is good. Honestly. I'm here and I'm ready to start over and make the best of it."

They both smile at me, and I reach for my coffee once more, bringing the mug to my lips and taking a sip.

"Enough about me, tell me all about the lives of two of the hottest Kings of Maddison."

***

"Okay... how'd you do that?" Ella whispers after both Luca and Leon walk me to my psych class after our coffee break.

"Do what?" I ask, following her into the room and finding ourselves seats about halfway back.

"It's your first day and the Dunn twins just walked you to class. You got a diamond-encrusted vag or something?"

I snort a laugh as a few others pause on their way to their seats at her words.

"Shush," I chastise.

"Girl, if it's true, you know all these guys need to know about it."

I pull out my books and a couple of pens as Professor Collins sets up at the front before turning to her.

"No, I don't have diamonds anywhere but my necklace. I've been friends with them for years."

"Girl, I knew there was a reason we should be friends." She winks at me. "I've been trying to get West and Brax to hook me up but they're useless."

"You want to be friends so I can set you up with one of the Dunns?"

"Or both." She shrugs, her face deadly serious before she leans in. "I've heard that they tag team sometimes. Can you imagine? Both of their undivided attention." She fans herself as she obviously pictures herself in the middle of a Dunn sandwich. "Oh and, I think you're pretty cool too."

"Of course you do." I laugh.

It's weird, I might have only met her very briefly this morning but that was enough.

"We're all going out for dinner tonight to welcome you to the dorm. The others are dying to meet you." She smiles at me, proving that there's no bitterness behind her words.

"I'm sorry for ignoring you all."

"Girl, don't sweat it. We got ya back, don't worry."

"Thank you," I mouth as the professor demands everyone's attention to begin the class.

The time flies as I scribble my notes down as fast as I can, my hand aching all over again and before I know it, he's finished explaining our first assignment and bringing his class to a close.

"Jesus, this semester is going to be hard," Ella muses as we both pack up.

"At least we've got each other."

"I like the way you think. You done for the day?"

"Yep, I'm gonna head to the store, grab some supplies then get started on this assignment, I think."

"I've got a couple of hours. You want company?"

After dumping our stuff in our rooms, Ella takes me to her favorite store, and I stock up on everything I'm going to need before we head back so she can go to class.

I make myself some lunch before being brave and setting up my laptop at the kitchen table to get started on my assignments. My time for hiding is over, it's time to get back to life and once again become a fully immersed college student.

"Holy shit, she is alive. I thought Zayn was lying about his beautiful older sister," a deep rumbling voice says, dragging me from my research a few hours later.

I spin and look at the two guys who have joined me.

"Zayn would never have called me beautiful," I say as a greeting.

"That's true. I think his actual words were: messy, pain in the ass, and my personal favorite, I'm glad I don't have to live with her again," he says, mimicking my brother's voice.

"Now that is more like it. Hey, I'm Letty. Sorry about—"

"You're all good. We're just glad you emerged. I'm West, this ugly motherfucker is Braxton—"

"Brax, please," he begs. "Only my mother calls me by my full name and you are way too hot to be her."

My cheeks heat as he runs his eyes over my curves.

"T-thanks, I think."

"Ignore him. He hasn't gotten laid for weeeeks."

"Okay, do we really need to go there right now?"

"Always, bro. Our girl here needs to know you get pissy when you don't get the pussy."

I laugh at their easy banter, closing down my laptop and

resting forward on my elbows as they move toward the fridge.

"Ella says we're going out," Brax says, pulling out two bottles of water and throwing one to West.

"Apparently so."

"She'll be here in a bit. Violet and Micah too. They were all in the same class."

"So," West says, sliding into the chair next to me. "What do we need to know that your brother hasn't already told us about you?"

My heart races at all the things that not even my brother would share about my life before I drag my thoughts away from my past.

"Uhhh..."

"How about the Dunns love her," Ella announces as she appears in the doorway flanked by two others. Violet and Micah, I assume.

"Um... how didn't we know this?" Brax asks.

"Because you're not cool enough to spend any time with them, asshole," Violet barks, walking around Ella. "Ignore these assholes, they think they're something special because they're on the team but what they don't tell you is that they have no chance of making first string or talking to the likes of the Dunns."

"Vi, girl. That stings," West says, holding his hand over his heart.

"Yeah, get over it. Truth hurts." She smiles up at him as he pulls her into his chest and kisses the top of her head.

"Whatever, Titch."

"Right, well. Are we ready to go? I need tacos like... yesterday."

"Yes. Let's go."

"You've never had tacos like these, Letty. You are in for a world of pleasure," Brax says excitedly.

"More than she would be if she were in your bed, that's for sure," West deadpans.

"Lies and we all know it."

"Whatever." Violet pushes him toward the door.

"Hey, I'm Micah," the third guy says when I catch up to him.

"Hey, Letty."

"You need a sensible conversation, I'm your boy."

"Good to know."

Micah and I trail behind the others and with each step I take, my smile gets wider.

Things really are going to be okay.

DOWNLOAD NOW TO KEEP READING

www.ingramcontent.com/pod-product-compliance
Lightning Source LLC
Chambersburg PA
CBHW050746190726
48285CB00005B/1547